THE ONE-WAY TRAIL

THE ONE-WAY TRAIL

by

Max Brand

The Golden West Large Print Books
Long Preston, North Yorkshire,
BD23 4ND, England.

British Library Cataloguing in Publication Data.

Brand, Max
    The one-way trail.

    A catalogue record of this book is
    available from the British Library

    ISBN   978-1-84262-904-8 pbk

First published in 1922 by Street & Smith's Publication

Cover illustration © Michael Thomas

The moral right of the author has been asserted

Published in Large Print 2012 by arrangement with
Golden West Literary Agency

The Golden West Large Print is an imprint of Library Magna
Books Ltd.

Printed and bound in Great Britain by
T.J. (International) Ltd., Cornwall, PL28 8RW

Acknowledgments

'Forgotten Treasure' under the byline George Owen Baxter first appeared in Street & Smith's *Western Story Magazine* (11/19/27). Copyright © 1927 by Street & Smith Publications, Inc. Copyright © renewed 1955 by Dorothy Faust. Copyright © 1966 for restored material by Jane Faust Easton and Adriana Faust Bianchi. Acknowledgment is made to Condé Nast Publications, Inc., for their cooperation. All rights reserved.

'The Man Who Forgot' under the byline John Frederick was first published under the title 'The Man Who Forgot Christmas' in Street & Smith's *Western Story Magazine* (12/25/20). Copyright © 1920 by Street & Smith Publications, Inc. Copyright © renewed 1948 by Dorothy Faust. Copyright © 1996 by Jane Faust Easton and Adriana Faust Bianchi for restored material. Acknowledgment is made to Condé Nast Publications, Inc. for their cooperation. All rights reserved.

'The One-Way Trail' under the byline George Owen Baxter first appeared in Street

Editor's Note

The texts used for the short novels that follow are based on a concordance between the author's own typescripts and the versions that first appeared in Street & Smith's *Western Story Magazine*. The reason for this is two-fold. Frequently texts appearing in magazines had to be cut in order to fit in the space allotted, or upon occasion editorial intervention occurred for a variety of reasons that ultimately corrupted the text.

Table of Contents

Forgotten Treasure

'Forgotten Treasure' was first published in Street & Smith's Western Story Magazine *in the issue dated November 19, 1927. Subsequently, it appeared in a somewhat altered form together with the short novel, 'Chip Champions A Lady,' in a double-action mass merchandise paperback published by Tor Books in 1990. A slightly abridged version of this story is currently available from Audio Renaissance as read by Barry Corbin. This story of a feud of long-standing appears now for the first time as its author, Frederick Faust, wrote it.*

I

In the beginning, every Quince was fair of hair, and every Dikkon was dark. Every Quince was tall and broad, and every Dikkon was narrow and small. Every Quince had eyes of green. Every Dikkon had eyes of black. He who had made them so differently set down the families side by side in the mountains of Kentucky.

War, of course, followed and, though the Quinces were bigger and wider and correspondingly stronger, they simply offered a fairer target to the guns of the Dikkons. Finally, a scattered handful of the fair-haired giants packed their belongings and started for the far West. On the way a cruel band of Dikkons swept down upon them and harried them so dreadfully that, in the end, only two small families gained their distant goal.

But even these were not left in peace, for fate led the Dikkons in numbers to the same spot, and the feud began again. At last the name of Quince was reduced to a single man, and that man was outlawed. He married and left a son behind him when five of the Dikkons cornered him in a nest of rocks and paid three lives for his one. It was considered that the price was small, for the more the Quinces were reduced in number, the greater became their strength. Now that this dangerous father was dead, it only remained to comb the mountains and find the boy who lurked somewhere among them. He was but twelve years old, and therefore, when he was found, the last of the viper breed would be wiped out. So they searched for young Barney Quince. Twice they found his bullets, but they did not find him.

He eluded them, and again and again he dodged their searchers. However, the game became so hot that he was forced to leave that district. For three years he disappeared from the Dikkon ken, and their tribe increased and flourished. They nearly owned the rich town of Adare with all the valleys for farming and the highlands for grazing which lay around it. The Dikkons, and those who had married into the clan, dominated this region. They controlled the county, elected the officials, and above all saw that the dignity of sheriff constantly should be vested in a person of the right Dikkon lineage.

Then in his sixteenth year Barney Quince came back and fell upon them like a plague. Their champions rode out against him and came back with weary horses and some empty saddles, but they could not get Barney. They might cut him with their bullets, but they could not cut him to the quick!

He looked upon as his perquisite all that the Dikkons had. If he needed money, it was always a Dikkon he robbed. If he were lacking a swift horse, it was from the Dikkon herds that he cut out the best and the strongest. If he wished for meat, a Dikkon beef or a Dikkon mutton was his victim. All of this he did with the price mounting upon his head but his heart free from the sense of guilt for, it was apparent, he had been nurtured deeply in the lore of the Quince family. His mother had lived long enough to teach him all the past, poisoned with her bitter tongue. So he preyed upon the Dikkons with the subtlety of a desperado and the boldness of an honest man. His known boast was that

15

never a man had fallen before him except one who bore the name of Dikkon, never a penny of money had been taken at the point of a gun except money made by a Dikkon, and never a morsel of food would pass his lips except what he robbed from the Dikkons. He scorned to labor on his own behalf and swore, so that all should know his resolution, all that fed and clothed him should be reaped in a broad and rich harvest from the possessions of his hereditary foes.

For ten dreadful years he was a scourge upon the backs of the Dikkons. They hushed their children at night with his name, and every young Dikkon grew into manhood with a single glorious goal before him – to find and destroy Barney Quince!

One question was asked repeatedly by the clan: had Barney Quince married? No, not yet! Therefore, there was no son and heir to his name and his terrors. The Dikkons might not capture him, but at least they drove him here and there like a swiftly glancing shuttle through the mountains and the valleys so that he could not mate. If they could not take him with their net, at least the peril would vanish with him. Yet others said that he knew this well and would choose his own good time to marry. Before he died surely another of his name would be riding and destroying as he had ridden and destroyed.

This was not merely an occasional theme

with the Dikkons, but it mingled bitterly with the bread of every meal that was eaten in the town of Adare. The sun never rose upon their rich valleys, their standing crops, their flocks, and their herds without bringing the thought of Barney Quince coldly upon their hearts.

Consider, then, what horror, wonder, joy, and disbelief were mingled in the souls of the clansmen when, as they sat at their supper tables one evening with the rose of the sunset time beyond their windows, they heard a startled rumor that Barney Quince had come down into the town itself. They rushed out – all the men. The women and the children cowered behind. The armed men, resolute and stern – for when was a Dikkon a coward? – formed a solid van with rifles ready, and then they saw the strangest sight that ever dawned upon their eyes.

For a tall man was walking lightly down the central street along which their houses faced and behind him stepped a magnificent horse, a gray that glimmered brightly in the rose of the evening. They knew the horse, and they knew the man. When it was a magnificent three-year-old, the hope and the pride of Harvey Dikkon, the colt had been stolen from him by the marauder, and for three years now it had served to whisk the evil doer away from his pursuers. That was the gray and before him was Barney Quince, with his long yellow hair shining as it had shone many a time before, blinding the eyes of the Dikkon clansmen. But at the back of his head it was stained and clotted with blood. That blood, and his gay and careless manner as he descended into the town of his enemies, made his coming something that chilled their very souls, because it was a ghostly thing beyond human understanding.

It was doubtless this sense of the unearthly that caused many a rifle, raised to cover him, to fall slowly again, while the gunmen gaped and shook their heads. When he came to the very center of the village, old Ned Dikkon, with a cry, started out into the roadway and brought his rifle to his shoulder.

There was no doubt in his mind. As for a sense of ghostliness in this proceeding, he was familiar with the sad touch of the other world, for his two strong sons had been taken from him, his two gallant boys who stood in the very forefront of the clan for manliness and skill in all that makes a Western rider formidable and famous. They had been taken from him, and there came the man who had stopped their lives – both in one sudden battle of an August afternoon where the trail turns on the gray shoulder of Mount Forrest.

He shouted: 'Barney Quince, think of Pete and Charlie Dikkon that you murdered!' He pressed his steady finger slowly around the trigger.

That bullet would have found the heart of Barney Quince without doubt, but Oliver Dikkon, when he saw his older brother start out, rifle in hand, ran after him and came in time to thrust the weapon aside and then wrest it from his grasp.

'Man, man!' he called. 'You wouldn't do a murder?'

That broke the spell. A flood of excited men bound the hands of Barney Quince – those terrible hands which now submitted passively – and they led him to the nearest house which, by chance, was the house of Oliver Dikkon.

It was an excited crowd, and savage voices began to rise in it after the first shock of the surprise had worn away. Oliver Dikkon took control, not only because he was one of the head men in the clan, but because he now could exert a doubled authority as the owner of the house in which they were crowded. He called together the half-dozen recognized leaders of his people. The rest, though sullenly and ill at ease, departed from the dwelling and gathered in the front garden, overflowing into the street.

They did not leave but remained there leaning on their guns. Behind them came the children swarming, and anxious mothers after them telling them in shrill voices to come home again, for where Barney Quince was, there was peril. It was hopeless to try to convince them, however. They swarmed out as they would have swarmed to see the giant Jack killed in the story, filled with fear but also filled with expectant delight.

In the meantime the grim voices among the men were raised now and again. There was not one among them who had not had a father, a brother, a son, a cousin destroyed either by this man or by his hardly less terrible father. There were none who had not ridden, at one time or another, upon his trail. There were men who were scarred by his bullets. There was gigantic Ben Dikkon, for instance, who had closed with the outlaw in single combat on one heroic and never-to-be-forgotten day when he had been left for dead. Now the scars of that dreadful fight were on his body and seamed his face. He towered above the rest of the smaller, dark-faced clansmen, and he alone said nothing, but his set jaw and his narrowed eyes told nonetheless plainly what stirred in his mind.

The others looked at him. Having met the destroyer and lived to tell the tale, he seemed to them like some primeval force, greater than other men, half god-like. They would have welcomed speech from him, but speech there was none. So silence gradually settled over the entire assemblage. Even the children were quiet. Anxious eyes looked up and noted that clouds were gathering heavily across the face of the sun, and a wind cold as night blew down from the upper mountains. Some great event, they knew, was about to come to pass, and gloomily they felt that it did not bode well for the clan of Dikkon.

II

Within the house they sat in a duly ordered semicircle. At its right tip was Randolph Dikkon whose beard had been white for twenty years. Next to him was Eustace Dikkon, almost as old as Randolph but who, instead of turning white, had remained gray and, instead of withering, had merely shrunk a little and grown harder and harder. Little Henry Dikkon, on Eustace's left, owned a farm in Windale Valley and was prosperous enough for that alone to account for his place on the governing committee. John, beside Henry, had been educated in an eastern university and, growing soft in professional life as a lawyer, he alone graced Adare with a frock coat and a gold chain looped across his increasing stomach. Oliver had his place in this high body, well earned whether as a fighting man, or a shrewd councilor, or as the proprietor of the lumber mill which, on the river just above the town, harnessed the stream and made it do his bidding. Last of all was Martin Glanvil. He had married into the clan and was the first of a foreign name ever to sit in this august assemblage and, there-fore, despite his advanced years, he ever had the seat most to the left from the acknow-ledged master of the Dikkons. He was looked upon, to a degree, as an interloper, but the strength of his broad and patient mind had been tested often, and never had he been found wanting.

So the six wise men sat together and focused their grim attention upon the last of their hereditary enemies. He who alone stood between them and a permanent peace was now helpless in their hands. A cloth was tied around Quince's head for Lou – Louise Dikkon, the daughter of Oliver and the woman of the house – had washed away the blood and found a ghastly wound ridged in his skull. This she had dressed, and now close to the fire which burned on the broad hearth she watched observantly.

'He's had his head broken by a fall,' she told them, 'and his wits are gone. If you do anything to him, you've done something worse than the murder of a baby.'

Eustace Dikkon parted his hard lips. 'I remember the story of how the Quinces came down on the house of Jerry Dikkon in Kentucky and murdered the men, then locked the doors and let the women and the children burn. There was a couple of babies inside, I've heard tell.'

He expanded his thin, flinty hands toward

the distant blaze and rubbed them slowly together, but warmth was something he never would get into his flesh or into his heart.

'What's been done before by man or woman against the Dikkons ain't of account here and now,' pronounced Randolph, his hand buried in his beard, 'but only what's been done by this here man before us. Barney Quince, you stand up and answer what's asked of you.'

The prisoner, when he heard his name, looked up with a pleasant smile which made his handsome face actually beautiful for an instant. But then the light went out of his face, and he remained for a moment with lifted eyes, staring past the heads of the circle as if into some vast distance.

'You see!' said Lou Dikkon, 'he don't know a thing. You'd better put him to bed ... and hang him when he gets his senses back.'

'Woman,' said Randolph, 'leave the room!'

She could not argue against such resistless authority, but for an instant she lingered beside the prisoner and dropped her hand upon his great shoulder.

'He's done his killings,' she said, 'but he's never fought foul. He's never shot from behind. He's never been a snake in the dark. Dad, you won't let 'em murder this poor half-wit?'

Thunderous silence greeted this appeal, and she shrank from the room, only pausing at the door to cast back a single earnest glance at the big man who sat before the fire with its light glimmering through his long golden hair and touching on the sea-green of his eyes.

Still the silence held. Then the hard lips of Eustace parted again. 'Out on my place,' he said coldly, 'I halter-break the fillies as well as the colts.'

Oliver colored under this rebuke, but he made no answer. Old Randolph brought the talk back to its proper subject.

'I've called on you to stand up here, Barney Quince. You hear me talk?'

There was no reply. Barney Quince yawned broadly, touched the back of his head as though it had been stabbed by a pain, and almost instantly fell into a deep study over a cricket that was crawling across the floor toward the heat of the fire.

At this, Randolph said: 'He don't answer. What's to be done?'

John Dikkon felt the eyes of the others turning toward him. He expanded a little. One hand he hooked in his massive golden chain. The other hand he laid upon his smooth knee. He depressed his chin a little and said: 'In such a case one might proceed by considering silence an affirmation. Threaten him, therefore, that you will proceed in that manner.'

'John,' said the chairman, 'I reckon that

you know what this Barney Quince is said to have done. You open up and ask him, all lawyer-like, if you please.'

John stood at once. He took a position in front of the captive and, thrusting one hand behind his back, he made the tail of his frock coat stand out like the tail of a rooster. Then, leaning a little, he waved a fat forefinger like a club above the bent head of Barney Quince.

'You, Barney Quince,' said the lawyer, 'standing before this bar for judgment and in your contumacy refusing to answer the questions justly put to you and yet being subject justly to its authority, are hereby declared to have returned an affirmative answer to those questions to which you return no answer except silence. Hear me and reply if you have anything to say against this judgment.'

The captive, during the latter part of this little oration, had listened to the speech with a sort of mild wonder, raising his head and regarding the orator with a wandering attention. But now he chuckled softly and, leaning forward, he picked up the cricket and placed it farther from the fire and in the long hair of a bearskin rug – a skin which Oliver Dikkon himself had brought home after a desperate battle with the original wearer.

John Dikkon turned and bowed to the reverend head of the court. 'The prisoner returns no answer and thereby accepts the condition,' he declared. 'Shall I proceed with the examination?'

'D'you know what you're talkin' about, John?' asked old Randolph.

'Sir,' said the lawyer, 'you forget that I am a Dikkon. No man is more familiar with the outrages which are attached to the name of this man.'

'Go on then.'

The lawyer returned to the charge. Again his fat forefinger impended in the air. 'At the tender age of twelve years,' he said, 'an age when most men are children and unacquainted with the dreadful profession of arms, did you not, when three honorable gentlemen of the name of Dikkon were riding through the mountains, willfully assault them with intent to kill, actually shooting one horse from beneath the person of William Dikkon and striking Harry Dikkon through the shoulder, so that from that day until his death he never had proper use of the afflicted limb?'

'Go on,' said Randolph, 'you got a good memory, but just leave out the age of him when you talk about what he's done to us!'

There was an affirmative stir in the court. Barney Quince was still rapt with the cricket.

'The prisoner returns silence,' said the lawyer, 'and thereby admits the charge of willfully and feloniously assaulting the persons of three men, killing a horse, and seriously

26

wounding one man. A serious charge!' affirmed John Dikkon. He went on: 'Did you not, just three months later, in the middle of the night when two men entered your room in a hostelry known as Larkin's Luck, at a crossroads between Elkhead and Lewis's Crossing, willfully and with malice afore-thought, with intent to destroy and take the lives of those two men ... did you not, Barney Quince, with a gun in either hand attack them, shooting Gerald Dikkon through the hip and neck, so that he lay for months near to death. And did you not at the same time shoot Lawrence Dikkon through the head and through the body, so that he did instantly fall down dead in that room? Answer ... on the peril of your life!'

The prisoner did not stir, and something between a groan and a growl was heard from the six judges.

'The prisoner returns no answer, and by the agreement already entered into with him,' said the man of the law, 'this silence is accepted as an acknowledgment of the willful assault upon and murder of Lawrence Dik-kon, together with the willful and malicious attack upon and the vital wounding of Gerald Dikkon.' He made a little pause then con-tinued: 'Three years elapsed and then, on a December night, did you not, Barney Quince, descend from the mountains and raid the ranch of Rathbone Dikkon, taking from him forcibly and at the point of a gun two horses as well as a whole pack of guns, ammunition, and food of various kinds, being all that was in the larder of the said Rathbone Dikkon? And when he with his two sons pursued you, did you not attack the three and willfully and with malice afore-thought, with intent to slay, fire upon them, wounding Rathbone Dikkon through the right arm and taking the life of Jerome Dikkon, his eldest son?'

He turned to the court.

'The prisoner remains silent,' said the lawyer, 'and thereby he pleads guilty to the second charge of having taken the life of a good and law-abiding American citizen, by name Jerome Dikkon, who had acted merely in defense of his just legal rights.'

He made another pause and was raising his fateful right hand once more for fresh accusation, when the sharp and brisk voice of Henry Dikkon broke in: 'I dunno that there's any use asking the rest of the list, unless you can hang a man higher for fifteen murders than you can for two. Suppose that we start figuring what we're gonna do with this gent?'

The mention of the round number of actual deaths among the clan which had occurred because of this man caused a shudder to pass through the circle. Then there was silence, and all heads turned to Randolph Dikkon for his judgment.

III

He of the long white beard combed it for a moment, intently eyeing the prisoner, and the latter, as though wearied of the cricket, now stood up and raised above his head his roped hands. He stretched, rising on tiptoe, and the ropes that bound his hands together creaked mightily. At that, six-guns appeared swiftly from beneath six coats, but the ropes held, and the prisoner's hands fell before him once more.

'I guess I'd better be going,' he said.

Oliver Dikkon met him and caught his arm. 'You sit down where you were,' he said sternly.

The big man looked down on the other without malice and, nodding his head cheerfully, he answered: 'All right, if that's what you want.'

He sat down. He searched with sudden care for the cricket, found it, and replaced it on the bear rug. Then he settled back to a more earnest contemplation of its peculiarities. At last Randolph Dikkon spoke.

'We've got our man at last,' he said, 'and John says that he's admitted what we all know that he's done. I dunno what more we could ask for, and I guess that we've got trees high enough to do what we want of them. Eustace, you'd better take charge of him, and the quicker you get the thing over with the better for him ... and for us.'

Eustace rose accordingly, with a slight hardening, if that were possible, of his features and approached the prisoner.

'Stand up, Barney Quince!' he commanded.

The prisoner rose, and he smiled his beautiful smile at the little, frost-bitten Eustace.

At this, Oliver Dikkon started out of his chair and crossed to the pair. He tapped his elder cousin, Eustace, on the shoulder.

'Hold on a minute, Eustace,' he said.

'You always was fond of talking, Oliver,' said the older man. 'But I dunno that talk will serve us now. There's a hanging to be got done with, Oliver.'

'I was just thinking ... you're a man who's always handled dogs a good deal, Eustace.'

'And there's only one way to deal with a mad dog,' said Eustace readily enough.

There was a deep-throated murmur of assent, and Oliver nodded agreement. 'Certainly, you're right. But tell me, Eustace, when a puppy comes into your house and tears up a hat or a pair of riding boots, what do you do to it?'

'Thrash it, of course, and teach it better sense,' said Eustace. 'Stand out of my way, Oliver!' He said the last with a tone of anger, for Oliver Dikkon had interposed between him and the prisoner.

'I still have something to say,' replied Oliver, 'and I guess it's the rule with us that everybody has a chance to talk out what's in his head until Uncle Randolph overrules him. Is that right, sir?'

He of the white beard nodded gravely. 'Go on and talk, lad,' he said. 'I guess that nobody could improve on what you sometimes got to say! What's bothering you now?'

'I say,' declared Oliver, 'that there's no more difference between a grown dog and a puppy than there is between the Barney Quince that killed our men and the Barney Quince that's here in front of us now.'

This speech made a sensation, and hard-bitten Eustace said with a sneer: 'You kind of like this giant, Oliver. You kind of take to him, it seems to me.'

To this Oliver said sadly: 'I hope I've proved myself as good a Dikkon as you have, Eustace, though you're a good deal older than I am, and I suppose that you're wiser in most things. But I want to point out that nobody has lost much more than I have through this man. It was he that came down and burned my whole wheat crop and barn on my river farm, as anyone can remember. And my two nephews that were raised about as much in my house as in their own ... I mean poor Charlie and Peter ... they both were killed by this man. I mean to say that

I've got reasons both of hard cash and blood to hate him, and I think that I hate him as much as most of you do. But I got a couple of things to point out to you.'

There was a restless turning of heads to Randolph Dikkon but, since the old man said nothing at once, Martin Glanvil spoke up in his deep and growling voice: 'Facts is facts, and blood is blood. Unless they can be swallowed, this here man has got to die, Oliver.'

'Wait a minute,' broke in Randolph Dikkon. 'We've got to hear everything that Oliver has to say, if he keeps us here all night. Go on, Oliver!'

'Thanks,' said Oliver. 'Then I'll talk up and say what I've got to say. I want to remind you of the time when Bud and Luke, Sam Dikkon's two boys, started out and swore that they'd never leave the trail until they'd found Quince. They found him, as you might remember. It was winter. They got to a shack, and there they found the signs of Quince. They stayed there until the dark came down, and they lay quiet, ready to kill him when he opened the door.

'Well, he did open the door at last, and they turned loose at him. He fell down in the snow with a bullet through his left leg and, lying there, he shot them both. They surrendered to him wounded like he was, and they...'

'By heaven,' cried Eustace, 'I'm not gonna listen to this!'

'Steady! Steady!' said little Henry Dikkon. 'We've got to take the bitter with the sweet.'

'Then,' went on Oliver, 'he crawled in and took their guns. Bud was drilled right through the body, and Luke was shot through the shoulder so bad that his arm ain't any good today. And Quince stayed there in the cabin with his game leg and helped to tie up their wounds. For two months he kept them, and then he turned them loose, safe and sound, and let them ride down to the valley again. And Bud and Luke to this day ... they never will say a word against him. Is that all a fact, or do I make it up?'

A gloomy silence answered this statement and appeal.

Finally the speaker went on: 'Now, here we got Barney Quince. Did we go hunting for him? We did not! Did we get him by a fair fight? We did not! Did we buy him from his enemies even? We did not! But he walked in and gave himself up, you might say, because he'd been hurt worse than through the body or the leg. He's gone in the brain, and there he is for any of you to see that he's got an empty brain. Now, men, I say that the killing of a man like that is worse than the murder of a baby, and I'll work and fight against it as long as I've got a thought in my head and a drop of blood in my body.'

'You think,' said Eustace bitterly, 'that,

because you stand in with him now, he'll stand in with you later on when he's better!'

'How can he get better, once his wits have left him?' asked Oliver. 'Look at him, will you? Studying a cricket while we try him for his life.'

'Maybe he's playing possum,' suggested Glanvil sternly.

'Did that bring him down into the middle of our town?' asked Oliver Dikkon.

'Speak up, Uncle Randolph,' urged Eustace in the greatest excitement, 'and tell 'em that they're gonna bring down blood on their heads if they let this gent live.'

But Randolph Dikkon said not a word. Finally Henry broke in: 'I dunno how it is, but I got to agree with Oliver. That ain't a man there. It used to be Barney Quince. It's the size and the shape of Barney Quince still, but it's just an empty shell, it seems to me. There's nothing inside of it because a man with his wits gone is like a nut with the meat out of it. Killing Barney, here, you ain't killing the man that done the shooting of so many of our clan. It's like killing a stranger that never lifted a hand in his life to hurt nobody.'

This speech made two on the side of the prisoner, and all faces became grave.

John Dikkon burst out: 'I say that I hate the face and the name of him, and no harm can be done by putting him out of the way.

Let it be done legally, if you want. But let it be done. Bring him up for trial then.'

'Bring him for trial before Judge Postle-thwaite,' said Henry Dikkon, 'and he'll send him to a home for the feeble-minded before the trial's a day old. Ask your own good sense, John, and you'll see that that's true.'

The lawyer was silenced, though he shook his head in a sullen denial that had no meaning.

'Uncle Randolph, will you give us a judgment, here?'

The old man sighed.

'There's no good going to come of it,' he said, 'but, when two and two is put together, you got to say that it adds up four, and the two and two that you name here, it looks to me that it adds up to what Oliver says. This man is no more than a baby. The Dikkons never have loved the Quinces, but we never have been baby-killers. I guess that's about the end of things. Call Louise, Oliver, and ask her to get me a cup of coffee. I kind of have a need for it before I go home in the cold.'

Oliver went gladly to obey the order but, before he reached the door, Eustace whirled upon the others and raised a thin hand above his head. It was quivering with his wrath.

'I hear you talk, you gents,' he said. 'I hear you talk, and it's all very fine what you got to say. You talk about babies and such. But I talk about Barney Quince, and I tell you that

35

you'll never again have the chance that you've got now. Here he is that's done all of the murders and, if you let him go, you'll never have the like chance again. God forgive you all if you set him free to start on the trail again. More of us'll be hunted down. For the fifteen that he's killed already, a hundred is apt to drop before the finish. Besides, he'll have the time and the chance to leave a son behind him to carry on for the name of Quince where he left off. I've got no part in this decision. I say that you're a parcel of fools. I'm going home, and I'll be damned if ever I come to another council of the Dikkons. Get another to take my place!'

IV

The head of Barney Quince healed in due time and never for an instant did it make him an invalid. He was constantly about the house of Oliver Dikkon, sometimes wandering into the fields and sometimes climbing about the great lofts of the barn, where he seemed to take a peculiar pleasure in getting as far aloft as possible. Then, sitting on a great cross-beam or dizzily poised on the derrick rod which projected above the door of the mow, he would fall into brooding. Time seemed to him of no more moment than it is to a roosting owl. At night he slept in the hay, and often on the coldest nights he stretched himself on a mat in the kitchen in front of the stove. His long life in the wilderness had made the softness of a bed apparently distasteful to him.

He was not altogether simple, even though it seemed impossible for him to understand most of the words which were spoken to him. For instance, he allowed no tear to appear in his clothes without sitting down at once to mend it with a scrupulous fineness of handiwork which no woman could have surpassed. His skill at this suggested to Louise Dikkon other means of employing him, so that he might be useful to the family which supported him now and also to himself. The doctor of the village of Adare could only suggest that constant occupation would be better for the poor, deranged, stunned mind.

Barney Quince was at the disposal of Lou Dikkon because, from the first day, he looked upon her with a great attachment – not as a man to a woman but rather as a dog to a master. He would follow her about the house for hours. If she sat down to her sewing, he sat down cross-legged on the floor nearby and seemed perfectly contented. If she went for a walk, he ranged with her, wandering with his rapid step here and there, sometimes running to a distance but always circling back. Her father was alarmed at this constant attendance, but gradually everyone came to understand that Barney Quince was utterly harmless.

So Louise began to employ this useless, mighty engine. She tried him at first at the woodpile where the dried oak, hard as flint from the seasoning it had received, had to be sawed into convenient lengths and then split. With her own hands she put the heavy and cumbersome cross-cut in position and guided it for him. For the greater part of a day she worked at the lesson before he could learn what was wanted. Then he sawed through a segment readily enough and, as he grew warm with the work and rolled up his sleeves, she watched the sinewy muscles playing snake-like up and down his fore-arms. Then she understood why the warriors who were the pride of Adare had been help-less in the hands of this giant, and she felt a great awe, much as may be felt by a trainer who compels lions to do trifling tricks.

It was very hard to make progress with him. When he had sawed through a log, he would come into the house bearing a ponderous section in his hands and offer it to her with a smile of childish joy. She had to lead him back and replace the great saw at the proper point. It was a week before he could understand the whole business of wood-sawing, but after that he advanced into the huge pile of timber like a fire. When the sawing was done, she taught him to split the chunks to appropriate sizes, and then with much patience she instructed him in cording the wood in the shed. He seemed to feel no burden in these labors; and sometimes she would pause in her kitchen work, hearing out of the distance a great voice that swelled into a phrase or two of song. Only a little moment of music and then a long silence, as though the fumbling brain had picked up a happy thread only to lose it again almost at once.

After this start had been made with him, it was increasingly easy to teach him other tasks. She taught him to milk the string of cows and pour the milk into the pans in the creamery. How to churn, and how to fork down the hay for the teams so that their mangers were filled when they came in from work at the plow. She even attempted to teach him to work the plow, but in this she failed utterly, for he persisted in leaving the team standing in the field while he came back to the house to her. At any distance from her he was unhappy, bewildered, and through the day he had to come to her again and again and stand silently by, reading her face with an expression half intent and half wistful.

She became fascinated by her duties as schoolmistress and tried him at reading and writing, but here she had no success whatever. For though he might sit down and write off a whole sentence at dictation with a rapid and flowing hand, yet in the middle of a word the machine might stop and refuse to start again that day. In the meantime, however, he had become a profitable worker and Oliver Dikkon, estimating his value with a strict sense of honor, paid monthly wages into the hands of his daughter to be used for her protégé as she thought best.

She was seen walking down to the store, with the giant stepping softly behind her. He stood by, vaguely pleased, while she bought clothes for him or shoes. There was one heart-stopping moment when he paused by the rack where the rifles stood and, taking out one of the best, opened the chamber and reached with an automatic hand for a cartridge, fumbling blindly when he discovered that he was not girt with the long-familiar belt. However, he let her take the weapon from his hands, and she led him away, past the pale-faced clerks.

She talked to her father about this incident, and he considered it for a long time before he made the most unexpected answer.

'You've got to let a man work along the lines that he knows,' said Oliver Dikkon. 'A fine cowpuncher may be a fool at books, and a bookman may be a fool with cows. A good miner might die of dry rot being a clerk. So with Barney Quince that has lived by the gun for his whole life, pretty near ... maybe one thing that keeps him back is not having a rifle, say, and plenty of chance to use it!'

'And...?' she began.

'And if he should ever use it on a man ... why the man would be dead, and we'd have to kill Barney. It's a hard chance to take. But I think that there's no danger in him now. There's no meanness, and there's no malice. I'm going to let you take him my best rifle tomorrow.'

She was full of fear, but she recognized sound reasoning behind this advice. That same day she placed the rifle in the grip of Barney Quince and put on him the cartridge belt. For two days he was helpless with joy, sitting with the gun in his lap, admiring its brightness, patting it like a living creature. The third day he was found cleaning it. The fourth day he disappeared!

Terror ran through the entire village of Adare. Swift messengers were sent to outlying workers in the fields. In dread and in silence they waited. But in the evening a giant walked from the shadows of the trees and strode across the fields carrying on his shoulders a deer which would have been well nigh a burden for a horse. He kicked open the kitchen door and laid it at the feet of Lou Dikkon. Then he stood by, panting with his vast labor, and laughing out of the joyous fullness of his heart. All Adare breathed once more.

After that, there was hardly a day when he

41

did not slip off from his other duties and hunt in the fields, in the woods, over the hills. He brought back rabbits, squirrels whose heads had been clipped off as though with a shears, deer, partridges. The larder of Oliver Dikkon's place was crammed with fresh meat, and his neighbors came to bless the gun of Barney Quince. It was at this period also, as the spring turned warm, that he was put on the trail of the lame grizzly which for three seasons had devastated the valleys, choosing with a nice taste the best of the yearling colts, dining once upon each body and then departing to come again.

For a week Barney Quince was gone, and Eustace Dikkon vowed that he would never be seen any more. He was seen, however. With a great bearskin rolled on the back of a burro, he trudged home to the house of Oliver Dikkon and laid the massive spoils before his mistress.

From that moment the attitude of Adare toward Barney Quince altered perceptibly, for up to this time the villagers had looked upon him as a public menace, a danger postponed but inevitably sure to fall. Thereafter it was felt that his old identity had been lost forever, and that he had become a public benefactor. Moreover, they derived a rather sinister satisfaction from the knowledge of what he had been, and what he now was. When they saw him striding down the street behind his mistress, resolutely refusing to walk at her side, they could not help smiling, one to another, for this was as it should be with a Quince! He was better than dead. His old self had perished. He lived only to serve his enemies like another Samson with bonds not upon his body but on his brain.

Lou Dikkon was aware of the public attitude, but her own differed. She took great and greater care that he should not be made an open show. When small boys formed the habit of running after them, her father was sent to call on their parents. Gradually people came to know that Oliver Dikkon and his daughter respected this hulk which once had been so great a ship, and for the sake of Oliver Dikkon the smiles were ended.

So the bright heat of summer came to Adare, and with it came the usual thin drift of Easterners, arriving for a vacation among the mountains. Most important of these holiday-makers was that great and good man, Dr. Mansfeld, from New York. On the very first day of his arrival he passed on the street the smiling face and the blank eye of the giant, and he stopped short and turned to look after him. Of course, he had already heard the story. And that night he came to the house of Oliver Dikkon and asked to see this stricken man.

He found Lou Dikkon at the piano, drawing accompaniments out of its untuned strings, while she sang like a bird. Leaning on the piano, stood Barney Quince. He allowed his head to be examined with perfect indifference. Afterwards, when Lou went to bed, he went after her to lie in the hallway across her door. The doctor remained behind with Oliver Dikkon.

V

The doctor went straight to the point. It needed no special skill, he declared, to tell what was wrong with Barney Quince. It was the fall which had stunned him, of course, that had made him a half-wit or something little better. The reason he remained in that condition was simply that a segment of skull had been permanently depressed and bore down upon the brain. Now, there was one chance in ten that an operation would kill the patient. There were four chances in ten that the operation would do him no good. There were five chances in ten that he would be completely cured and made as intelligent a man as ever he had been before.

Oliver Dikkon listened, growing more and more tense, and his brown face lengthened with gravity. Finally he said: 'Suppose you win with him, Doctor Mansfeld. Then what'll he be?'

'An intelligent, alert man once more.'

44

'D'you know what kind of a man he was?'

'I've heard that he was a rough character, but his experiences recently, no doubt, will have tamed him. You have been kind to him, Mister Dikkon. That kindness can't be forgotten.'

Oliver Dikkon mused: 'When he got the blow on the head, it wiped his memory clean. Lift the bone and probably he'll go back to the time when he had the fall. Ain't that possible?'

'It is,' agreed the doctor unhappily.

'Fifteen men have been killed by Barney Quince,' said Dikkon. 'They were all my kin. Ten of 'em lived in Adare. I say that if you bring him back to his wits, so's he'll remember his own name, then he has to stand trial for fifteen killings, and the trial will be before a jury of Dikkons, and there ain't any doubt of what the verdict would be. You'd only be saving him to hang him, Doctor! If he didn't hang but got away, there's many a strong and brave man alive today that'll die under the guns of Barney Quince before he's ended with a bullet through his head.'

All of this the doctor considered, and he could see the strength in the argument. Yet he was pushed on by earnest devotion to his art. He argued: 'Quince is already dead, and this poor creature who fills his body is neither man nor beast.'

'He's a man!' insisted Dikkon. 'He does a

45

man's work, too, and he's worth his pay. I'd rather have him the way he is than any other two men on my ranch. What more do you ask for him? He's happy. He loves my daughter. She can make him do anything. She's teaching him a little more and more all the time. Maybe he'll wake up entire, one of these days, except that he won't know he's Barney Quince and born and raised to kill me and my family. Ain't there a chance ... that he'll get pretty normal, I mean?'

'There is no more chance of that,' said the doctor, 'than there is that he'll walk to the moon. I leave this matter on your conscience, Mister Dikkon. If I were in your place, I should not like to have on my mind that I've stood between this man and his true self.' With that, he left.

Two days later Dikkon came to the hotel where Mansfeld was putting the finishing touches to his preparations for the mountains.

'I've talked it over with my daughter,' he said. 'I didn't call in the older heads of my people because I knew beforehand what they'd say. I've talked it over with my daughter, and she's been driving me on to it. If you say the word, she'll bring Quince in to you whenever you wish.'

So that matter was arranged, and the doctor hurried on with his work, arranged for a room that would serve for the operation, found by keenest good luck a skilled assistant, and prepared his instruments.

Early the next morning, Lou Dikkon came to the hotel, and behind her walked Barney Quince. She stood in front of great Dr. Mansfeld and said to him, all pale and still of eye: 'If ever Barney Quince kills another man, Doctor, what will you think about it?'

The doctor did not like this view of the matter. He said something about the necessity for serving the will of nature with the skill of science. But he was so ill at ease that he rushed on with the preparations, and soon Barney Quince was alone with the doctor, his assistant, and half a dozen strong fellows who were to help during the anesthetizing process.

That process had hardly begun before there was a violent disturbance in the operating room. Wild cries were heard. The door was split clean in two, from top to bottom, and Barney Quince rushed out, shaking off the last man to cling to him. Lou Dikkon blocked his escape and, taking his hand, she led him back into the operating room. At sight of it his nostrils flared, and a dull light glowed in his eyes. But at her direction he lay down again on the table, and he allowed her hands to tie on him the bonds which had driven him frantic before. Then she explained the process of anesthetizing as well as she could. It was plain that all was a cloud to his weak understanding, but he clung to her hand and fixed his great, dog-like eyes upon her.

'It's all right, Lou?' he asked her.

'It's all right,' she said.

She stood by with her hand resting upon his shoulder, and so stood while he lay without the slightest motions of resistance. She grew dizzy with the fumes of the ether. The doctor pronounced the state of unconsciousness complete, and she was allowed to leave the room. But as she reached the door, a shout and a sudden struggle called her back.

The giant had ripped across the cloths which tied his hands, and four men vainly were striving to keep him from sitting up. Lou hurried back, and in a few seconds the patient lay passively under her hand.

'It seems,' said the doctor in deep bewilderment, 'to be rather hypnosis than ether. You'll have to stay here, my dear young lady.'

Stay there she did and closed her eyes to keep out the sight of what was being done. But she could not keep out the sound of hammer on chisel head, or the hideous dull noise of chisel on bone, or the sound of the saw, or the low voice of Dr. Mansfeld pointing out details to his assistant as he proceeded.

Once, indeed, she opened her eyes. There was a whirl of confusion, in the midst of which the doctor raged with terrible fluency and volume. Black mists rose before her eyes. But then she steadied herself and clutched her fingers into the quivering muscles of Barney's shoulder. After that, there was quiet again. She began to reel with weakness.

Still the work went on, and the long silence continued. Still she dared not look. Perhaps this doctor with his demonic skill was taking her out of the soul of poor Barney Quince with chisel and saw.

'Lou!' said a choked voice.

'Steady, steady!' she murmured.

The giant was still once more, and her heart leaped with a wildly selfish joy. He had spoken her name – her memory, then, had not been wiped out!

She felt there was something of devilish magic in this labor of Mansfeld's. But in the meantime, she was chained to her post, though her knees began to tremble. Then a hand touched her shoulder, and a voice said quietly: 'Drink this, Miss Dikkon!'

She looked up into the face of the doctor. His bristling, wax-tipped mustache, his glittering eyes, and his pointed beard made her feel that she was staring at some devil incarnate. She drank what he held at her lips – something pungent and stinging.

'Courage!' he said. 'Without you, we can do nothing! Courage and strength, my dear child!'

He patted her shoulder, but she knew that

there was no kindness in the touch. It was totally perfunctory. She happened to be, for him, a necessary instrument at this moment, and therefore she was worth conciliation – until the work had ended. But the drink gave her fresh strength.

Another long, dreary interval passed. A buzzing came in her ears and, through the buzzing, a voice boomed distantly: 'She's going to faint, I think.'

'Let her faint ... the job's finished!'

That was the voice of Dr. Mansfeld, like the booming of a cannon. Afterwards, faint she did and felt arms receive her. She shook off the weakness instantly as she heard a groan from the man on the table. That was the shock that cleared her brain again and enabled her to stand to her task. Someone was explaining something to her

Ah, yes! The operation was finished. It was successful! Now, if she would walk beside the stretcher as they carried the patient only into the very next room...? She walked beside it with fumbling steps. Fresh, untainted air blew about her from the open windows, and then she was sitting beside the bed of the patient.

Up and down the room walked Dr. Mansfeld. He was speaking. She heard only snatches, as he talked about difficulties – uncertainties – pressure on the brain – the brain itself – the mystery of thought. She hardly knew what all these long combinations of words meant, but she knew that she was ordered to sit quietly there. She was willing to do that, for the face of the sleeper wore, in flashes, the same beautiful smile with which she was so familiar. When he awakened, surely he would be the same. He stirred.

'He's going to waken,' snapped the incisive voice of the doctor. 'Now, my girl ... you're fond of this fellow. Then lean over him. Imagine you're facing a camera. Look pleasant, please, and...'

The eyes of Barney Quince opened. They were no longer blank but filled with a wildly delirious light. 'Steady, Jerry ... steady, you old fool.' And then the voice rose to a great shout. Barney Quince sat up in bed. 'Hello, hello!' he murmured. 'That was a crash and ... who are you?' he asked and looked straight into the face of Lou Dikkon.

VI

Somehow she was out of the room and feeling her way blindly down the stairs. At the bottom brilliant sunshine blazed before her. She put her hand to her face and found it wet.

'I mustn't cry,' she said aloud, and feebly. 'I've got to be steady, steady!'

So she took a firm hold on herself, and

made her step light as she reached the street. A shadow came up beside her and took her arm.

'What happened?' asked her father.

She clung to him weakly. 'Get me home ... I'll try to talk there,' she said.

So they hurried together, but it seemed that the little village street had been stretched out to weary, stumbling miles before the familiar door of the house opened to them. She lay on the parlor couch, her eyes closed and her father holding her hand.

He was saying very gently: 'It was too bad. I didn't want the chance to be taken. But he said it was only one in ten, you know. And, after all ... poor fellow! What was there in life for him, Lou? I'm sorry too, though. It chokes me actually. There, there, honey. You cry. It'll do you good.'

She shook her head. 'It isn't what you think,' she managed to say. 'He's alive, but he's worse than dead to all of us. He's forgotten me. He's the old Barney Quince!'

In the hospital, the doctor ordered quiet and, when he heard that sharp incisive voice of the patient, he leaned above him and said in a tone of command: 'Quince, you're all right now. You've had a bad accident. You'll have to lie still. In two weeks, perhaps, you'll be able to leave. Perhaps a month. Perhaps ten days. You seem to have the strength. But now, you'll have to lie still. Do you understand?'

Barney Quince looked at him from thoughtful eyes and said nothing at all. But he obeyed the orders with the strictest patience, and for many and many a day he lay still and studied the ceiling and spoke not at all, except to say good morning and good evening.

Then the doctor came back. He had been away on a brief excursion, and he visited his patient before the next mountain trip was undertaken. He came in cheerfully and found himself looking down into a pair of stern and quiet eyes. It seemed to the doctor that never before had he looked at a face so heroically formed for strength or so beautiful in feature.

'Well, Quince,' he said, 'how are you?'

'Able to ride, thank you,' said Barney Quince.

'As soon as this?'

'I'm able to ride,' repeated the patient.

'Perhaps in a short time but not yet. Has the time gone slowly with you?'

'No,' replied the other, 'because I've lain here and had a chance to think things out ... only there's a lot that I can't piece together.'

'Have you asked any questions?'

'No.'

'None?' exclaimed the doctor in astonishment.

'People always tell you what's really worth

hearing and good for you. And the other sort ... why, it ain't worth asking for, is it?'

The doctor smiled a little at this rather profound philosophy. Then he sat down and lighted a cigar.

'What do you last remember ... before you came to?' he asked of the patient.

'I remember my horse sliding down a bank and losing his balance when the pebbles began to slip under him. Then I crashed. It was like being hit hard on the point of the chin. That was all. After that, I woke up here.'

The doctor nodded. 'Nothing in between?'

'No.'

'Not a thing, then?'

'No, it's a blank.'

'Shall I fill in the blank for you?'

'If you want to.'

The doctor began to drum the tips of his fingers against the arm of his chair, always regarding the sick man with an intent gaze. 'You'd better find it out for yourself,' he said then. 'It may be a lot better that way. Do you know where you are now?'

'I got an idea.'

'What is it?'

'It's a thing that I don't like to talk about.'

'Ah?'

'Because I figure that I'm in Adare.'

'It's true.'

'And I'd rather be in any other place.'

The doctor nodded. 'I've heard a little bit

about the trouble between you and these townsmen,' he admitted. 'But now I want to give you a little advice that isn't exactly medical. You can't leave this place, Quince. They've put guards under your window and at your door. You have no weapons. The thing for you to do is to stand your trial like a law-abiding citizen. Face justice, Quince. It's always the best way. Forget your old life and prepare yourself for a new one.'

Barney Quince smiled, but his only answer was to ask quietly: 'Where would I be tried?'

'Here in Adare, of course.'

'The judge would be a Dikkon,' he said, 'and all the jury would be their men.'

Dr. Mansfeld rubbed his chin and found no more to say. He received the thanks of Barney Quince, and presently he squared his shoulders in the outer day and turned his thoughts to the upper mountains. He had done his work, and he had done it well. As for the consequences, after all he could not pretend to be both a doctor and the body of the law.

So Barney Quince was left alone and, now that he knew the situation he was in, he adapted himself to it as swiftly as he could. The doctor had ordered another fortnight of absolute rest for his patient, and the men of Adare were not prepared to arrest their enemy until the medical man had pronounced him fit to go to jail. This much they would make sure of, lest afterward the law should be brought down upon their own heads. In the meantime they kept their guard in place, changing it at regular intervals.

It was a costly business to tie up so much man power, but the expense of it and the trouble were small things to them. The important point was that Quince lay in their power, and therefore they made the net strong and waited with unwavering patience for the appointed day.

Barney Quince was laboring to bring back the strength which he had lost by lying so long prone. It was no easy task, for a dozen times by day and a dozen times by night the door of his room would be softly opened and someone would look in upon him silently, and silently the head would be withdrawn after making sure that all was well. He could not even be sure of the intervals between these espials. Sometimes he might have two hours free from disturbance. Sometimes not two minutes elapsed between the spying glances that were turned upon him.

To circumvent this crafty observance, he used the utmost patience. Lying in his bed, he went regularly through small movements which would exercise his muscles – such as arching his body on head and heels, or thrusting himself up from his spread arms, or lifting both legs and keeping them raised until the great thigh muscles shuddered with effort. All of these things he could do with movements which were utterly noiseless and which needed hardly the slightest disturbance of the covers of his bed. The result of these patient exercises was that the discarded mantle of his strength gradually returned to him, his chest arched, and power tingled down his arms to the tips of his fingers.

Yet, with the strength regained, it was no easy matter to use it for his escape. He lay on his side at the edge of his bed and scanned the ceiling and the wall. They were of smooth, newly made plaster and could not be broken without noise. Then he stole to the window at midnight and looked down to the street. It was a sheer descent of twenty feet, much too far to be jumped, and just opposite he saw two riflemen seated, waiting patiently, should he attempt to climb down, both wide awake even at this hour.

The window and the ceiling and the walls were hopeless as outlets, and beyond the door waited the second guard. There remained the floor. It was of tough strips of pine, held down with new nails, and covered, in part, with a rag rug. Through that floor, nevertheless, he knew that he must go, and constantly it was in his thoughts. He had one tool: a pocket knife which they had disdained to deprive him of because the longest blade was well under two inches in length. However, with that tool he had finally determined to attack his problem.

To be sure, the blades were short, but they were wide and strong and made of the very finest steel, with chisel edges. He fell to work. Lying on his side, the cot was so very low that he could reach the floor with either hand. He turned back the rag rug and began. If three of the sections of the boards could be cut through and lifted out, then there would remain beneath him the lath and plaster work of the ceiling below. But the laths could be cut through quickly enough, he could be sure.

He started, conscious that there were two great dangers to its consummation. One was the fear that the spies at the door might look in upon him and find him at his labor. The second was the terror lest the rag rug should be stripped off the floor and taken out to be beaten. On Saturdays that work was usually done. This was Tuesday on which he was commencing his work, and he must trust that the daily sweeping would be done without disturbing the rug too much. As for the constant spyings, he trained himself to baffle the spies. He never worked except during daylight, and then with one eye he constantly regarded the knob of the door. It was kept so well oiled that it could be turned without the slightest sound, but it could not be turned without the motion becoming visible. Watching that, the instant there was the slightest disturbance the rag rug was jerked back into place, and the prisoner-patient was discovered lying on his face on the cot.

This required that his nerves should be drawn to the breaking point at all hours of the day, but it was a price which he had to pay, and he paid it willingly. As for the cuts he made in the boards, the long strips of the tough wood that he whittled away were tucked into the mattress on which he lay, for he had made an opening in a seam for that very purpose. He made the cuts very wide, which facilitated rapid cutting, but the instant the rug was moved he would be discovered. It was a peril which he had to accept.

He did the cutting, first, at the point which he had chosen farthest down from the head of the bed. It required until Wednesday night to complete that work. Then he attacked the upper cut and went through it in a single day of hardly interrupted labor. And still he had all Friday before him – his escape he planned for Friday night.

As he tucked the last shaving into the mattress and with a smile patted down the hard little lump of wood which had been formed there under the seam, the door opened with its usual softness. Eustace Dikkon entered and came to the bedside, and with him was a spectacled gentleman. The latter set out stethoscope, thermometer, and the rubber tubing of the instrument for taking blood pressure. Then he began his examination and went over every inch of the leonine body of the sick man. Eustace Dikkon stood by with no expression in his rock-like face.

'Temperature normal,' said the doctor. 'Pulse normal and strong. Heart excellent. Blood pressure normal. Muscular condition excellent. In fact, I've never heard of a man in bed so long whose muscles retained their temper so well. I should say, Mister Dikkon, that this man is perfectly sound in every way ... infinitely above the average. He's in a super-normal state of health.'

Eustace Dikkon let his eyes rest for a single instant on the face of the captive and never was malice and determined hatred more plainly visible. That single, glowing glance and then he withdrew from the room.

Young Barney Quince lay rigidly in the bed. Somewhere out of the distance a clock was striking. He never had heard it before, but now all his faculties were roused by excitement to a super-sensibility, and he tolled off the faint pulse of the sound. It was ten o'clock and, as fast as Eustace Dikkon could prepare adequate quarters in the jail, Barney Quince would be brought there to wait for his death.

VII

A stir began in the hotel – a passing of many feet to and fro, the sound of subdued voices in the halls, and the sharp creaking of the stairs under the weight of people who hastened up and down. Barney Quince slipped softly from his bed, from the closet took shirt and trousers, and stepped into them. As for shoes, he was better off without them for his purposes. As he turned from the closet, the door of the hall yawned open swiftly and silently, and a great shaft of light beat into the room. His first impulse was to leap straight at the spy; but softly the door was shut again. He heard no sound of hurrying feet or any exclamation.

Might it not be that, glancing at the ruffled clothes of the bed, the watcher had told himself that Barney Quince was still there? A thousand times they had looked in, in this fashion, and a thousand times all had been well. However, there must be no such sudden interruption as this in the moments that followed.

He picked up the one chair, stole close to the wall – where there was far less chance that a floor board would creak under foot – and then to the door. With the greatest care he braced the back of the chair under the doorknob. Returning to the side of the bed, he threw back the rag rug. There was a dim light faintly filling the room, from the great gasoline lamp which burned until midnight over the entrance to Whitney's Stables across the street. By that light, as he raised the pine board through which he had cut, he could examine the work which remained under his hand. The lathing was wide but the strips were thin, as if made to order for his purpose.

All the great power of his wrist went into his work as, making the notches wide, he labored around the edge of the gap in the floor. There were a hundred grittings of the knife against the grains of the plaster. Twice the blade squeaked in the wood, but the disturbances continued throughout the hotel and the noises he made were apparently confused with what was heard elsewhere.

Once or twice he paused to listen and, in those pauses, he was aware of subdued murmurs in the hall outside his room, murmurs of many men gathering there. It was certain that Eustace Dikkon was making surety doubly sure by marshaling a little army to conduct the prisoner to the jail. Then came a sharp crunch of wood against wood. The door had been thrust inward, but the chair stuck at once and yielded, screechingly, only a bit.

'What the devil is this?' exclaimed a roaring voice. 'What deviltry is up here? Some of you boys put your shoulders against that door!'

Barney Quince was in a whirl of rapid

action. The upper layer of the laths he had cut through. What remained below, beside the tough plaster, he could not guess. He swept the spread from his cot and wrapped it around his bare feet. Then he leaped into the air to the full of his power and brought down his two hundred pounds and the drive of his stamping legs in the center of the hole.

There was a crash in answer and a great sagging beneath him. At the same moment the door was struck by the weight of several strong men, yielded, then jerked open, the chair skidding before it. Half a dozen of the posse men spilled headlong into the room. Again Barney Quince leaped, and this time he drove straight through the lathing and the plaster work beneath him. Down he dropped as through a trapdoor. The rough edges of the lathing rasped at his clothes, ripped his body, but he fell headlong on the floor of the room beneath.

It was an unoccupied bedroom, as he saw when he sprang to his feet and shook the dust from his face. Above him, pandemonium was breaking loose. Feet were thundering on the stairs, voices shouting. He leaped to the door. It was locked! Glancing upwards, he saw an arm ending in a revolver reach down.

It was like the flash of a spur in the eye of a frightened horse. Sideways Quince sprang at the door, and it split before him as though it were thinnest cardboard. Into the hallway he stumbled and lurched straight into the arms of two men who had turned onto the landing of the stairs at full speed.

They clung to him valiantly, but his impetus carried all three over the brink of the stairs and brought them whirling and crashing down. In a way it was as though Barney Quince were the core of a rolling ball. The impacts which he might have received were muffled by the bodies of those who clung to him and, as that spinning mass of humanity crashed against a lower, angling wall and lay still, Barney Quince rose from it to his feet. The other two remained motionless.

Something glimmered on the landing. He scooped it up, and now he stood armed with a loaded Colt. Half the barrier between him and freedom was already crossed. He was in a place of utmost peril, however. From the stairs above him a flood of armed men was descending, swerving around the landing places, thundering on the steps. Just below him the narrow lobby of the hotel was alive with men who had rushed in from the street. There was no escape by turning and striving to shoot his way through the numbers above him, but in the confusion beneath there was some hope.

The central light which hung from the lobby ceiling was quivering back and forth in a slow arc, so greatly had the old building been shaken by this turmoil. One shot from his Colt shattered it to bits, and a shower of burning oil flamed wildly down over the heads of those beneath. Yells of terror and pain went shrieking up. To either side the men of the clan split apart and, through the narrow channel between them, Barney Quince fled on racing, naked feet.

Straight in his face, and from either side, half a dozen guns belched fire at him, but those shots were aimed by guess and from quivering hands, and the target was running like a stricken deer. He leaped through the doorway, swerved, but the speed of his going made him lurch over the side of the front verandah. He landed in the soft, pulpy dust and so darted around the corner of the hotel.

Before him rose a tall board fence, a wall of blackness. A bullet jerked past his ear with a rising whine. With a bound and a throwing of his body to the side, Barney Quince rolled over the top of that fence and dropped into one instant's freedom from peril in the dark beyond.

VIII

No, hardly a single instant of safety was his. Around the front of the hotel the pursuit was spilling and, though these clansmen had been unsteadied hitherto by the surprises with which they had been confronted, he knew that thereafter their aim would be almost as deadly as by day. Also he heard the back door of the hotel crash wide and the heavy impact of many of the pursuing men who leaped clear of the rear stoop and landed on the ground beyond. A brief instant of confusion covered the eyes of Barney Quince as with a veil. Then his head cleared, and he ran onwards.

He could run fast and far, but just beyond the village lay rough ground that would cut his feet to ribbons. Besides, what is the speed of a man on foot compared with the speed of a running horse? And horsemen would begin to rush out from the town of Adare to find him. They were mounting now in the street; the thunder of hoofbeats was beginning and the yelling of the riders!

He went straight on, crossing the vegetable garden in which his feet drove ankle-deep through the soft sod. Swinging in a high vault over the fence beyond, he found himself in a little corral. Half a dozen horses leaped and rushed to the farther side of the enclosure.

Out of the distance behind him yelled a voice: 'He's at the horses! Chuck! Toby! Come on, boys! Don't give him time to saddle!'

Time to saddle? No, there was not a second to be spared for that but, crouching in the shadow of the fence, like a panther in a cattle yard, Barney Quince eyed that frightened knot of horseflesh. He saw one arched crest that lifted above the others, and he knew that whether he lived or died it must be upon the back of that horse.

There was no time for a hesitating, gentle approach, no time for a soothing word. He had to accost that group of horses like a charging beast. If he reached his target with his spring, then a ghost of hope could rise in him once more. If he missed, he was a dead man, and he knew it well.

So he leaped from the fence shadow and darted forward. They split before him, rearing and squealing in their haste, but past a snaky head that snapped savagely at him he swerved and saw his chosen horse plunging to get through the mass and escape. He aimed for the mane with his hands and missed it but, as he leaped, his legs coiled around the shuddering loins of the horse, and a squeal of terror answered him.

He was nearly torn from his place by the lunge of the great animal. A smaller gelding went down before the big mare. Barney Quince was in the seat now, and one hand was twisted deeply in the flying mane as the horse hurled herself into the air.

'He's got a horse! By heaven, he's got Christie!' shouted someone from the fence top.

A gun flashed, and a bullet sang. Aye, they

shot close to the mark by day or by night, the clan of Dikkon, but the great glimmering bay whirled Barney Quince around the corral like a flying comet. She crashed through the scattering herd again, and he was nearly torn from his place as she plunged clear, bucking madly still. No stirrup or girth or pommel to cling to, no spurs to lock in the cinches, no cantle to keep him in place, still he clung like a bit of her own flesh, and she flashed around the circle again.

It was a maelstrom of wheeling, squealing horses. A thick cloud of dust darkened the air like a fog. Guns flashed through the mist, and there was the groan and fall of a stricken horse. What purpose, however, in milling here, while the clan gathered around the corral? Yet how to break free? Certainly no kind hand would set the gate ajar for him!

He transferred his gun to the hand which was tangled in the mane. Then he reached back with his free fingers and sank them in the soft flesh of his mount's flank. He closed his hand and turned it. The result was a veritable scream of agony from the tortured mare, and she flung straight away at the fence. It was built high to hold wild creatures from the plains and none wilder than she had ever stood within it, yet she soared toward it like a bird. Her heels cracked in a sharp tattoo on the upper bar, and then she was over and rushing faster than the wind across the open ground beyond.

Bucking could not dislodge this torturing devil that clung to her. Then she would daze and bewilder him with the sheer speed of her flight. Yes, like an arrow she drove through the darkness. A black cloud rolled before them – trees and no reins to turn the flying mare. Clinging close, Quince leaned far over and prayed for luck. Boughs reached him like tearing hands, branches scourged his face like the lashes of whips, but then they were through.

Before them water flashed, but the mare rose nobly at it. A broad, pale face, it gleamed below them – then she was across with a shock on the farther bank that nearly tore Barney Quince from his place. Scrambling cat-like up the slope, she broke through the farther screen of trees – and before them rolled the hills and the sacred heads of the mountains high against the stars.

Still she flew, and Quince laughed with savage joy as he felt her speed. Let them try to follow, no matter how light their weights, how good their saddles, how keen their horsemanship. For where is there a saddle so good as fear? Where is there a spur so sharp as utter terror?

Then he began to soothe her with a gentle voice, his hand on her neck and passing gently back over the flank which he had torn at with his grip of iron. She heeded nothing.

She was sleek, dripping, slippery from sweat; foam flew whitely back from her mouth, open as though a cruel curb were tearing at it.

They rocked over the hilltops and pitched wildly down into the hollows. Not till the first long slope of the upper mountains rose before her did the mare's gallop slacken and fall first to a staggering canter, then to a trot. She was beaten at last, but only after such a burst as those hard-riding men of Adare never could match with their best and bravest. From a wall of the gulch up which they were passing, Quince tore a long arm of trailing vine. From this he made a rope which he knotted about the mare's neck and then slipped to the ground.

She came to a dead halt, head down, ears falling loosely forward, legs braced. He felt her heart. It thundered with a rapid hammering against his hand, jarring his whole arm and body. A little more and she was dead!

He had to beat her down to the edge of the boiling creek. Once there, she stood shuddering, sagging at the knees, untempted by the cold water that foamed under her very muzzle. He began to wash her down, whistling a little, to occupy her attention while he swished cold water over her legs, over her neck, and then gradually rubbed down her body. For a long and aching time he labored over her, until at last she gathered her legs under her and reached for the water.

He allowed her only a swallow then dragged her tired head away and walked her up the cañon floor. Every few minutes he paused and rubbed her vigorously again. Then he passed on, tugging her after him. There was not strength enough in the vine rope. He had to drag her by the mane and sting her flank with his open hand to keep her in motion. It seemed that she never would come back to herself.

The gray of the dawn began as they climbed wearily out of the cañon and reached an upper tableland which made one mighty shoulder of old Mount Chisholm. There he paused, regarding the mare anxiously as the light grew. She was a red bay, long necked, deep of barrel, with, it seemed, Herculean quarters fit to bear the burden of the world. She seemed to have forgotten already, in her great and generous heart, the terror which she had felt for him. When he stood close, she laid her head against his breast and sighed like a weary child.

It seemed to Barney Quince, as he stroked her wet neck, that all the adventure of his stay in Adare – that strange and cloudy stretch of months of which he had no memory – and the fall in the mountains and the labor of his escape with all its perils had been preordained merely to bring into his hands this peerless creature. He tore up some bunch grass and offered it to her. Twice she sniffed it and turned her head away. He ripped up a bit more choice, dew moistened. This time she nibbled at it with feeble interest, and her ears raised and stiffened a little. Barney Quince stood back from her and laughed aloud. For he knew that that long battle for her life was ended, fought and won!

From the next runlet he let her drink but not her fill. Instead, he pulled her head away and went on slowly. In the back of his brain there was a great weariness, but he kept it out of his consciousness. All that he could be aware of was freedom, sweeter than wine to his taste.

He kept steadily on but, when he came to a tempting bit of pasture, he paused a little and let the mare graze, which she began to do greedily. She was coming back to normal rapidly. Her back no longer was partly arched, her belly no longer tucked up and gaunt and, though she stumbled now and then, when he had rubbed her down with twists of grass as the sun rose, nearly her whole strength seemed to have come back to her.

He turned now, high on the shoulder of Chisholm, and looked far down into the valley of Adare. He could not see the town because it was blanketed with blue morning mist, but the church steeple rose like a narrow blade of light. Barney Quince stood in the flaring face of the sun, and he laughed again.

IX

There were five shots remaining in the revolver of Barney Quince. With those five shots he killed a partridge and a rabbit the first day. The second day two more rabbits had to go to fill his hungry maw. On the third day he ate nothing at all but stalked ceaselessly to find bigger game. On the fourth day he slipped like a snake through a thicket and put a bullet into the heart of a deer just as it gathered its legs to leap.

For a week he lived on that meat and nothing else, and he lavished his time on Christie. It had taken her several days to recover entirely from the terrible strain of that flight from Adare, but now her full strength was back. She had forgotten the agony of her fear with which that ride began. She remembered instead the care and the kindness and the deep, soothing voice of the man in the time of her exhaustion. For let no one think that a horse cannot respond soul to soul, the animal to the man, both linked together by one common element of the divine. Christie had found her master, and she knew it with a profound certainty.

It was easy to teach her. She would follow

Quince uncalled by the end of the second day; by the end of a week she would stand where he left her, grazing only in a small circle. At the pressure of his hand on her neck and the sound of a certain whisper, she would lower her sixteen-three of might and muscle to the earth and lie still, head stretched forth from the ground.

He trained her for mountain work. Indeed, mountain bred, it was not difficult for her to walk on a narrow ledge, or slide down difficult slants, or pick her way among the sharp-toothed rocks. But though she improved greatly under his tutelage, still he knew that with that length of limb, that mighty bulk, she would never be a true mountaineer. She lacked that deer-like activity which is essential. The quick ups and downs broke her. Her wind left her in the labor of handling her own weight. No, she was meant not for dodging in and out along the coast, fighting the tidal roughs, clipping up narrow rivers and bays, skimming through shallows, turning in her own length, tacking like a restless midge. Instead she was meant for the open, like a great square-rigged clipper cleaving a way from China to the Thames. When once her swinging stride was driving her without effort, regardless of two hundred pounds on her back, running at half her power she could leave gasping and heartbroken behind her the very same cat-like mustangs which would catch her in no time among the hills.

These things Barney Quince pondered darkly. Those mountains were to him as home or home grounds are to most men. They were to him walls of safety, and the narrow and twisting ravines, and every cave, and every pothole, and the condition of every run in dry weather and wet, and all states of the passes according to the seasons, and all the upper trails, iced or piled with snow, were printed legibly in his memory. As it were, he turned the pages of a book and read at will. Should he abandon this, it was much indeed that he gave up.

He knew the valleys also, and the wide deserts and the rough, inhospitable plains into which they merged, chopped with sharp-edged draws, broken now and again by the high, ragged head of a mesa. But traveling there was different. He knew the water holes, and he knew many of the people, but the region was not so thickly dotted with his friends as were the mountains, where a few dollars spent with wise caution here and there ensured him of safe harborage and true friendship. On those perilous plains below, his enemies could hunt him glass in hand and dull beyond imagining would be the eyes that failed to recognize the looming outline of Christie with such a rider on her back!

There would be need of all her speed, down there, he had no doubt. They would bring out their Thoroughbreds, their flashiest speedsters to catch him. They would send afar off to experienced manhunters and mount them with the best and send them out to run him in relays.

Lying on the edge of a tableland that jutted out like the prow of a ship on the ridge between Lorimer Mountain and the Little Standup, he studied the lowlands for a hundred miles beneath him. Then he sat up and set his teeth. He was going down and let the Dikkon clan beware of his coming.

He started straight back for Adare, reached a thicket a few miles from it an hour before sunrise, and camped there for the day. Then he went on again when the night had gathered. It was the first time that he had come to pillage in the town itself. He had struck here and there on the outskirts. He had plundered outlying ranch houses of size. But he had not made his mark in the center of the town itself. The danger had seemed too great.

However, on this night he walked on into the village, with Christie left in a clump of poplars on the verge of the place. He looked about him with a calm eye of possession. To his distorted reason, all that he saw was as good as his. For, surely, it was true that the clan of the Quinces once had been stronger in numbers, richer in horses and land, than ever were the Dikkons. Yet in the bitter warfare back in Kentucky, by craft, by cunning guile, by the subtlety and the silence of Indians, by gathering in numbers and striking at few, the Dikkon clan had beaten down his own, harried them out of the country, sent them almost beggars into the West.

Then, with deathless malevolence, they had followed, and once more the Quinces were ruined. It was something like the story of Hydra – and, when one head of a Dikkon was cut off, two new ones came to take its place. Where he'd killed some famous fighting man of the Dikkon name, two stalwart sons now were growing to maturity, seasoning their hatred for him and practicing with their guns. For nearly fifteen years no target had seemed worthwhile to any Dikkon save the target of the living Barney Quince. All his wounds of knife and bullet burned in him and printed their pattern anew with an electric tingle.

He went straight down the middle of the central street. There were lights in the hotel and saddled horses standing in front of it – no doubt a late game of poker was dragging on there. The long rays gleamed upon him as he went past. He felt the lightness of his empty Colt. Still he did not dodge into the shadows – skulkers are the first seen and the first shot at.

He came before a big store, calmly turned the corner of the building, and at a side window he tried his hand power. The window was latched, but the latch was weak and rusted. It gave with a sudden snap and squeak under the pressure and slid up. He waited, his head canted toward the ground, but he heard no sound.

He slipped through the window and carefully closed it again. It was pitch dark inside the room, so he lighted a match and, by its first glare, he scanned the nearby counters and the loaded shelves behind him. Clothes – but he could attend to clothes and shoes later on. What he wanted now were guns and ammunition, and he began weaving back and forth among the counters straight to the far end of the store. There he laid his hand upon a barrel of cold steel.

He stopped and straightened, struck with a sudden wonder. Surely he never before had been in that store. How did it chance, then, that he found the gun racks? These were the rifles. Then where were the revolvers? In his mind a picture seemed to rise – the revolvers were ranged on a rack just opposite, behind his back. He turned, groping in the dark, and laid his hands instantly upon them. Sweat stood on the forehead of Barney Quince. It was, indeed, as though some ghostly voice had guided him and guided him aright.

Ammunition, then? Well, try the second counter over to the right and under it in cases. His hands were instantly upon the boxes. He loaded the two new Colts – he was so perfectly familiar with the weapons that he could take them apart and assemble them in utter darkness – and then he sear-ched for a cartridge belt – two rows of pockets in it, the lower for rifle cartridges, the upper for revolver. Somehow he knew that he had seen them lying on a counter – yes, just behind the ammunition layout. There, indeed, they were. He filled the belt. He gathered up his revolvers, and the comfortable length of the rifle, and went to the clothing department again.

He had more difficulty there, and he had to risk the lighting of a dozen matches before he had found what fitted him. Shoes were even a greater labor. The lapse of time began to tell upon him, and the nerve strain made his hands tremble. But he was equipped from head to foot at the end of an hour. Slicker, boots, underwear, socks, shirts, a pair of good blankets, a Stetson, some silk bandannas, and the guns. He went back to the other counter and dropped some extra cartridges into his pockets. One never could have too many. Then he heard the noise of a key fitted ever so quietly into the lock of the door.

The new and heavy boots made no diff-erence to him. Silently he stole across the store and shoved up the window without a noise equal to a whisper.

'Who's there?' called a frightened voice.

Gun poised, he turned. He heard a stumble

79

and a faint curse in the distance. Some nerveless watchman had seen, or thought he had seen, the flare of one of the matches that Barney Quince had lighted. Now, like a fool that holds a lantern for his enemy to shoot by he came, announcing his coming. But Quince was already through the window and standing safely on the ground outside when there was a flare as the big gasoline lamp of the store was lighted. He peered in and saw the poor watchman crouched, his rifle at the ready, peering around him at the shadows and apparently frightened almost to death.

Barney turned away with a chuckle and started to return to Christie. But the way was to be longer than he had planned.

X

As he reached the back yard of the store, he heard the double explosion of two shots fired in rapid succession from the interior of the big building. A window slammed wide, and a voice shouted loudly into the night: 'Robbery! Thieves! Help! Help!'

Barney swung himself up to the top of the board fence and hung there, regardless of the dangerously clear silhouette which he cast against the stars for any watcher, any chance prowler. He waited, listening eagerly for the result of his mischief-making to become apparent. Presently there were answers from up and down the street and almost at once the spatting of rapid hoofs in the dust. No doubt the gamblers at the hotel had responded to the call. Windows began to open, and doors were slammed. He heard distinctly fragments of conversation as men strode up the street, and he heard deep cursings. The men of Adare seemed incredulous. It was not possible in their eyes that any man should dare to invade their precincts, their innermost circle, to plunder.

Very clearly he heard one prophet cry out: 'If it's anyone, it's Barney Quince! It's him, come back to cover his nakedness!'

Barney dropped down on the farther side of the fence and jogged comfortably on down the line of back yards. He was passing a vine-covered stretch of wire netting when he heard the crunch of footfalls, too soft and light to be more than half guessed at and, before he himself could swerve, a man of Adare swung around the corner. They were so close to one another that Barney had not even time to whip out a gun. Instead, he darted a long left into the face of the man and then chopped a heavy right-hander on his jaw.

After that, he slipped back a little to give the man room to fall, since fall he must – for nothing living and calling itself human, surely, could resist two blows from the fists of Barney Quince. The other fell, decidedly, but he fell inwards and cast his arms around Barney as though to support himself. He was a Dikkon. Barney could be certain of that by the silence and the malevolence of the fellow's fighting. He was not tall. There was no giant in the clan. But the man was exceedingly broad and, when he fell against Barney's chest, it was as though a pillar of iron had dropped against the taller man.

Then the thick, slow arms of the unknown man moved around Barney Quince. He found that his left arm was bound against his side by the encircling pressure. The other arm of the stranger was biting into his ribs. There seemed literally no end to the strength of the man. He kept throwing in fresh power until Barney felt the wind going from his great chest. He knew with a sense of terror and of awe that for once in his life he was overmatched in sheer, Herculean strength.

His right arm was only partially imprisoned. He managed to tear it free and, then poising it, he struck. The trip hammer does not need to fall far, and neither did the leaden fist of Barney Quince. Twice and again he let it fall on the face of the squat man, and three times he felt his knuckles bite deep and jar against bone. But the man did not stir. He merely freshened his grip with a might that threatened to crush Barney's spinal column.

The latter changed his aim and, drawing

82

back that lethal weapon, his right hand, he drove it home behind the ear of the stranger. The latter slackened his hold. One thrust and Barney was away from him, but still the enemy, though staggered, had not given up the battle. As a bulldog, having lost a grip, waddles steadily, resolutely in toward his foe, so this vast, squat, ape-like creature came waddling toward Barney Quince.

Something like fear came into the proud heart of Barney then, for half a dozen times he had smitten this fellow, and still the man had not gone down. He was almost tempted to draw a gun and fire, but he saw that his assailant, as though stunned, thought of nothing but hand-to-hand combat, and Barney Quince disdained to refuse a meeting on any grounds to any foe.

He fell back a little from the silent advance. Stepping in, deftly and lightly, he brought to bear the full weight of his body and the full smash of his active arm and wrist – and felt his hand jar home on that spot known as the button. Solidly and with all his strength he smashed. It was almost like hitting a rock. There was merely a small sagging of the head of this monster, while the half-broken hand of Barney Quince dropped back to his side.

It was unreal and ghastly. Quince felt his blood turn cold with the awful conviction that this could be no man after all, but some vast and horrible gorilla which presently would leap on him and bury its fangs in his throat. For still the monster did not fall but slowly waddled toward him, extending his arms like something without sight, feeling octopus-like for his prey. Wild terror arose in Barney Quince. He could, of course, whip out a gun and end the struggle with one well-planted shot, and against this beast-like creature he felt that gun powder alone should be used. Yet, doubtless, it was a man, and like a man it should be battled. So, his heart in his throat, he plunged swiftly in again, his teeth set and his eye narrowed.

His right arm dangled almost uselessly at his side, so terribly had the shock of the full stroke numbed it to the shoulder, but with the left he was well-nigh as strong, and with the left he smote now to the full of his power. Once again there was the true finding of the jawbone; and once more there was a shock as though beating against a house timber. Quince's numbed arms swung idly, foolishly at his side. He hardly could have drawn a weapon now if he had tried, and certainly he could have struck no mark with any gun.

So, scorning to fly, he stood before the squat shape. Indeed wonder and horror made it quite impossible for him to move from his place. A hundred times before, in his adventurous youth and in his manhood, he had fought with his bare hands, whether wrestling, or rough-and-tumble such as the miners delight in, or else standing off and fairly squaring away at an antagonist. In all those years, since he was a half-grown youngster, he had not known the man, no matter how vast of bulk, who could retain his senses after being struck fairly on the jaw by his fist. Yet here was one who had withstood two such blows as never before had he dealt – blows which he felt must have crushed the heads of normal men.

Half a dozen mortal seconds that squat bulk stood before him, its arms still outstretched, but its advance ended. It seemed more terrible than all else to Barney Quince that the figure made no outcry, no shout for help but simply stood uncertain. Then slowly, heavily, down upon one knee it slumped, both ape-like arms fell and supported it, and Barney Quince could see that the whole bulk was wavering a little from side to side.

The second punch, then, had told the story but, with a true fighting instinct, the stranger had still presented himself as if for battle. Barney hesitated. If he went on, this colossus might arise and follow him. If he remained long, he would have to resume the battle. There was nothing that Barney Quince wanted less than to taste the power of those arms a second time.

He jerked out a gun, for a tap with the

long barrel of the Colt might be decisive. But he found that the weapon hung in air. It is no easy thing to strike a helpless man. So he turned away and ran straight toward the nearest trees – but then changed course at sharp angles behind the screen of them and hurried down the line of the village houses, anxious now to get back to Christie, where that good mare waited for him, still without a saddle. He cut in closer to the houses.

There was no such uproar as he had expected after the robbery was discovered. Instead, the people of Adare appeared to be returning to their houses. Only, in the distance and scattering here and there, Barney Quince made out the separate poundings of many riders, as they went on their way through the night. He was pleased by this. In all things the Dikkon clan worked sensibly, quietly, never making a vast uproar. Indeed, they were efficient men, efficient fighters. Though his blood boiled at the thought that they should have destroyed another clan of such men as himself, still he knew that there was a mighty force in them. Often it is easier for a hundred men to beat a hundred than it is for them to beat one. At least, one mounted on such a creature as the mare, Christie!

He dipped back toward the line of the houses, bent upon gaining a saddle fit for the mare. The first place that caught his eye was discarded for the sake of the second which was now made out against the stars in the near distance. He examined it as he came up with an odd feeling, as though he had seen it before.

As he came closer and saw the peculiar sway in the back of the barn, he told himself that this had been observed long before. Yes, he could swear to it. To the right and below that sway, on this side of the roof, there was a broad patch of new, unpainted shingles. Would that he had the daylight now to test the truth of what he had guessed. With his hand on a corral fence, he bowed his head and let his half-wakened memory work.

Down at the left hand was the granary – then the great barn with the work horses ranged upon the one side and the mules upon the other. There on the right was the feed shed for the winter cattle, when they were kept up, and for the milch cows. That smaller structure was the creamery where the flat tin pans stood in long, waiting rows. And yonder, above the trees, arose the pointed roof of the house itself. Beneath that roof was some delightful, some wonderful, some heart-devouring thing of beauty! What could it be? On that point his mind was blank.

XI

Like some creature that cannot see but is

drawn on by another sense, like that of scent, Quince drew nearer to the house. It was very dangerous, he knew, to linger too long close to the village of Adare, now that it had been roused against him, but he could not resist the temptation. It forced him back from the barn, through the rear gate of the yard, and through the narrow path that pierced the vegetable garden.

He found himself taking the close turns by instinct, as though this were a place long familiar to him. Again and again he paused and tried to shake from him the impulse which urged him on, and still he was forced ahead with an invincible power that led him under the edge of the outhouses which lay behind the main buildings, across the soft lawn, and so beneath a window outside of which was a little balcony overhung with a vine. He knew that vine was starred with small pink blossoms as clearly as though the sun now shone upon it, and the sweet frarance was also familiar to him. With every breath of that perfume the emotion drew deeper into his very soul, and he stared at the open window above him as a thief might stare at the entrance to a king's treasury.

It was not wealth of money that lay within. What it was, indeed, Barney Quince could not tell himself, but he actually laid hold upon the stout stem of the vine as though about to venture up the stalk. Then reason overcame the emotion. He forced himself back from that house with a reeling brain, telling himself that he was turning mad indeed. For what could lie inside the house of any Dikkon except hatred for him, guns prepared, and bullets straightly aimed?

He made a little detour, driving himself ahead, but every step he took away from the house was a step of pain. Still he made reason command him, and so he reached the next premises, and there he searched for a saddle and the proper equipment for Christie. He found it with the same unerring prescience which seemed to give him sight in the dark.

He passed the barn and went to a little adjoining shed, opened the unlocked door, and found within a range of saddles. He selected one that suited his purpose, took blanket, bridle, and all necessities. With the considerable burden he started back toward the spot where, so long ago, he had left the mare. It required skulking across the main street, but this he ventured over safely with not a sound or a sight to alarm him. He came eventually close to the little poplar copse where Christie should be.

Nearby, he flattened himself against the ground and listened. For the ground is a sounding board which sends out vibrations more distinctly than the thin air. Yet he heard not a sound except a faint gritting and grinding, and he took that to be the mare grazing quietly in her small preserve. He stalked closer, on hands and knees, thrusting his new rifle before him, when suddenly the tall form of Christie appeared out of the wood, and she whinnied to him in a whisper.

Very glad was Barney Quince to spring up and throw the saddle on her back, while she sniffed at his new clothes and tried to nip them away, to get at the man she knew beneath them. He made wild haste, for it seemed to him that he had been wandering through a region of ghosts and that the instincts which had been guiding him were such promptings as witchcraft, say, brings to light in the heart of a man. Badly frightened indeed, he could not recall ever having been so happy as when at last he could leap into the saddle and thrust his feet into the stirrups. He cast one wild glance around him and then headed Christie for the open ground.

He had half feared that the new burden might clog her speed, but he was reassured by the first stride she made. She floated away with him and all his equipment as though the whole were thistledown and she a wind to carry it. Then the wide valley received them, and the stretching darkness lay deep and thick between them and the lights of Adare. He drew her back now to a soft trot, and still he rode with his face toward the village, for a strange debate was raging in him.

Reason, sternly and steadily, told him that Adare was thronged with enemies who would laugh as they killed him, as dogs pull down a wolf. Yet that blind, strange instinct with a powerful hand checked him and almost turned him back, seeming to say in the clearest of voices that behind him, in Adare, a treasure beyond counting waited for him, a treasure that was neither gold nor horseflesh nor weapons. What it was then he could not imagine, but he knew that his heart leaped wildly, and a frantic joy took him by the throat. It was as though he rode on some lofty and dizzy mountain ledge and were tempted to fling himself into the air, assured that wings would bear him up and carry him swiftly over the white summits beyond. That temptation raged like a fever in his blood, and yet common sense told him that such a flight was terrible, unavoidable death.

At last he turned a resolute head to the front, and yet in five minutes he had turned again and brought Christie to a halt to stare at the dwindling rays of light that shone out and reached after him like hands through the darkness. Desperately, he gave Christie his heel and, while she rushed at full speed ahead, he set his teeth and closed his eyes. When he opened them again and glanced over his shoulder, all was darkness around him. He was in the silent heart of the desert with the feeling that he had escaped from fate. He had carried off a full accouterment at the expense of aching ribs where those terrible arms of the stranger in the dark had crushed him. Rarely had there been a more profitable and easy adventure.

Yet Quince was not at rest, for he told himself that fate, after all, cannot be avoided. If he dared to question his heart, it told him that surely, before many days had passed, he would be led back blindly to Adare – and to what awaiting him?

By the stars and by the dim front of Mount Chisholm behind him, he laid his course with surety now and came at the end of two hours of easy travel to a small house between the glimmering face of a great tank on one side and the shadowy bulk of a string of cottonwoods on the other. Behind the house was a ragged line of sheds and a tangle of corrals, but all was on a small scale, so that even in the night the house seemed a pitiable thing, scarcely able to endure the withering heat of the sun and the sweep of the winter winds. He went to the front door and kicked heavily against it three times. He reined back and waited. Almost at once, a voice called from an upper window.

'Who's with you, Hilary?' asked Barney Quince.

'Hey, Barney,' shouted the man of the

house. 'I thought we'd never have the luck to see you again. It's all safe here. Nobody but me and the girl. Feed your horse in the shed. I'll be down...' As he turned from the window his voice was heard more dimly calling: 'Marjorie! Marjorie! Hey, wake up! It's Barney come back to us!'

It soothed the puzzled heart of Barney Quince to hear this cheerful welcome. He fed Christie in the barn, and then he came back to find Hilary Clarkson hurrying toward him in the starlight.

His hand was wrung. He was led by the arm into the house, and there was pretty Marjorie, her eyes dancing, her nose a little more freckled than ever, dressed in a blue gingham wrapper. She gave him both her hands – which is *not* the Western way! – and then she made a tremendous racket at the stove and half filled the air with dust as she shook the ashes from the grate. Immediately the fire was blazing, the coffee pot was on, the frying pan began to smoke – as, with lightning hands, a place was laid on the clean oilcloth which covered the table.

'She's great, ain't she?' said Barney Quince in admiration to the father. 'What a woman she's turning out, Hilary!'

'Tell it to her,' grinned the father. 'She'll listen to you ... maybe. Now lemme hear about yourself ... and what happened to you, Barney, in Adare?'

93

But a shadow fell over the mind of the guest at that word. He set his jaw and frowned. Then he shook his head and made answer: 'I'll talk about anything else. I don't want to talk about that.'

'Hey?' cried Clarkson. 'But smashing your way right through the whole mob of them ... and getting clean off, bareback, on Steve Dikkon's best horse! The finest mare, they say, that ever stepped inside of Adare. Man, you mean you won't talk about that?'

'I'll talk about that,' said Barney slowly, 'but nothing else about Adare ... it makes me a little sick, Hilary. I ain't myself. My nerves are turning upside down ... and I dunno what's wrong with me.'

The rancher nodded sympathetically.

'You take the life that you've been leading, and everything that's happened to you lately' – here he touched the back of his head and nodded significantly – 'and it's sure to upset you some way. I tell you what, Barney, there's only one thing for you to do.'

'Well, lemme hear?'

'It's simple and plain as the nose on your face. Change your name. Go north. Go somewhere on the range where nobody ever has seen your face. Start life over again, dead quiet ... and ask a woman to be your wife ... one that ain't afraid to rough it with you.'

'Ah?' cried Barney Quince. 'A woman? A woman?'

There was such a strange note in his voice that the girl by the stove started and then bowed closer over her cookery, a deep crimson flooding her face. But Barney Quince was looking far off at his thoughts, and he saw nothing that lived in that room.

XII

Now, in the dark of the room which was assigned to him, he sat at the window and looked across the plain, wide and level as a sea. These faithful friends, he knew, would watch over him and guard him like a member of their family. He could remain here safely until the next evening, when again there would be danger that the pursuit from Adare, passing out from that village in increasingly great circles, might reach as far as this. Yet safety from the pursuit of his enemies was not his concern. Safety from the assault of his own mad impulse was what haunted him.

For still he could breathe the fragrance of that shower of unseen bloom beneath the window of the unknown house in Adare, and still the memory of that perfume went into his mind like the rarest wine, and the house itself rose before the eye of his imagination, like something not once but a thousand times seen. Yes, it seemed to him that he could have opened the side door – he knew well that the key was kept beneath the mat – and he could have passed silently, even in the darkness, from hall to hall until he came opposite the door of that same chamber whose window he had stood beneath.

He buried his face in his hands, for the mere thought of the door, like the memory of the window, made his pulse leap wildly. It was only by a vast effort of the will that he was enabled to force himself into his bed. There he lay face down, his arms wrapped around his head to shut out the world of sight, the world of sound, the world of all imaginings.

He slept at last but a wild and broken sleep in which he dreamed that he dreamed, and the dream became reality, and reality became the dream, so that he sat up in the morning, pale, faint, with a heart that fluttered weakly in his breast, as though he had been climbing mountains all night long.

Marjorie was already up and at work in the kitchen. She gave him a smile from an open heart, but he walked past her with a nod and went to the barn. On the way he passed Clarkson, who hailed him cheerfully. Christie, at least, would be something actual, a sunlight reality. No, when he saw her, though she filled his eye as a perfect mount, he could not help remembering that he had won her from the semi-fabulous town of Adare. Therefore, she was a part of the dream, she was the ever-present link that connected him with the past! How had he come by her? Where would she bear him? Back, of course, to the town. Back until he stood once more beneath that fascinating and dangerous casement, clad with vines and with immortal fragrance.

Barney Quince felt his brain reeling. He harnessed the mare. The saddle was in his hand when he knew what he must do, and he hurried out to find Clarkson milking his one cow.

'Hilary,' he said, 'have you got a pony here?'

'You mean something to carry you?'

'Yes.'

'I was in and looked at the mare you borrowed from Steve Dikkon,' grinned the rancher, 'and you'll never need a second while you've got her to carry you.'

'I want to change with you,' declared Barney Quince. 'I'll trade her for any good mustang that can pack me through a day's march.'

Hilary stared. 'I wouldn't have enough cash in a year's income,' he said, 'to pay you the boot you'd need.'

'I want no boot,' said Quince bitterly. 'I'll give you the mare. You give me the mustang. We'll be quits.'

Clarkson shook his honest head. 'What I've done for you is too little, old man,' he insisted. 'You want to give me something. You ain't got the cash, so you offer me your horse. Well, that's like you. But I couldn't take her. You don't owe me a thing. Why, Barney, you've always overpaid me.'

Barney Quince grew wroth. 'I tell you,' he exclaimed, 'that all I want is to leave that mare behind me! I don't want her. I'm finished with her. She... I'd rather ride hellfire than ride her!'

The rancher stared again but with a vastly different expression. 'If that's really the way of it ... well, there's my string in the little pasture. You go and take what you want.'

Barney Quince took a roan. It was a lump-headed creature, with little wicked eyes, but he felt that that humor would suit him exactly. So he packed that sturdy mustang, with the inward assurance that, if the little horse could not go fast, at least it could go far.

He returned to the house and, pausing near the door to scan the wide plain with a joyless eye, heard the rancher saying: 'I dunno what's wrong with him. He talks sort of crazy. It's the fall that he got, I suppose, and he'll never be the same man again!'

'Fall? No,' said Marjorie, 'it's a woman. I know! When they get that wild, sad look ... they're crazy about some girl. Poor Barney!'

Again, as on the night before, an electric shock leaped through the body and soul of Barney Quince. A woman! He felt as though a prophet had spoken out of a holy text; there could not have been more truth. There was a woman at the base of all his trouble. At the back of his brain, if he could make some vast effort, he would be able to visualize her features. It was the terrible and joyous hope of seeing her in the frame of the window above the balcony that had made his heart swell. It was the thought of her that had brought him to the door in the house of the stranger. Fate again! Yet, what a black curtain of uncertainty had fallen across his eyes.

He went in and had his breakfast and, when it was finished, he paused at the door, his quirt coiled in his hand, and leaned above pretty Marjorie.

'Marjorie,' he said, 'I heard you telling your father what's wrong with me. Are you sure of it?'

She, crimson, trembling, could not meet his eye, and her glance wavered from side to side. 'I don't know, Barney,' she managed to say. 'I don't know ... you ought to know ... best ... yourself.'

'God bless me!' said Barney Quince. 'Are you crying, really? Why? Look here, honey. The next time I come near a town, I'll find a present for you and bring it back.'

The unbidden tears still streamed down her cheeks, but she clenched her hands and stamped. 'I don't want your presents!' she cried at him.

Barney shrank awkwardly out of the house. He did not understand. Neither did he know, indeed, why Hilary Clarkson smiled grimly on one side of his face as he bade his celebrated guest adieu. But he was sure enough that all was not well between the family and himself.

He rode across the desert, aiming his course toward the pools which stand between Claverhouse Crossing and the Little Run. There he would water, rest his horse a day, and then start on through the real heat of the desert and its long, flat marches. He had only one direction in his mind and that was away from the town of Adare on the straightest line. He was putting between him leagues which, he felt confident, would blot from his mind the temptation which kept swelling there. He realized that Marjorie was right. He was in love and for the first time. In love with a nameless thing, a ghost, a thought, a nothingness.

Squaring his shoulders, he continued on the march, only turning now and again to scan the horizon behind him and all around. It was in one of those moments of observance that he saw a group of small black spots against the sky. He paused and looked at them with the greatest care. They gradually grew larger. He made sure by the rate of their approach that they were horsemen. With strange troops of riders he must take no chances, so he sent the mustang into a gallop and rocked steadily along over the loose sands.

For half an hour he kept up the pace and then looked back to make sure the four specks had disappeared. By no means! Instead of disappearing they had grown vastly larger, and he could distinguish them now without the slightest trouble. Four riders and undoubtedly mounted on blooded horses. Where could they come from except from the town of Adare? Who could be in those saddles except men of the clan of Dikkon?

Quince trimmed himself in the saddle and gathered in the slack of the reins. He worked the roan hard in a straight line ahead. Now and again he threw a backward glance. The roan was running hard and true, but the four were gaining with alarming rapidity.

What were those stories of mustangs capable of dropping behind them, in the uncertain footing and burning heat of the desert, all the well-bred horses of the world? Here was the chance to prove it, for the roan was a good one of his type, hardened by constant work, with every advantage except grain in his feeding. Yet he could not stand against these rushing riders on horses with a stroke that seemed twice as long as the bobbing roan's.

They drew nearer and nearer until Barney Quince unlimbered his rifle and calculated the distance for a long-range shot. Anger and scorn began to rise in him. For surely someone among them must have a pair of glasses – and they must know that they were riding in the pursuit of Barney Quince. Since when had four of the Dikkon clan dared to venture on the trail of Barney Quince?

Turning to view them more steadily, he saw that one was a strangely broad fellow. In the distance he seemed twice the size of any of his companions. Suddenly he knew by a certain premonition that this was his Hercules, his unknown warrior of the dark. A touch of coldness ran through the blood of Barney Quince. Though why he should have felt fear he could not say. The odds, at least, were not enough to disturb him. Let them come within the range of his rifle, and quickly he would reduce their fighting force.

XIII

They came fearlessly on. He drew the mustang back to a soft canter and, turning in the saddle, he raised the rifle to his shoulder. At once the four split and spread out fanwise, though they made no effort to fire with their own weapons, frankly admitting that at such range they were helpless. Barney Quince was not helpless, and he fixed his grim eye on the squat and powerful form of his night foe. That man gone, the three would surely think twice before they pressed him closer. He stopped the mustang altogether, covered his man, and drew the bead so firmly that he felt as if a line were drawn from the muzzle, arching through the air, leading the bullet to the mark.

The other three were weaving their horses to and fro as they galloped, but the squat form of the stranger drove straight on, disdaining such maneuvers. Barney Quince, feeling in his heart respect for such dauntless courage, pressed the trigger and lowered his rifle to watch the fall. But the man did not fall. He rode on, and the wind curled and uncurled the brim of his wide sombrero.

Quince, stunned, blinded, was sure that the four could not be other than an empty mirage, still galloping closer, for it was not his wont to miss a human target. With an oath, he jerked the rifle once more into the hollow of his shoulder, took aim even more carefully – and at a target how much nearer? – then fired a second time. But still the squat and mighty horseman drove on, disdaining to weave from side to side, disdaining to draw his rifle for an answering shot, though his three companions had their weapons out now and were pumping a shower of lead at their foe. Barney was agape, half unnerved.

They were near enough now for him to see them turn in their saddles and point to the side and, following the gesture, he saw yet another rider sweeping over the sands, far swifter than the others. No, not a horseman, but a riderless horse which ran valiantly. The four swept to one side, waving their hats, shouting, as though they wished to cut off the advance of the strange horse. They might as well have striven with a thunderbolt for, arching out a little from the straight line of its coming, with the sun flashing on its polished flank, the great runner came for Barney Quince, and suddenly he understood. It was Christie, broken away from her new keeper and coming for her real master. Somewhere in the past he had heard of horses able to work out a trail – and no doubt she had seen the direction of his going. Here, at least, was the miracle sweeping toward him and the four riders hot behind her. He turned the mustang and rode with red spurs, as fast as the short legs of the sweating horse would carry him. But the whinny of Christie was coming up behind, and soon her shadow shot over the sand beside him.

The four were hopelessly distanced by her, but still they gained fast on the mustang, and Christie began to circle around her master in great loops, her ears flattened, curvetting high as though she threatened to dash the life from the mustang in one of those charges of hers. So Barney Quince, to take a gift that had fallen from the sky, undid the throat latch, undid the girths and, as they were dangling, he jerked the mustang to a halt, tore off saddle and bridle, and flung them on the mare.

The four behind knew well what that meant. They had their guns out, even the squat and formidable warrior. They clipped the air about the ears of Barney Quince as he jerked the girths up and then flung himself into the saddle. Let them ride their best, for Christie was away like a happy arrow driven toward a mark of its own seeking, and in the saddle Barney Quince turned and dropped a pursuing horse with his first shot. The rider rolled headlong, then got up staggering in a cloud of dust, and in another moment the remaining three drew rein, dropped from their saddles to the ground, and opened fire. The very first bullet cut through the crown of Barney Quince's hat, but luck favored him. Before him opened a draw just deep enough to swallow horse and man from sight and, dipping into it, in five minutes he was safely out of range.

He came back to the upper level and, looking to the rear, he could see the enemy gathered in a group as for consultation. With that, he put them from his mind. They had done their best, and their best was very good but not good enough for Christie.

He reached the water holes in the middle of the afternoon and gave the mare to drink.

Then he rode on and made dry camp that night in a belt of greasewood that ran out down a shallow draw, creeping like smoke on the face of the desert. It was the loneliest night in all the life of Barney Quince. For in the other days – save long, long ago when his father lived – there had been no human interest in this world for Barney. Even that father had been rather more of a name than a flesh-and-blood reality. He had been seen by flashes, coming and going, save on a few occasions when he returned wounded and sick. The great work was all that occupied the mind of Barney's father – that great work of stinging the Dikkon clan like a gad-fly, to madden them if he could not destroy them. In turn, Barney himself inherited the labor of his kind and made the feud a greater thing than happiness. For happiness, indeed, was only on the Dikkon trail, gun in hand. The record of his glory was the number of notches which he was entitled to file into the butt of his gun.

That was what humanity meant to him – gun fodder! There were, to be sure, certain so-called friends who were scattered here and there through the mountains and the desert. He had bought their kindness, and Hilary Clarkson was the best of them. But even Hilary, Quince well knew, could not be trusted past a certain point. His price could soon be reached.

There was no real tie between this wanderer and the whole human race. He looked upon himself not as a man, indeed, but as a highly perfected instrument of vengeance, and there was never a time when he would not gladly have laid down his life to take half a dozen lives of the Dikkon clan. However, there was another responsibility before him, for he must not only strike in person, but also he must leave another behind him to strike and to bear the name which he had borne. So one day he must have a wife – he looked forward to marriage as a necessary evil, a vast evil, and a trouble.

He who has no friends, and wants none, cannot be alone. But now it seemed to poor Barney, as he lay in the black hollow of the night, that one half of his soul was gone from him and stood again beneath the window of the house of the stranger in Adare. If there were a woman, a Dikkon she must be, and how could he exchange so much as a kind word with one of that infernal breed? Yet there was a pain in his heart, aching like an old wound in cold weather until he sat up with a groan, and Christie came softly toward him and snuffed loudly at his face.

He fell back again and closed his eyes to shut out the brightness of the stars, for they too were a part and a portion of the enigma in which he found himself. The world was strange to him, but far more strange than the world was the riddle of his own new-found soul. Fate, he was sure, had taken him in her hand. All things served to show it. No doubt what fate meant was that he should fall soon at the hands of the clansmen. For that matter from his earliest boyhood he never had conceived any other end as possible, proper, or desirable. He merely had hoped to extend the blood trail through many years. Now he knew that that trail was drawing to a close.

All things pointed to it. Men have premonitions before the end. So had he. Odd things begin to happen as a stormy life draws toward the final port. Lights glimmer from the unseen shore. So with him. With invisible noose he was drawn back toward Adare. Here was the mare from which he had separated himself now, as it were, by a miracle restored to him. Above all, there were those strange encounters with the unknown warrior who had wrestled with him in the dark, who had pursued him, and had been immune before his bullets.

The eyes of Barney Quince closed a little before daybreak, but his sleep was short and troubled. When he wakened, he rose with the gloomy air of a man who knows not where or to whom to turn. Like one who throws all burden upon chance, he let Christie take the lead that day and would go whithersoever she would, and very glad was he that she had turned away from Adare. He let her journey on, and he was gladder still when he lost his bearings altogether, for it was a pleasant relief to cast himself upon the broad shoulders of his fate. Let it guide him where it would.

A dust storm struck them in the afternoon and gave horse and rider three wretched hours, but Christie kept steadily on, dog-trotting with a stride that made the miles drift by. The wind fell, but now the sky was overcast, and the air still so filled with un-settled particles that it was like a dense fog through which the traveler could not see a half mile in any direction.

Darkness began, and the visibility became less and less, while Christie moved cheerfully on her self-appointed course. At last, at the top of an upgrade, in the middle of a pleasant wood, Quince made his halt for the night. In this darkness he could risk a fire with little chance of being seen, but no sooner had the flame begun to take in the wood than he looked up and saw the clouds widely parting across the arch of the stars, and then a changing wind began to clear the lower air. With haste he put out the fire and scattered earth carefully over the embers. He went to the edge of his little grove to look over the countryside and gain his bearings if he could.

Straight before him rose the mass of Mount Chisholm, with its familiar square shoulder, and in the valley beneath was a huddle of gleaming lights. Christie, swinging through a great circle, had brought him fairly back upon Adare!

XIV

All that Barney Quince had dreaded before now he knew to be the truth, and the destiny against which he had vainly fought now overmastered him. The very animal which had come into his hands and which loved him was now an instrument which brought him bodily back to his enemies. She had saved him twice only to destroy him in the end. In a cold despair he surrendered his last hope and prepared himself to die.

He would not go down to the enemy as a ragged vagabond at least. He stripped and bathed in the starlight in a little runlet of water. He shaved in the darkness, an operation to which he was long accustomed. Then he dressed, brushed his clothes with care, and rubbed up his boots. Finally, he rubbed down Christie, resaddled her, and rode to meet the destiny which had been hounding him.

On the way, he looked to his guns and made sure that every chamber was loaded. There were fifteen shots in the rifle. There were six apiece in the revolvers. A heavy knife hung in the front of his belt and, as he drew nearer to the lights of Adare, he merely asked of fate that he might be allowed to empty his guns and then to die knife in hand, working what harm he could before the last of the clan of Quince fell under the hands of their ancient enemies. Indeed, it seemed to him that it had long been pre-ordained that the clan of Dikkon should triumph over its foes.

Let come what might, he turned Christie along the back of the town until he was opposite the great outline of the barn which arose behind the house of mystery. In a thicket he left her, and for an instant leaned his head against her sinewy, silken-surfaced neck. Then he went straight toward the house.

Like a cat he walked, pausing now and again and staring through the darkness. But no trap seemed laid for him and, if he were walking upon his fate, at least the Dikkons seemed unaware of the good fortune that was about to come to them.

He crossed the fences and the gardens once more. He passed beneath the trees which made a cool belt of shadows around the place, and again it seemed to Barney Quince that he could name them in the darkness – here an oak, there an elm, and there a holly bush beside the wall. He went to them and touched their leaves and then shuddered as he realized that his guesses had been utterly correct.

111

A curtain was drawn up suddenly, and a column of light flared forth at him. Out of its path he leaped and crouched in the darkness, with two guns ready in his hands. This, surely, was the end.

But no, the window was raised, creaking a protest. The sound of the voices of men came clearly out to him. One was a deep, husky rumble; one was clear and pleasant of tone, so Quince approached stealthily and stood to listen by the window. When he cared to risk a glance, he could see their faces. He knew them both.

One was a man of middle age, with a brown, kindly, shrewd face which, Quince was sure, he had seen a thousand times before, though he could give it no name. But in some other incarnation, in some other life, by some division and rejoining of his spiritual being, in whatever mysterious manner, he had known that man, and the very sound of his voice, and the small white scar which flecked his right cheek.

He knew all this and besides he knew well the second partner in that conversation. Enormous of head, bull throated, with shoulders as wide as a door, this was that night-fighter who had closed with him and so nearly crushed the life from his body. This was that same rider who had followed him over the desert with such remorseless courage and made his shots fly wild.

All this great power was not his now. There was a neat white bandage around his head, and his body, when his coat fell open, seemed oddly bundled. He lay back in a big easy chair. His face was pale, and his eyes were sunken in deep hollows.

Indeed, the first word that Barney Quince heard referred to the condition of this arch-enemy, for the older man was saying urgently: 'You'd better go to bed, my lad. You shouldn't be sitting up like this. You'd better turn in and rest. The doctor...'

'I tried bed and couldn't stay there,' said the rumbling voice. 'I've got to be up and around. Besides, I'm only scratched not really hurt!'

'A slash along your head and a furrow down your ribs ... is that nothing, Jim? By heaven, you touched hands with death a couple of times today, old fellow.'

The other leaned backward in his chair, his face disturbed a little with pain as he stirred.

'He's beat me twice,' he said slowly, staring before him with unseeing eyes. 'I never thought I'd find the man that could do it. He's beat me twice!'

The older man was silent. Barney Quince, his heart far lighter, listened eagerly. For, after all, his bullets had not missed. Each of them had touched the target, and each of them would have turned back any other man than this.

'Twice?' said the first speaker slowly. 'Twice, Jim?'

The big fellow pointed to one side of his face, swollen and discolored.

'You mean where you tripped and fell into the lumber pile, Jim?'

'It was no lumber pile.'

'What? That night the thief...'

'I met the thief.'

'Do you mean it?'

'I met him. He was Barney Quince. I put my glass on him today, and I knew it was him. And then we came closer, and I was surer. I've never seen him before except in the night, but I knew the cut of him. It was Barney Quince, and he was the thief. We fought, and he got in the first blow ... he had that advantage.' He paused, his lips working a trifle and his big jaw muscles bulging. 'Afterwards, I managed to close with him, and I got my arms around him...' After another of those eloquent pauses, he added: 'I've had my arms around men before, cousin, and I've worked through their strength, big and small, and had 'em turn to pulp. Well, I tried to break Quince in two, and I put more power into it than I'd ever tried to put into another thing. I had a reason to want him out of the way, for the minute I saw him loom in the dark, I knew that fate had put Barney Quince in my way, and if I got rid of

114

him...' He paused again, and then lifted his head and looked keenly upwards.

'I understand,' said the other. He nodded in perfect sympathy.

The man continued: 'I was putting out my full power on him, Cousin Oliver.'

That name startled Barney Quince, for now he remembered it perfectly – once it had sounded in his ears. Oliver! Oliver Dikkon – a kind and a just man! How could he know both the name and the nature of this man?

'But it was like...' continued Jim Dikkon, 'it was like hugging a cask. The bones of my forearms ate into the ribs of him. They were like the ribs of a ship! But still I had trust that I'd break him down. Then he tore one hand free and beat it into my face three times, and three times it was like being hammered in the face with a maul. I laid my head on his shoulder, where he couldn't get at me and, at the same time, I felt his body begin to sag. I thanked heaven. I told myself that I had won. I had a flash, maybe, of how fine it would be to bring in that grand man a helpless prisoner. Taken by one man, eh?'

He stopped again to laugh bitterly.

'But he wasn't taken,' continued the narrator. 'He clubbed his fist. It was like a lump of iron, and he brought it in behind my ear. Well, it got him loose from me. Afterwards I tried to rush in, but he stood away and his fists were like cannon balls.

115

They seemed to hit straight through my head. He dropped me and stunned me. That was the lumber pile I stumbled into, Cousin Oliver ... Barney Quince!'

Down Oliver's face great beads of perspiration were rolling. 'It was as near a thing as that, Jim!'

'Aye, it was.'

'But at least you got away from him. He didn't have a chance to use a gun on you.'

'I lay on my knees, sick and seein' nothing. He could have finished me then. With a gun ... or a knife, maybe. Or he could have choked me. I was that soft.'

'It's not his way, after all,' observed Oliver Dikkon. 'Give the devil his due – he fights fairly.'

'He does,' agreed the warrior. 'There's no murder in him. I'll give him his due. That night he outfought me. Today he beat me again. Still I tell you that I have confidence, Cousin Oliver.'

'Would you meet him again, Jim?' asked his cousin curiously.

'I'd meet him again, and I will meet him again,' replied Jim Dikkon. 'I've got a sort of feeling about it. I'm gonna have him at my mercy, the way he's had me at his. And then...' His face grew savage.

'And then?' asked Oliver Dikkon, leaning forward in his chair.

'Why,' began Jim savagely, 'why I'd...' His

voice trailed off but, rallying fiercely, he said: 'I have reason enough for wanting him dead, I guess?'

His glance again flashed upwards, and again Oliver Dikkon nodded in understanding as he answered: 'So have we all ... reasons a little different from yours perhaps.'

'And still,' murmured Jim Dikkon, 'I dunno ... I dunno ... somehow I don't see the end of it!'

XV

It occurred to Barney Quince, as he stood by the window, that had a Dikkon been in his place at such a point of vantage with two of the clan's enemies helplessly seated before him, their moments of life would have been short indeed. But he was not tempted to assassination, for like his father before him his battles were straightforward struggles in the open.

But, however interesting might be the conversation between Oliver Dikkon and his companion, it was not to listen to talk that Barney Quince had ventured into this danger. He left the window and returned beneath that vine-hung balcony which had clung like an obsession in his thoughts for days. The window above was open, but all was black within, and yet it seemed to him that a transcendent joy poured out to him from above. He laid his hand on the stalk of the climbing vine. He tested its strength, and a shiver ran through the foliage above, but all held fast.

Softly as he could manage it, he began to climb, and he drew himself up little by little until his hand could grip the lower edge of the balcony. Then, swinging once or twice like a pendulum, he lifted his leg over the railing and presently stood on the little platform, stifling the sound of his breathing.

In the dark square of the window he saw a form of glimmering white, like a ghost it stood before Barney Quince, and like a spirit it called to his soul. He heard a frightened cry: 'Who is there?'

He answered, half stunned with fear and wonder: 'It's me ... it's...'

'Barney! Barney!' cried the voice of a girl, and he thought there was both terror and joy in it. 'Oh, Barney, you've come back ... why are you here?'

She came closer. She stood in the window so that the clear starlight fell on her face, and he could see her. He knew that he had seen her before. This was the lovely mystery which had remained within the room, this was the thing for which he had been brought back. It was the weight of awe that dropped upon his heart that made Barney fall upon his knees.

'Who are you?' said Barney Quince. 'Who am I? And in the name of heaven have I ever seen you before? And where? Because my brain's spinning like a top!'

'I'm Louise Dikkon. Of course you've seen me a hundred times ... when you were living here.'

'Dikkon!' he breathed, and the name stabbed him with a dreadful pain. 'Dikkon!'

She leaned from the window, drawing a dressing gown around her shoulders.

'Barney, do you remember at all?'

'I begin to. It's all in shadow. But I begin to remember... Lou!'

'What brought you here?' she asked of Barney.

'You!'

Her breath caught.

'They have ten armed men in the house, ready to start for you in the morning. They hate and they fear you, Barney, and if they found you here, I couldn't save you. Do you understand? You're standing over powder.'

'A man has to die some day,' he answered her gravely. 'I can't keep on living forever, Lou. I've tried to ride away. I've had to come back. I've had to come back to you, Lou. I won't leave. If they find me ... then let it be the finish. What finer place could I get to die?'

She stepped through the window and stood by him, and he rose, towering above her. She caught his great arms and shook them in nervous desperation.

'I mean what I've said. They'd shoot you down with no mercy! There's nothing on earth that they'd rather do ... they hate you ... except my father and me. They all hate you, Barney. They don't know your kindness and your gentleness...'

'Kindness?' murmured Barney Quince, amazed. 'Gentleness? Lord it ain't me that you've known but some other man.'

'Don't speak,' said the girl. 'They'll hear you. They'll hear you even if you so much as whisper, I think. Jim Dikkon will hear. He's not like other men!'

'Who is Jim Dikkon?'

'The man you wounded today. Don't you know?'

'He's going to ride after me?'

'Yes, yes!'

'He came here to hunt me?'

'He came here to marry me, Barney.'

'Aye,' murmured Barney Quince, 'I guessed there was a real reason why he needed killing.'

A door slammed heavily somewhere in the house. Footsteps came up the hall and paused.

'Lou!'

At that, overcome with terror, she swayed into the arms of Barney and clung to him. He drew her closer and felt the warmth and tremor of her body.

'Lou!' called a voice from the hall.

Distinctly they heard another say more quietly: 'She's sound asleep. Let her be, Cousin Oliver!'

The footsteps retreated.

'Go now!' gasped Lou Dikkon. 'You see? Jim Dikkon suspects something, and he brought my father up to see if anything were wrong! He's like a hunting dog. His brain isn't like the brains of other people. Go now, Barney. In another minute it will be too late.'

He leaned above her and kissed her forehead, and then her lips. When she tried to speak again, he kissed the words away. That fragrance which he had breathed before now entered his very soul never to leave it until his death day. She, faint and pale, swayed in his arms.

'Lou, if they were to find me now and kill me, I'd laugh as I died. Why do you try to send me away? It ain't the years a man lives that counts. All the rest of my life, compared with this, why, I'd chuck it away and laugh as I chucked it. It ain't worth thinking of. I tell you, Lou, heaven or the devil or something sent me back to you, and I'm helpless. I can't leave you!'

'Barney,' said Lou, pushing herself back to look up into his face, 'I know that you love me.'

'Love is a fool word,' said Barney Quince.

'There ain't any word that could name what I feel for you, if you understand that.'

'Barney, I know that I never can care for any other man. Even when your brain was stunned and you were so like a poor child, I loved you, but I didn't know it until the doctor took you away, and the operation...' Her voice failed.

'I'm beginning to understand things,' said Barney Quince. 'I'm only beginning to understand. This was where I stayed when I was out of my head.'

'Yes, yes, yes!'

'And I lived right here among the Dikkons?'

'My father wouldn't let them hurt you. Afterwards ... I think everyone grew fond of you, Barney. Only when they knew that you were getting well and had forgotten everything here ... they tried to take you.'

'I begin to see it. Your father kept me here?'

'More than eight months, Barney.'

'If I'd met him afterwards, not knowing, I would have shot him down not thinking. I tell you, Lou, let them do what they want with me, because they've had me in their hands once, and I owe them a life. D'you understand?'

'But for my sake, Barney? Go away for me, because I do love you, dear! Will you listen to me? We can arrange places to meet ... and then something may happen so that we...'

'I stay here,' he answered calmly, 'because I know that I've come to the end of one life, Lou. I can count the seconds of it running away from me like blood ... d'you think that I'll give up my time with you to spend it anywhere else?'

She said in desperation: 'If you'll go, Barney ... I'll do anything! I'll go with you. I'll stay with you. I'll live with you in the wilderness, Barney. Will you go now?'

'You go with me?' he said, holding her head in his great hand. 'How would you live as I live, Lou?'

'I'd find a way. You and I together would find a way. I'm not the least afraid of that. I only know that if you stay here, they'll surely kill you. I'll never live after you're dead, Barney. I'll never live a day!'

He stood rigid.

'Me like a sneak and a thief,' he murmured hoarsely, 'stealing you away! But maybe this is the end of my old life and the beginning of the new life. I'll trust my chance to it and you, if you're willing to try. Lord knows ... some way may turn up. Lou, go dress. I'll wait for you at the bottom of the balcony.'

'I'll be there in one single minute.'

'Good bye, dear.'

He saw her vanish in the darkness of the room; then he swung lightly over the edge of the balcony and lowered himself, cautiously, carefully, to the ground. There he stood, looking up. She like a white flower would lean from the vine shower above him, before long. She, too, would climb down, and his arms would receive her. How plain it seemed to Barney that God directs all things in this world.

For a single instant a shadow crossed his mind. She was to him like an angel, with all the indescribable air of holy things about her, yet her name was Dikkon. She was of the enemy clan. If she became his wife, the long war would be ended. He could not raise his hand against her kindred and the blood relations of their children, if children came to them. So it would be, as he could see, the end of the old life, and the beginning of the new the instant that he received her in his arms.

Something, he thought, stirred softly behind him, and he was about to whirl, gun in hand, when an object was thrust sharply into the small of his back and a deep voice said in a subdued tone:

'Barney Quince, Barney Quince, say your prayer if you got a prayer to say, because you're dyin'. Barney, you're almost dead.'

XVI

It would be folly to attempt to make any

movement. Quince's hand closed on a tendril of the vine and crushed the delicate leaves to nothingness.

'You're Jim Dikkon?' he said.

'I'm Jim Dikkon.'

'I should have killed you the first time I met you,' said Barney Quince. 'I was a fool ... I was a rank fool!'

'I'd give you a fair fighting chance,' said Dikkon, 'except that there's the girl mixed up in this. You've got to die for her sake, man.'

'I'll ask you for one thing.'

'Well, ask.'

'Walk me back into the trees and finish me there.'

'Aye,' murmured Jim Dikkon, 'because otherwise she'd know who...'

A whisper floated down from above: 'Barney, Barney, darling!'

'Yes?' whispered Barney Quince. He raised his head and barely could see her.

'Are you ready for me?'

'Aye, ready.'

'I'm coming down.'

She slipped over the edge of the balcony, and Barney heard a faint murmur behind him: 'Lord forgive me! Lord forgive me! *She* never will...'

The reaching arms of Barney received the girl and held her closely to him. Only then she saw and turned rigid in his arms.

'I can't do it,' said Jim Dikkon suddenly.

'You ought to die Barney Quince, for her sake. But instead, if you'll go with her into the house and face her father and tell him what you would have done for her ... do you understand?'

They sat in a family circle around the fireplace, though the hearth was black and empty. Oliver Dikkon had his daughter on one side of him, and Barney Quince sat on the other. In the background sat the captor, contributing no word to the discussion but keeping his burning eyes fixed solemnly upon the face of the enemy of his clan.

Oliver Dikkon said at last: 'I had a sort of an idea of what might come the first night that we had you here. I had an idea,' he went on, leaning as though he were watching a rising flame in the fireplace, 'when I saw Lou caring for you. Because there's nothing that softens the heart of a woman like seeing an enemy helpless. Lou, here, isn't the sort that is apt to open her heart twice. Afterwards, I was pretty sure of it. All the time that you were here was a time of hell for me. I saw her growing to care about you. I couldn't send you away. I couldn't send her. She wouldn't have gone! You remember, Lou, when I wanted you to visit your aunt in Chicago?'

'I remember,' she answered softly.

'Well, then the doctor came and did his work. It seems to me that heaven has taken charge of the rest. We've hunted Barney Quince with our best men. We never could take him or hold him. Jim nearly died on the trail today. If I go to the family council and ask them, face to face, if it isn't worthwhile to have you as a friend and the husband of my girl, I guess they'll rage and curse a little, but in the end they'll take you. Once you're in the clan, there'll never be a hand lifted against you by man or boy that wears the name of Dikkon. Jim, am I right?'

But Jim had stolen from the room.

Then, for the matter could not wait, Oliver Dikkon left the house to bring the family council together to decide this grave matter. Barney and Louise were left sitting, staring wide eyed at one another.

'I begin to remember, sort of,' said Barney Quince, suddenly closing his eyes. 'I remember a saw ... a cross-cut saw, Lou, that you gave me to work with.'

'Yes!'

'And the cows! And the hunting! And the woodchopping!'

'Barney, Barney, it's all coming back to you!'

'It looks to me,' said Barney with the broadest of grins, 'as though you'd been sort of training me for the job of husband, Lou, right from the start.'

THE MAN WHO FORGOT

Faust's first appearance in Street & Smith's Western Story Magazine *was 'Jerry Peyton's Notched Inheritance,' a serial that began in the issue dated November 15, 1920. It was published under a new pseudonym – George Owen Baxter – and in succeeding years Faust would add to his string numerous other* noms des plumes. *He was so prolific an author that during the 1920s he might have a serial by David Manning, a serial by George Owen Baxter, and a novelette by Max Brand all running in the same issue of* Western Story Magazine, *and this remained the case as late as the issue dated 4/2/32. Frank E. Blackwell, editor of the magazine for all the years Faust was a contributor, once recalled: 'How did I get hold of Faust? Bob Davis was over-bought. Munsey found it out, told Bob he'd have to shut off buying for as long as six months, and use up some of the stuff in the safe. Faust, always in need of money, no matter how much he made, came to me with a story. I bought it. He was mine, and mine only from there on.' This wasn't completely true. Faust did write for other magazines as well. But for nearly fifteen years he did write better than a million words a year for Blackwell. A short novel titled 'The Man Who*

Forgot' by John Frederick marked Faust's second appearance in Western Story Magazine. *It was published in the Christmas issue dated December 25, 1920. This new byline was necessary because the same issue carried the final installment of George Owen Baxter's 'Jerry Peyton's Notched Inheritance.'*

I

It was snowing. A northwester was rushing over the mountains. As the storm wind shifted a few points west and east, the mountains cut it away, so that one valley lay in a lull of quiet air, with the snow dropping in perpendicular lines; or else the mountains caught the wind in a funnel and poured a venomous blast, in which the snow hardened and became cold teeth.

The two men lying in a covert saw Skinner Mountain, due south of them, withdraw into the mist of white and again jump out at them, blocking half the sky. The weather and the sudden appearances of Mount Skinner troubled Lou Alp. In his own way and in his own time, Alp was a successful sneak thief. He had been known to take chances enough; but that was in Manhattan, where the millions walk the street and where mere numbers offer a refuge. That was in Manhattan, where a man may slip into twisting side

130

streets with a dozen issues through alleys and cellars. That was in Manhattan, where a fugitive turning a corner is as far away as though he had dropped to the other side of the world.

Far different here. Of man there was not a trace, and the huge and brutal face of nature pressed upon the sensitive mind of Lou Alp; the chill air numbed his finger tips and made his only useful weapons helpless. Lou Alp depended upon sleight of hand and agility rather than upon strength. This whirl and rush of snow baffled him and irritated him. He kept repeating to his companion: 'Is this your sunshine? Is this your happy country? I say, to hell with it!'

His companion, who lay by his side in the bushes and kept a sharp lookout up the road at such times as the drive of the snow made it possible to see fifty yards, would answer: 'It's a freak storm, Lou. Never saw it come so thick and fast so early in December as this. Give the country a chance. It's all right.'

Alp would stare at him in amazement. From the time of their first intimacy Jack Chapel had continually amazed him. That was in the shoe shop of the penitentiary where they had sat side by side on their stools. The rule was silence and, though there were many opportunities for speech from the side of the mouth in the carefully gauged whispers which state prisoners learn to use so soon, Chapel had never taken advantage of the chances. Lou would never forget the man as he had first seen him, the clean-cut features, the rather square effect given by the size of his jaw muscles, the prison pallor which made his dark eyes seem darker. On the whole he was a handsome chap, but he had something about him more arresting than his good looks.

For the most part the prisoners pined or found resignation. Their eyes became pathetic or dull, as Lou's eyes became after the first three months. But the eyes of Jack Chapel held a spark which bespoke neither resignation nor inertia. He had a way of sitting forward on his stool all day long, giving the impression of one ready to start to his feet and spring into action. When one of the trusties spoke to him, he did not stare straight before him, as the other prisoners did, but his eyes first looked his questioner full in the face and flashed, then he made his answer. He gave an effect, indeed, of one who bides a day.

These things Lou Alp noted, for there were few things about faces which he missed. He had learned early to read human nature from his life as a gutter urchin who must know which face means a dime, which means a cent, and which means no gift to charity at all. But what lay behind the fire in Jack Chapel's eyes he could not say. Alp was cunning, but he lacked imagination. He knew the existence of some devouring emotion, but what that emotion was he could not tell.

He was not the only one to sense a danger in Chapel. The trusty in charge of the shop guessed it at the end of the first week, and he started to break Chapel. It was not hard to find an opening. Chapel had little skill with his hands, and presently job after job was turned back to him. He had sewed clumsily; he had put in too many nails; he had built up the heel awry. After a time, he began to be punished for his clumsiness. It was at this point that Alp interfered. He had no great liking for Chapel, but he hated the trusty with the hatred of a weasel for a badger. To help Chapel was to get in an indirect dig at the trusty.

Because Lou Alp could do almost anything with his agile fingers, he began to instruct Chapel in the fine points of shoemaking. It was a simple matter. He had only to wait until Chapel was in difficulty, and then Lou would start the same piece of work on one of his own shoes. He would catch the eye of Chapel and work slowly, painstakingly, so that his neighbor could follow the idea. Before long, Chapel was an expert and even the carping trusty could find no fault.

Now charity warms the heart; a gift is more pleasant to him who gives than to him who takes. Lou Alp, having for once in his life

133

performed a good deed, was amazed by the gradual unlocking of his heart that followed. He had lived a friendless life; vaguely, delightfully, he felt the growth of a new emotion.

When the time came, he had leaned over to pick something from the floor and had whispered sidewise: 'What's the charge?'

The other had made no attempt to reply guardedly. His glance held boldly on the face of the sneak thief, as the latter straightened again on his stool. There was a slight tightening of his jaw muscles, and then Chapel said: 'Murder!'

The word knocked at the heart of Lou Alp and made him tremble. Murder! Looking at the strong, capable, but rather clumsy hands of Chapel, he saw how all that strength could have been applied. Suppose those square-tipped fingers had clutched someone by the throat – an ache went down the windpipe of the thief.

If Lou had been interested before, he was fascinated now. In all their weeks of labor side by side, only four words had been interchanged between them, and here he was in the soul of his companion. He was not horrified. Rather, he felt a thrill of dog-like admiration. He, Lou Alp, had wished to kill more than one man. There was the 'flatty' who ran him down in 'Mug' McIntyre's place. He had wanted to bump that man off.

There were others. But fear, which was the presiding deity in the life of the sneak thief, had warded him away from the cardinal sin. He respected Chapel; he was glad he had helped his neighbor; he felt even a touch of reverence for the boy.

And later on he had said: 'How?'

'It was a frame,' answered Chapel. 'A dirty frame!'

And then Alp knew the meaning of the spark behind those eyes. It took some of the thrill from his feeling for Chapel, but now he understood that undying alertness, for it sprang out of the hate of a man who has been wronged. After all, it is almost as exciting to be seated beside a man who has been wrongly convicted of murder as it is to sit beside a man who is really guilty.

A little later Chapel put his first question.

'And you?' he said.

'They framed me, too,' said Alp, and with marvelous skill he was able to put a touch of a whine even in his whisper. 'The dirty dogs framed me, too!'

He hardened his face in lines of sadness, prepared to meet unbelief in the eyes of the other, but there was no questioning in Jack Chapel's mind. Instead, he sat rigid on his stool and his eyes flamed at his companion. Then he smiled. The last bar was down between them; he admitted the sneak thief into his friendship.

Events came swiftly to a head. About his past Chapel was reticent. He had come from the West and he was going back to some part of his own great country when he was out. He was not going to attempt to get even for the double-cross which in the first place had brought him East and then lodged him in prison for a ten-year term. His vengeance was barred, for it was a girl who had engineered the whole scheme to save her lover. Alp learned of this reticence with amazement. If a strong man had injured him in a similar manner, he might well have postponed his vengeance as he had often postponed it in times past; but to withhold the heavy hand from a woman, this was a thing which he could not comprehend. As always when a thing passed his understanding, he remained silent. In the future he was to find that silence was often necessary when he talked with the falsely accused murderer.

A new event came. Chapel was planning an escape and he confided his plan to the sneak thief. That night Lou sat in his cell and brooded. If he took part in the attempt, it meant a probable recapture and a far heavier sentence for breaking jail. The other alternative was to tell the prison authorities everything. They would make him a trusty at once, lighten his service, and cut his term as short as was possible. On the other hand a still, small voice kept assuring him that if he betrayed Chapel, he would sooner or later die by the hand of that man. There was a third possibility, to remain quietly in the prison, say nothing, and take no part in the attempted escape.

Lou Alp had not sufficient moral courage to be reticent. As a result he found himself dragged into the plan. On the appointed night, after five minutes of quiet work and murderous suspense, he stood outside the black walls a free man, with Jack Chapel at his side. Instinct told him, as strongly as it tells the homing pigeon, safety lay in the slide across country to the all-sheltering labyrinth of Manhattan, but the voice of Jack Chapel was stronger than instinct and Alp started West with his friend. They had aimed for a district safely north of Jack Chapel's home, had ridden the beams as far as the railroad would take them, and then plunged into the wilderness of mountains on a road that led them here. The night before they had spent in a small village and there, with his usual ferret like skill, Lou learned of the payroll which was to go the next day from the village up to the mine in the hills under charge of two armed men. He had told Chapel, and the latter insisted on a holdup.

'I'll take what's coming to me, and no more,' he said. 'What's my time worth for two years? I don't count in the pain or the work or the dirty disgrace, but write me down for a thousand a year. That's two thousand. Then you come in. A year and a half at the same rate. That's thirty-five hundred the world owes us and here's where we collect. Thirty-five hundred, no more and no less. We use that to make a new start. Tell me straight, is that square? And we take it from old Purvis's payroll. God knows Purvis can afford to spare the coin. He's so crooked he can't lie in bed. How'd he get his mines? By beating out poor devils who hit hard times. So he's our paymaster. Something is coming to us. We're both innocent. We've both been hit between the eyes. Now we can get something back. Is that logic?'

There had been a sort of appeal in his voice as he made the proposition to Alp early that morning.

'Sure it's justice,' nodded Lou.

Then Chapel drew a little breath and his eyes flashed from one side to the other. 'I ain't much on a holdup,' he faltered.

'You never stuck 'em up before?' cried Lou, horrified by such rash inexperience.

'Sure I never did. That doesn't make any difference. I know how holdups go. You step out and shove a gun under the nose of somebody. He jerks his hands over his head. You go through his pockets or whatever he has the coin in. You take his guns. He rides into town like a shot. A posse starts out after you. You go one way and they go the other way.

138

Haven't I seen it work out that way a hundred times? I tell you there's nothing to it, Lou.'

Once more Lou had been drawn into the dragnet of the other's commanding will.

II

Alp did not like it, no matter from what angle he looked at it. It was foreign to him. The game was not his. He was used to playing a lone hand and now he lay like a rabbit in a covert, not knowing what was expected of him, or if he would have courage to carry through the part assigned him. If it had been spring weather, he kept saying to himself, with a good, clear sky to pour content through the mind of a man and air through which one could see, things would have been very different with him. His one comfort was the bright eye of his companion. Cold had turned the fingers of Jack Chapel purple around the knuckles, but for some reason Alp could not imagine him stopped or even seriously embarrassed by such a thing as cold.

Yet he asked to make assurance doubly sure: 'Pretty smooth with a gun?'

'Me? Smooth with a gun?' asked the heavy-shouldered young fellow. 'Why, Lou, I couldn't hit the side of a barn with a rifle, let alone a revolver.'

The terror which had been reined up in Lou Alp's vitals now burst loose and flooded him. The chill which swept through him was a mortal cold that had nothing to do with either wind or snow. It was fear, horrible, strength-devouring fear. He could not even speak, as he heard his companion continue carelessly.

'But what does gun work have to do with it? I wouldn't hurt those two fellows if I could. Their boss is a skunk. He deserves anything that comes his way, but I don't hold any grudge against those two fellows. Not me! But there'll be no shooting. No, all you need for a game like this is a little bluff and some sand.'

He followed his statement with his usual chuckle. Alp was seized in a fresh amazement. There were qualities about this man which never grew old. There was a surprising freshness, a nearness to the soil. Two things about him spoke the two sides of his nature. There were the bright, steady, and dangerous eyes. Lou Alp had been among the defiers of society long enough to recognize that glance. On the other hand, there was that ready chuckle. It came deeply out of his throat; it was musical, changing, and redolent with good nature. It was a laugh which instantly made a roomful of people smile and turn around. It was a laugh which never offended because there was not the slightest suggestion of mockery or derision or self complacency in it.

Yet it failed to warm the trembling heart of the thief at this juncture. He continued to stare as though at a revelation of madness.

'But for heaven's sake...' was all he could say. Then: 'I've been wonderin' about your gun, where you been keepin' it all this time?'

'Here,' said the other and, reaching above him, he snapped off a twig, shook the snow from it, and presented to Lou Alp the frost-blackened, curved fragment of wood. The sneak thief threw back his head and began to laugh wildly. The sound came up through his slender throat cackling. It was singularly like the wind-shaken scream of some bird of prey.

'That!' he cried. 'Man, don't you know that you got two armed men to handle? Don't you know that they're lookin' for trouble? That's why they're with the coin! And even if you had a gun...' he broke off, unable to continue. Then: 'Let's get out of this. I'm froze clear through.'

'What's the matter?' asked Chapel. 'Don't you trust me?'

Again Alp was staggered. He had dragged his cold-cramped body to his knees and now he paused, agape. He was about to say, 'What has trust got to do with powder and lead?' but he checked himself. It occurred to him that this singular fellow might be angered by

141

any doubts cast upon him; already there was the queer, thoughtful flicker in his eyes, and Alp dropped back into his bed of leaves and snow. It came to him that much as he dreaded the storm and the coming of the armed men, he dreaded Jack Chapel even more. He knew now why the twelve good men and true had looked into the face of this man and had believed all too readily, with only the most circumstantial evidence to back their belief, that he had been guilty of a murder. Aside from the escape from the prison he had never seen Chapel meet danger or perform any violent act, and yet he was ready to premise the most tremendous things of this bright-eyed man.

He lay back in the snow without a word and began to massage his lips with his knuckles, so as to be able to speak when he had mentally framed his argument. He must prevent this incipient act of madness that would destroy them both. His agile brain began to turn and twist around the subject, looking back on a score of arguments; but, when he was on the verge of beginning, there was a low exclamation from Jack Chapel.

'They're here!'

He cast one wild glance down the road, but a whirl of snow rose and closed the way before him. Then, like the coward that he was, he looked to his companion, prepared with the protest, prepared with the plea, to let the danger and the money pass. He was stopped by the singular expression of happiness in the face of his companion. Somewhere he had seen such a look. Now he remembered. It was when he had taken a girl out of the slums to the theater; when the curtain slipped up, in the dim glow from the stage, he had turned and watched the face of the girl, her lips parted, her eyes at once dreaming, wistful, and eager.

Such was the face of Jack Chapel. The same hushed expectancy, the same trembling alertness, the same love of the unknown that lay before him. Now, through the curtain of the snow, the heads of two horses thrust out, powdered and unreal. Instantly the whole of the buckboard and the two men who rode in it came out upon Lou Alp. They were humped into bunches of flesh, shrinking from the cold, made numbed and sleepy by it. Looking up at them they seemed huge and formidable to Alp. A shudder went through his meager body when he thought of a single man, armed with a bent twig, trying to halt that on-sweeping force of horses and wagon and fighting men.

Chapel was on his hands and feet like a runner at the mark. The wagon rushed nearer, rattling above the hum of wind and the soft crushing of the snow among the naked trees. Suddenly the man leaped out from behind his screen with a deep shout.

The horses stopped and veered to one side, cramping the wagon dangerously. The men in the wagon sat and stared stupidly at the apparition. There stood Jack Chapel before them, crouched a little, with the twig in his hand not extended at full arm's length, but drawn back close to his breast. For the moment Alp forgot that it was simply a crooked piece of wood. He expected to see fire flash from the end of it.

The guards must have expected the same thing. For they made no attempt at resistance, but slowly – or was it the feverish activity of Lou's mind that made it seem slow – they put their hands up to their shoulders and then, inch by inch, above their heads.

Chapel was barking orders. Obediently they climbed down and turned their backs, still with hands above their heads. Jack went to them at a run, still speaking swiftly, cautioning them not to make a suspicious move. He jerked a revolver out of the holster that hung at the hip of one of them and tossed his twig away.

Lou Alp stood up. The blood was beginning to run freely again in his veins. A spot of red stood out in the hollow of each sallow, thin cheek. For the madman was turning his madness into sane matter of fact. With his twig he had rendered two stalwart men helpless. With a cry of encouragement, Lou was about to step out and render such help as he was

144

capable of when the second of the guards, whose revolver had not yet been taken, jerked down his arms, whirled, and fired.

It happened with incredible suddenness. Lou felt his left leg go numb, but he forgot that, giving his whole attention on Chapel. He expected to see that broad, strong form topple to the earth. Instead, his friend smashed the fist that carried the revolver into the face of the man who had just fired. The fellow tossed up both arms, staggered back, and sank slowly into the snow. His companion, turning at the shot, grappled the bandit. For a moment they swayed and twisted and then were torn apart. The guard came close again, his arms reaching out. He was met by the lunging fist of Chapel and dropped loosely upon his face.

By the time Alp's brain began to work, he felt the numbness in his leg give place to a sharp pain, as though a red-hot knife had been thrust into his calf and left there to burn the flesh. Not until then did he realize that he had been shot through the leg by that first wild bullet from the gun of the guard. A red trickle was running out over his trousers. He watched it, fascinated.

Chapel was tying the fallen guards. Now that the danger was past, Lou attempted to go to him, but his left leg crumbled beneath his weight. Lying on his side, he saw his friend climb into the buckboard, take up a box, smash the lock with a bullet, and then drop to the snow with a stack of what he knew to be money. Chapel was counting it. Was it possible that the fool was only taking the thirty-five hundred? There must be at least twelve thousand in that payroll!

He dragged himself out from the covert at the same time that the other finished dumping his loot into a sack. Chapel was instantly beside him with an exclamation while tears of self-pity rose into the eyes of Alp.

'The dirty swine,' he moaned. 'Look what they done to me? Will you? And what harm was I doin' 'em?'

Before he answered, Chapel knelt beside Lou, ripped up the leg of his trousers, and examined the wound. 'It's an easy one,' he said. He was tearing away his own coat as he spoke, and now he ripped his undershirt into strips and made a swift and skillful bandage. 'Clean as a whistle, Lou,' he went on re-assuringly. 'You won't lose a tablespoonful of blood hardly. Keep your chin up, will you?'

A hot rage sent a mist across the vision of Lou. 'Pump 'em full of lead !' he said through his teeth.

'Why ?' asked Jack Chapel.

'Didn't they do this? You ask me why?'

Something in the face of his companion cleared Alp's eyes again. He saw that Chapel was looking at him with a curiously cold glance.

'It was just a chance that you got hurt,' he said. 'Besides, do you blame 'em for tryin' to protect the stuff they were sent out to guard? No, they showed they had ... courage. I like 'em all the better for it, but the luck was against 'em. And that's the only reason why we're not blown full of lead, the way you want me to fix them now that they got their hands tied.'

Lou Alp forgot the pain of his wound as he met the new glance of Chapel.

'Say, bo,' he grinned feebly. 'You don't think I meant it, do you? The leg was hurting like fire and it peeved me for a minute.'

'Sure,' said Jack Chapel slowly, 'I know what you mean. Only...' He did not finish the sentence.

III

Somehow that incompleted sentence tied the tongue of the sneak thief even when he saw Jack Chapel take up the box with the gold coin and drop it in the snow beside the guards. There went close to ten thousand dollars perhaps. Yet Lou Alp merely writhed in silence. He dared not speak.

Lou was lifted in the strong arms of Jack Chapel and placed in the rear of the buckboard. Looking over the side, he saw Chapel search the two guards for weapons, and then in amazement he saw him cut the bonds of his enemies. Such faulty procedure took the breath of Lou Alp. Still he attempted no advice, and even flattened himself on the bottom of the buckboard.

He felt quite sure that up to this point his presence had not been noted. He had not issued from his hiding place until after both guards had been stunned by the blows of Jack Chapel and, as they lay face downward in the snow, there was small reason to think that they had heard his voice over the screaming of the storm, or that they had seen him during the very brief interim before he was placed in the bed of the wagon. He lay still and said nothing while the two struggled to their feet and went with uncertain steps down the road. The circling, thick eddies of the snow covered them from view quickly. Jack climbed up to his place in the driver's seat. He turned and looked down to Lou Alp, bedded in feed sacks with his injured leg cocked up to break the jar of the bumps. As he turned, Lou saw Chapel's right hand laid on the rail of the seat, with the knuckles scraped bare and bleeding. The blows which knocked down the guards had done that work, he knew, and he felt once more that surprise, tinged with fear, with which he had already discovered so many unsuspected accomplishments in his companion. He knew enough about boxing to recognize the snapping, straight-armed power of the blows which had stunned the guards. He felt again that there was more to Jack Chapel than appeared on the surface. The man was hiding something.

'Are you going to be all right, there?' asked Jack.

His voice was cold, and Alp winced under it. 'I can stand it, pal,' he said conciliatingly.

He watched to see the face of the other soften, but with a curt nod Chapel turned and started the horses on. He swung the wagon about and sent it along the valley with the storm at their backs. They made good time up the road, jogging steadily on for the better part of three or four hours. Before the end of that time Lou Alp had squirmed into a dozen positions and was finding ease in none. How fervently he blessed the moment when the buckboard was brought to a halt. Chapel climbed down from the seat and stood over his companion.

'We've come to the end of the road,' he said.

'This wilderness? Where in the name of heaven can we put up? Jack, I can't stand much more!'

'Look over there.'

Lou strained his feverish eyes and made out the vague form of a house ghost-like in the storm, a big house of which he saw more the longer he stared.

'But how'll I get there?' he groaned. 'Must be half a mile, Jack.'

'I'll get you there.'

Something of restraint in his voice made Lou wince again. He broached the vital question. 'Will ... will you be safe there?' he asked. 'Suppose the posse turns along this road?'

'I dunno,' replied the other. He turned as he spoke and looked into the teeth of the storm as though danger were at that moment riding upon him out of it. 'I dunno. But I've got to get you to that house before you get a cold in your wound.'

Lou could see his friend hesitating, and that hesitation drove him into a panic. Would he be abandoned here in the snow on the meager chance that someone from the house should happen on him, or that he could drag himself to the shelter? He was on the verge of breaking into a frantic appeal when he checked himself and thought of new tactics.

'Jack,' he said, 'listen to me. I've done you no good. First to last you've started everything and finished everything all by yourself. You got me out of jail. You brought me West. You planned the job down the road. You pulled it off. And all I've done is to clog up the works and gum the cards.' He paused a little to study the effect of his words. It was hard to read Jack Chapel with the wind turning up his hat behind and the snow

150

spattering on his shoulders. He seemed so self-reliant and self-possessed that again the shivering took Lou Alp. Yet he persisted in his singular appeal.

'Leave me be where I am, Jack,' he went on, his voice shaking. 'If you come up there to the house with me, they'll have you sure. Before ten hours somebody'll come along this way and the folks at the house'll tell 'em that you been there to leave me.'

The larger man grunted. 'What'll you do without me?' he asked harshly. 'You don't know these folks around here. You don't know their ways. You ain't like 'em and they'll see the difference. They'll start askin' questions and you'll be fool enough to start tellin' 'em lies. Inside of five days they'll have the sheriff out here to look you over as a queer one.'

The sneak thief looked into his wretched soul and shook in acknowledgment of the truth. 'Let them come and get me,' he said hoarsely. 'Let 'em come. But if they get me, I'll have this one satisfaction, that I didn't drag you into it. Jack, pal, you take the horses and go on. I'll take my own chances.'

Through a heart-breaking pause he saw the other hesitate, and even turn partly away; but at the very moment, when a wild and craven appeal was about to break from the lips of Lou Alp, Chapel turned again and caught the meager hand of the thief.

'I thought you were bluffin' me,' he said with emotion. 'I thought you were yellow and were just bluffin' me. But now I see you're straight, partner, and I'll tell you where I stand. Back there when you were peeved and wanted me to bump off those two gents, I figured that you meant it, and it sort of riled me a little. Speakin' man to man, I thought you were a skunk, Lou. Been thinkin' so all this time right up to now. But a gent that plays square once, can't play crooked the next minute. Here you lie, helpless, but not thinkin' once about yourself.'

The emotion in his voice had a powerful effect upon Lou Alp. Tears of self-pity for the sacrifice which he had shammed began to gather.

'And now I feel like a skunk,' said Jack Chapel. 'If you can take my hand and call it square in spite of what I been thinkin' about you, here it is. If you're still mad at me, why, when you get on your feet again, we'll fight it out. What say?'

Lou Alp, trembling at the narrowness of his escape, clutched the proffered hand eagerly and wrung it.

'That's good,' said Jack Chapel simply. 'That's mighty good!' He seemed to brush away the remnants of the situation and turned to new things. 'Give me your arms and I'll get you on my back,' he directed.

'But what about the wagon and the horses?'

'Don't you see what'll become of 'em? With this storm at their backs, they'll drift straight down the road. I don't know a whole pile about this country, but I know there ain't more'n one road for 'em to take down this valley. As long as the wind blows, they'll keep moving and they may wind up fifty miles from here. The posse, if they start one out right away, will go straight for the place where the horses and wagon, or what's left of the wagon, are picked up. They'll start combing the hills for me around that place. They'll never think to look for me in a house. Even if they find me, they won't know me because I had my handkerchief over the lower part of my face and my hat pretty well down over my eyes. And it's a cinch that they'll never dream of lookin' for two of us!'

It was all so logically reasoned that the sneak thief nodded in admiration. The fever which had been gathering in him, and the waves of weakness, began to make his head swim. Yet he followed Jack Chapel's voice.

'First thing they'll do will be to look over the list of their old employees. Why? Because I only took part of the coin. On account of that the big boss will think that somebody he'd wronged, or somebody with a debt he wouldn't pay, tuned up a gun and came out to take what belonged to him by rights. And I'll tell you what they'll do. They'll be apt to send the posse right to the house of the first

153

man around these parts that the big boss owes around thirty-five hundred dollars to. When they get all through with that sort of lookin' ... then, and not till then ... they'll take the back trail. By that time anything may have happened. Ten days ought to make you fit for a saddle, and most likely it'll be ten days before anybody bothers us here.'

'And so?' queried Lou Alp.

'And so I'm goin' to take you up to that house, and I'm goin' to stay there with you. I dunno who lives there. But if it's white folks, and you don't talk too much, we won't be bothered. You hear me talk?'

The sneak thief smiled feebly as he was raised into the arms of Jack Chapel. 'Jack,' he said, 'you're riskin' your life for me. I know you could make a get-away into the hills if you wanted to. You're riskin' everything to save me. You're givin' me everything. Some day I'll give it all back in a chunk!'

'Forget it,' answered Chapel. 'You talk a pile too much, partner.'

Again he began to breathe hard as the strain of the steep hillside told on his legs and the weight of the limp body told on his arms.

IV

The half mile up that grade was no easy walk under any circumstances. With a staggering storm from one side, with the rocks slippery from snow, and with the burden of another man weighting him, it was a terrific task for Jack Chapel. Looking up into his face, Alp saw the fighting jaw thrust out and the muscles over the angles of the jaw harden. Yet he took the half mile with only three brief pauses for rest. Finally, just a brief distance from the house, he deposited the wounded man in a bank of snow and leaned over him, panting.

'I don't know what our story is going to be till I see the people of the house,' he said. 'The thing for you to do is to keep your ears open and your eyes shut. You understand?'

'You want me to faint?' grinned Lou Alp.

'Sure. Soon as I come close up to the door, I'll give you the word and you go limp. That'll bring me to the door with an unconscious man. As soon as I go in, they'll rush around until your senses come back. I'll have a chance that way to size up the gang in that house and frame a story. I'll tell the story so you can hear it. It won't be long, and you hang on to what I say. Will you do that?'

'I'll turn a flop,' said the sneak thief, 'that'll have the real thing beat a mile. Lead on!'

Where it was a mere matter of stratagem, Alp felt at home. His head cleared and his pulse strengthened as matters approached this new crisis. Once more he was taken up and they came in full view of a square-built ranch house whose tall windows promised capacious rooms within.

'Now!' cautioned Jack Chapel, and the thief made himself limp.

He became so perfectly inert that his left arm dangled toward the ground, his head dropped back and allowed his hat to fall off, while his long black hair blew in the wind. He heard a grunt of satisfaction from Jack Chapel that was music in his ears. Then he closed his eyes.

He was too much of an artist to attempt to look through the lashes at what passed around him. He remained in darkness, his mouth agape, his head dangling, his whole weight utterly inert. He felt Jack prop him up on one knee and then heard the clatter of knuckles against the front door; it was opened. Warm air rushed out around them.

'Hello, there! What you got? Not dead, man?'

It was a deep, strong bass voice.

'No. But drilled through the leg. Accident. Hunting.' The reply of Jack Chapel was a tumbling mass of words panted out. 'Lemme get him to a bed, will you?'

'Of course. Let me carry him.'

'No, I'll manage him. Not serious, but he's played out. Lost a lot of blood.'

'Up this way, then, son. Hello! Mother! Kate! Come here. Hurry up. Hurry, I say!'

A scurry of voices and footsteps in the distance, and then Lou felt himself being carried up a flight of stairs. The feminine rustling and voices came from behind and below and poured up around him. A young, pleasant voice had cried: 'Poor fellow!' The voice of an older woman had screamed.

'Now, none of that foolishness,' said the man who led the way. 'Keep your head, Mother. He ain't goin' to die. Just a scratch. Lost a little blood. Kate, I want you to stand by to help. Get some water and bandages.'

They reached level flooring, turned, and a door was opened. Lou could tell by the changed temperature of the air.

'I'll have a fire going in a jiffy,' said the big man's voice. 'Kate, get that hot water. But how did you get him here? How far'd you carry him?'

Lou felt himself laid upon a bed and then Jack Chapel was answering: 'Not so far. We'd been hunting through the mountains. The storm got us, and we started down for lower levels. Coming along fine when this accident happened just in the hills, there above your house. And mighty lucky we were so close. Barbed wire is a curse, sir. Climbing through a fence got my holster caught ... tried to get it loose ... reached to pull my gun out ... and somehow the thing went off and drilled Lou through the calf of his leg.'

All the time he talked brokenly, he was

working swiftly, taking off Lou's clothes. Presently Lou Alp found himself slipped in between chilly sheets. In the meantime, a pair of massive fingers closed over his wrist.

'He'll come along all right,' said the deep voice after a moment. 'Lucky it wasn't higher. Lucky it didn't hit the bone. Men of this generation don't know how to handle guns any more. No sense for 'em. Don't mean to hurt your feelin's, my young friend. By the way, my name's Moore, Roger Moore.'

'My name is Jack Chandler and this is Louis Angus.'

'Glad to know you. He ain't one of the Barr County Angus family, is he?'

'Might be related. I dunno.'

'No, he ain't got bone enough to be one of 'em. Well, son, lucky you landed here. And you're welcome as long as you'll stay, and that'll be ten days anyway before he's on his feet. Come on in, Kate. Meet Jack Chandler. This is my daughter. Put that basin down over here, Kate. There's a good girl. Nothin' to be white about. The gent ain't goin' to die. Got a .45 through the calf of his leg, though. Was it a .45?'

'A .32,' said Jack Chandler.

'What! Never seen a .32 tear things up like that, but bullets are as tricky as guns. Never know what they'll do. Look at that scar on my wrist. Bullet went in there, twisted clean around my forearm, and come out by the elbow. Didn't break a bone or tear a tendon and my arm was as good as ever inside three weeks. That's one of the queer things a bullet'll do. Luck, eh? Hello! He's comin' to!'

Alp had felt a covert nudge from the knee of his companion and he took it as a signal to open his eyes. He did it very well. First he blinked. Then he glared up at the ceiling and murmured: 'It's all right, Jack. You couldn't help it.'

'Delirious a little,' muttered the deep voice.

Alp sat bolt upright in the bed and stared wildly around him. 'What the devil!' he exclaimed.

His words met a pleased chuckle from half a dozen faces, and each with shining, kindly eyes.

'The snow,' said Lou vaguely, rubbing his eyes. 'The wind ... I...'

A silver-haired woman with a youthful, beautiful face came beside him and laid her hand gently on his shoulder.

'You lie down, my boy,' she said. 'The snow and the wind and the trouble are all left outside. And now we're goin' to take care of you.'

He allowed himself to be pressed back into the bed, but still his eyes went the rounds of the room. He saw Jack Chapel standing over him, his face grave with well-simulated trouble. He saw behind the woman the owner of the deep, bass voice. From the hand and the voice, he had expected a giant. Instead, he saw a stubby fellow, middle-aged, with a prodigious pair of shoulders and a not over large head set between them. His arms were very long, and the hands in exact proportion to the shoulders. Yet the small face which topped off this clumsy body was so filled with energy and penetration that Lou Alp forgot the lack of proportion.

Rattling at the fireplace at one side of the big bedroom was evidently a woman servant, and close to her stood a girl with sunny hair and earnest blue eyes, still darkened with the shadow of her recent fright. Her head was framed by the snow-crusted window beyond, and against that cold background the brown of her hair seemed golden and the olive skin took on tints of rich life. Upon Lou Alp she broke as light breaks upon deep darkness. Only the knee of Jack Chapel, striking his ribs, made him rouse himself enough to turn his glance.

'You'll have this room to yourself,' the rancher was saying to Alp. 'And you can take that smaller room next door, Mister Chandler. I suppose you'll want to be handy to your partner, eh? That way he can call you plumb easy.'

He accepted the thanks which Jack Chapel proffered with a negligent wave of his massive arm.

'It ain't a thing,' he said. 'We're glad to have you. Lonely life we lead out here. Need company. Take Kate in particular, over there. She gets blue from bein' alone so much. Don't blame her. You try to cheer her up and I'll thank you for it.'

The girl flushed and parted her lips to protest, but her father, laughing uproariously, drove her and the others out of the room.

'You boys make yourselves to home,' he said from the door. 'I'll see that you're kept quiet. If you need anything, just holler. We chow in about half an hour. We'll send up some broth and chicken for Mister Angus. S'long, boys.'

He banged the door after him and went down the hall with a thunderous step.

The moment he was assured that there was no danger of being overheard, Lou Alp cried: 'Did you see?'

His companion turned moodily. 'See what?'

'The girl!'

'Huh?'

'The girl, blockhead!'

'Forget the girl.'

Chapel began to pace the floor slowly. Once he stopped and kicked at the fire so that a shower of sparks went snapping up the chimney.

'Don't cuss women,' said Alp, his face darkening. He was a good-looking fellow in his lean, dark way but, when he frowned, his face became savage to the point of venom.

'Cuss women?' said the other with a start. 'Who cussed them? I didn't mean to.'

'What a girl,' sighed Alp. He looked hungrily at Chapel but, seeing that he could not confide in the larger man, he changed the topic reluctantly. 'I guess we landed on our feet well enough.'

'I guess we did.'

'You don't seem terrible cheerful about it.'

'Maybe I don't,' growled Chapel.

'What's wrong?'

'They're clean,' said Jack. He straightened, and took a deep breath. 'They're clean!'

The sneak thief gathered the bed-clothes a little closer around his throat. 'But ain't ... ain't you clean yourself, Jack? Wasn't it a frame that put you in jail?'

There was a sort of acid eagerness in his query, a bitter longing to hold his head as high as his companion's.

'I s'pose I'm all right,' said the big man dubiously. 'But I've been in jail, and I bring the scent of it with me. I've been in the shadow, and now I don't feel right. Understand?'

The thief merely stared. His mind came near enough to comprehension to be disturbed, but no more.

In the meantime Jack Chapel paced up and down the floor thoughtfully. 'Did you

162

notice their eyes?' he kept repeating. 'Nothing behind them. Did you notice their eyes? Straight as a string. You can look a mile into eyes like that. Nothing to hide in 'em.'

'What have you got to hide?' asked Lou, rather viciously.

'Nothin' much. I'm just a supposed murderer and an uncaught highway robber. I'm a jail breaker and a bum. Outside of them little things, I guess the doctor'll give me a clean bill of health.'

He began to laugh in an ugly manner. Then the laughter broke off short, and he stood beside the fire with his elbow resting on the mantel. Over his downcast face the light tossed up bursts of yellow and bursts of red. It made the lines deeper and the strong jaw became a cruel, dominant feature. Lou Alp, looking on, saw as from a distance there was some inner struggle going on in the man. But he did not speak. He could not even silently name the trouble to himself.

'Nobody'll ever get anything on you,' he ventured at length.

'But what about myself?' cried Jack Chapel. He threw out his hand, but there was no oratorical suggestion in the gesture. It was simply the appeal of one seeking aid. 'They took us in and didn't ask any questions. Why, if the old man had asked questions, he could have punched my story full of holes. But he's so honest, he doesn't bother himself doubting. Well...' He stopped.

The sneak thief once more huddled deeper into the clothes. 'Well?' he echoed faintly.

'Don't talk. I'm filled full of something ... deviltry, I guess. I'm about ready to bust, Alp!'

V

A still small voice warned Lou Alp to be silent and let the mind of his companion work by itself. As one sees lights through a fog and cannot tell whether they mean ships or land or danger, so he stared at the gloomy face of Jack Chapel and wondered what passed behind his eyes. Secretly he rather despised Jack. Such exhibitions of emotion seemed ludicrous to Lou Alp.

Only one thing could extract any great display of his own inner self, and that was his overlord: fear. Yet, at the end of the chase when he found himself hopelessly lost, he could display the stoicism of an Indian. No third degree could make him betray the secrets of himself or of a confederate. Nothing under heaven could make him talk when he was helpless. The consequence was that each arrest was for a new and different crime, and not once had the police been able to link together a complete record of his doings from his testimony.

That day, for instance, up to the time when he was shot he was a coward, a trembling, rank coward. But the moment the bullet plowed through his flesh and made him helpless, he became brave. He had endured the torture of the ride with few murmurs, and only the new danger of Chapel's imminent desertion had shattered his nerves.

He was, indeed, the exact opposite of Chapel. To Lou Alp the exciting moment was the approach to this house where they knew no one, and where they might be betrayed and exposed. Once they were inside the place, helpless, hopelessly consigned to one course of action, fear departed from Lou Alp just as the fear which made the Indian flee in battle left him when he was in the hands of his enemy. On the other hand, Jack Chapel was perfectly at home meeting active danger, but this house closed around him like a new prison. The storm had been nothing except sound and fury, against which one could battle; but the silence of the house lay heavily on him. He was tormented by thoughts which could never enter the cramped forehead of Lou Alp. Under the sting of those thoughts he writhed. One room held the two men, but a world separated them.

In a few moments there was a tap at the door, which Jack Chapel answered. Katherine Moore entered with a steaming tray of food and her glance went pleasantly toward the wounded man, so that Lou Alp raised himself on one elbow, expectantly, and smiled back. Chapel took the tray.

'Thanks,' he said. 'But I'll take care of Lou.'

The girl glanced at him in bewilderment, his tone had been so sharp. She apparently struggled against a touch of irritation, and then the feeling of a hostess overcame her scruple of anger.

'We'll see that he's comfortable,' she suggested, 'and then we'll both have to go down to dinner. Everything's about ready.'

Chapel, on the way to the bed, turned back on her. 'I'd better stay here till he's through. He might want something.'

She paused, then, 'We can leave the door open and hear him if he calls.'

'If you don't mind, I'll bring a tray up for myself and stay with Lou.'

This stark bluntness astonished Lou. It was almost as if Jack Chapel considered the girl an enemy. Katherine Moore continued to examine their strange guest in silent surprise. She said at last, laughing a little: 'It will be a terrible disappointment to Dad. He's been congratulating himself on having someone to talk to. As a matter of fact, he's waiting for you now in the front room.'

'Then I'll go,' said Jack sullenly. He eyed his companion with a hopeless eye. 'Get along without me, Lou?'

'Sure,' said the other. 'Sure, I can get along

without you. 'S a matter of fact, I'd kind of like to be alone, not meanin' no offense to you, Jack.'

Jack favored him with a brief glare and turned on his heel. The girl took the tray and placed it on the table beside the bed while she stacked pillows behind Alp. He watched the movements of her hands in a happy trance. Sometimes as she leaned her hair came close to his eyes, and the firelight was in it. She hummed a little, working over him, and the sound completed the charm for Lou. It seemed to him that he was swept outside of himself and carried away. Something was taken from him, and in its place a light and heady happiness began to run into him. She built up the pillows behind him; she took him under the shoulders and helped him to sit up higher; she put the tray across his knees.

'Are you comfortable?'

'Yes.'

'Need anything more?'

'Nope.'

'You must eat as well as you can. Mother says that's the thing for you. Have to build up lots of blood, you know, to take the place of what you lost.'

Under his eyes she uncovered the dishes. The fragrance spoke strongly to the famished Lou Alp, and still he could not eat.

'Let me see you start,' she was saying.

The sneak thief folded his hands and

smiled vaguely at her. 'Somehow, I can't,' he murmured.

'It's the pain,' nodded the girl. 'I know how it works on one's appetite. You're mighty brave not to complain about it. Never a word all this time.'

Lou Alp was dazed. He, brave? Since his earliest recollection he had been kicked about by stronger men. Brave? One flash of fire in the eyes of another man had always made him sick at heart. Brave? He looked sadly at the girl, for she seemed so bright, so clean eyed, so beautiful, that the old rhythm ran into his head: 'None but the brave deserve the fair.'

'Oh,' said Lou Alp, 'I don't mind the pain, hardly. I'm kind of used to it, you know?'

A little impulse of sympathy moved the girl to lay her hand over his and press it warmly. 'You're the sort of man my father likes,' she declared, and her smile went through the eyes of Lou Alp and embraced his whole soul with warmth. Something akin to fear was in him and an enormous happiness wavered in front of him. A dream-happiness, and he trembled for fear the delicate illusion should vanish. The world-shattering truth came home to him. He, Lou Alp, was respected and admired as a brave man.

She was speaking of something else. What she said did not matter. The important thing was to keep her talking.

168

'Your friend is a little shaken up, I guess. Must have been an awful shock to hear that gun explode and see you fall!'

'Him? Shaken up?' gasped Lou Alp. He laughed faint and shrill. 'Lady, you don't know him.'

He observed that she was frowning thoughtfully, and began to regret what he had just said.

'He wasn't nervous?' she asked.

'He ain't got any nerves,' declared Lou Alp.

'Hmm,' said the girl.

Lou Alp gathered that in some cases she considered nerves a commendable possession. He felt that she was forming a strong prepossession against Jack Chapel, and for some strange reason this fact pleased him greatly. Indeed, Lou Alp would gladly have destroyed her good opinion of every man in the world except one.

'I'll tell you how it is with Jack,' he said. 'He's hard. You see?'

'Ah?' said the girl.

It occurred to the thief that he must not go too far, for a suspicion of one would embrace them both.

'But he's square,' added Lou. 'He's terrible square in spite of the fact that he's hard.'

'Terrible square is a good way to put it. He surely has a cold eye.'

Lou Alp became alarmed. 'You don't see under the surface,' he declared. 'In a pinch he's the best pal that ever stepped. No boastin', no braggin', but when the time comes he steps out and does his part. Steady as a rock, true as steel, honest as the day, that's the sort of a gent Jack is.'

If he praised his friend, was he not removing the foundation of any suspicion she might have? Was he not, by allusion, strengthening his own safety and good repute in this household? 'Birds of a feather,' etc. Then he observed that readily as the girl had been prejudiced against Jack Chapel, she was equally ready to be prejudiced in his favor.

'Is he all those things? In fact, I guessed at part of them.'

'Look at the way he done for me,' went on Lou Alp. 'It wasn't his fault I got shot. Then, when a lot of gents I know would of sat down and let me freeze to death, he starts right out to carry me and get me to some sort of help. Tears up his own shirt, makes a bandage, starts the long pull up that hill...'

'Up hill?' echoed Kate Moore.

'Down hill, I mean. I got my tongue twisted. But he took me a long way. Most men would of buckled before they carried me half so far. Then he saw the house. Didn't leave me there in the snow to freeze while he went and got help, but he carried me right down, with his breath comin' more like a rasp every step. That's the sort of a gent...'

His voice faltered and died away, for he

170

looked more closely at her and saw that her eyes were on fire.

'It was a fine thing to do,' declared the girl. 'It was a fine thing. Sounds simple, but I know how hard it was. No wonder he was gruff after all that hard work. And he wanted to stay with you! Why, he has a lot of affection for you, Mister Angus.'

'Him and me ... pals,' murmured Lou Alp.

He felt, miserably, that the light was gone for him. She stood up. 'I'm going down, now. They'll be waiting for me.'

'I'm sorry,' said Lou.

'For what?'

'I'll explain later.'

She went lightly out of the room, smiled back at him from the door, and was gone. A weight settled on the heart of the thief.

VI

Alp had that surpassing mortification, the feeling that he had been defeated with his own weapons, that he had overreached himself. He had talked so hard to remove her dislike of Jack Chapel that he had overshot the mark and made her just as keen in an opposite direction. Before she left she had been looking at Lou through a film, and he knew perfectly well that on the other side of that film was the face of Jack Chapel.

171

He writhed in his bed and forgot the tray of food before him. If he had only dismissed Jack with a careless word of reassurance, but he had drawn a clear and strong portrait. Even now she would be downstairs studying the man. This thought led on to further misery, for Lou felt that there was much to be studied in Jack. If she once seriously turned her attention upon him it would be long before she finished the examination.

Turning restlessly in his bed, he saw that the last light of day was gone and the early winter evening, almost as black as night with the storm, had come. The window was white and sparkling with the crusted snow, but behind it was a field of dark. The fire, dying toward a bed of coals, no longer held the room in shadow but sent a steady glow over the opposite wall and kept the ceiling dim. It was a big, square, old-fashioned chamber with plenty of reach overhead, yet for all the solidity of the wall, the storm pried through crevices, perhaps around the window, and sent probing, cold fingers about the room. These icy touches of the air chilled the heart of the thief. He began to eat but without tasting his food.

Perhaps in all his life Alp had never seen a thing he desired to possess in another manner than taking it in his hands. The pinnacles of his life had been the moments when a weight of gold glided over the tips of his

172

fingers, or when the cold surface of a rare jewel set the skin of his hand prickling with delight. He looked at those agile, lean, pale hands of his now with dumb lack of understanding. They were his weapons, his only weapons. They were his 'open sesame' with which he set ajar the doors to his desires. They were his livelihood. They comprised his profundities and his subtleties. They were almost detached intelligences. They could glide over human skin without alarming the person he touched. They could gesture with the speed of a camera shutter, eluding the most trained and vigilant eye. The nerves of those sensitive finger tips informed him of the mechanism of a lock at the first turning of a knob. In the center of his palm a mind seemed to work.

Now Alp sat in his bed staring wistfully at the capable hands and realizing that the new thing which he desired was beyond the power of instruments ten times more gifted. In a word, it was something which could not be grasped, which eluded the usual methods of acquisition, which could not be bought or traded for, or stolen. Lifting his eyes again, Alp heard the storm go whining past the house, a lonely sound, and he felt here was music made to order for him.

What was the matter with him he did not know. Indeed, in all matters of emotion he was younger and less developed than a child. He knew fear from the ground up, but beyond that he was uneducated in matters of the soul. In a vague way he knew that the girl was at the root of his trouble; and yet in what way he could not tell. He had known other girls before. There was the one whom he had taken to the theater out of the slums, where she lived a soiled, small life bounded by the reaches of a dozen streets around one central place of noise, scrambling children, drunken men, scolding women. To that girl he had been a superior power, a voice of all knowledge. They had had a few weeks of intimate companionship, but he soon tired of her and made it very plain to her that she had become an annoyance. The effect of this experience was the crushing of all her ideals and aspirations to lead a life of the better sort. If Alp had been told that he was connected with her failure, or even to blame for it, he would have been the most astonished man in Manhattan. But of such experiences his knowledge of women was built, and therefore it was no wonder that he found a new world in Katherine Moore. She possessed a combination which upset and startled him. He finally sank into brooding over his half finished tray of food.

How long he remained there without lifting his head he could not tell, but it must have been a long time. When he was roused by the entrance of Chapel, he felt as though he had been wakened from a deep sleep. He instantly straightened among his pillows. Into his thoughts of the moment before, the growing pain of his leg had entered, but now the pain was clean forgotten. An air of excitement had entered with the form of Chapel, and Alp, with his usual sensitiveness to changes, shared the unexpressed emotion.

It showed in the light, quick step of the larger man. It showed in the manner in which he walked swiftly back and forth through the room. Now and then he stopped in the midst of his pacing, and then went on again. Not gloomily, but as one rapt in a happy mood. Now and again a smile flashed on his lips and his eyes danced. The light murmur of his humming came to Alp in the bed. For some mysterious reason he connected that humming with the humming of the girl. He listened again. It seemed to be the same tune. It went through the heart of Lou Alp with a bitter pang.

As a matter of fact for the first time in his life he was jealous. In his small soul each emotion was over-mastering. In his narrow heart every desire was a cloud-sweeping thing. Before Chapel spoke, the sneak thief knew that the girl was at the bottom of this sudden mood, just as he suddenly realized that she had been at the bottom of Chapel's previous depression.

Suddenly the larger man started and became aware of his companion. He hurried across to him and took the tray. He was filled with concern that his friend had been left alone so long. He apologized because he had not seen that the tray was still burdening his knees.

To all of this Lou listened in silence. He felt that something was beneath the rush of good feeling. It impressed him as penny alms thrown to a beggar by a newly-made million-aire. He had to cast a film over his eye to keep its coldness from being apparent. Chapel carried the tray out of the room and, when he had done that, he hurried back and sat down on the side of Lou's bed.

'Been lonely up here, old man?' he asked, and then without waiting for an answer: 'Pretty clubby supper we had downstairs. These people are all to the good. Fine crowd. No dog. Plain, straight from the shoulder, don't turn corners when they talk. The old man is a world-beater outside of his stale yarns. His wife is a lady ... a lady!'

He repeated the word with a singular soft-ening of face and voice, but Lou Alp waited for something else, and presently it came.

'You dropped some pretty good words for me with the girl, didn't you?' he said, and his eyes were actually moist with gratitude. 'Tell you what, Lou, you're such a silent gent that sometimes I hardly know how to make you out. About as noisy as a snake, not meaning that in an ugly way.'

''S all right,' said Lou quietly.

He felt like a snake at that moment, and he would gladly have struck Jack Chapel with poison fangs.

'I made a fool of myself when I met her,' went on Jack. He rocked back on the bed and gathered his knees within his strongly interlaced fingers. 'But she dazed me a bit. I wasn't set for her, you see, and she made me feel that I'd been a skunk. You know how a good girl makes a gent feel?'

Lou did not know, but he kept his ignorance under a discreet veil. He knew only one thing now, and that was a raging hatred.

'I guess you made up for the way you met her later on,' he suggested, and smiled for fear that he could not control a sneer.

Chapel flushed at the memory. 'I dunno how it was,' he said, nodding. 'She seemed to sort of like me. Kept looking at me in a bright sort of way. You know?'

Alas, Lou Alp did know, and inwardly writhed in pain. 'Go on,' he said rather hoarsely.

'What's the matter?' asked Chapel.

'Matter? Nothin'. I've got a bit of a cold, that's all,' replied Alp.

'Hmm!' murmured Chapel. Every now and then he forgot what he was about to say and sat smiling into space. 'What a girl!' he said at length. 'Anyway, she began talking after a while. Sat next to me at supper, you see? I ain't much at talking, and I had the handicap of knowing that I'd almost insulted her when we first met. But it don't take any sense to talk to her. She leads the way and a gent can just sort of follow along easy on the trail she makes. She sure carried the lantern for me and told me where to step. Right off she spilled out all the nice things you said about me, partner. Mighty decent of you, too. Fine of you to come out with a bunch of stuff. Somehow,' he paused, and his glance flicked across the face of Lou with a shade of its old coldness, 'somehow I didn't expect anything like that out of you.'

The sneak thief grunted.

'Well,' said Chapel after a pause, in which he appeared to be stumbling with incoherent mind over the memories of that evening, 'I wrote down in red what you said about me, and I ain't going to forget it. You're solid with me for life, Lou Alp.'

Alp said nothing at all. Outside the window a fresh gust of the storm went rattling and howling by and, if he could have done so, Lou would gladly have transformed his companion into a dead leaf and thrown him to the mercies of that wind. He began to ask questions and, though every answer was a fresh probing of this new and acute inner wound, he could not desist. He took a perverse pleasure in torturing himself.

He learned that Kate and Jack had talked together a good deal during the supper. Old man Moore had broken in for a few snatches of talk. When he found that Jack had no pronounced political views, was not an expert cattleman, had no intimate knowledge of guns and gunnery, he lost interest. He confined his own share in the conversation to a few threadbare anecdotes at which the family had faintly smiled, as at old, familiar faces, and at which Jack had made an effort and had been able to muster a laugh at the correct times. 'Kind of jokes my grandfather told,' said Jack.

Then, after supper, they had drifted into a big, dark room with a fireplace of gigantic dimensions, filled with great logs that roared and snapped like musketry. Here Mr. Moore had fallen asleep in his easy-chair, Mrs. Moore had gone up to her room, and Jack and the girl had the time and the silence to themselves. He appeared to have made great progress in the direction of securing information. He knew the schools to which she had gone. He knew the names of her friends and particularly of one Ross Kirkpatrick, of whom Chapel spoke with a concentrated venom, which it was easy for Lou to understand. He was a wealthy mining man. He had built up his own fortune. He was an Eastern 'college gent.' Chapel referred to him with the polite endurance a Puritan would show for the devil. In the middle of this talk the door was suddenly flung open, and without any warning Katherine Moore flung into the room.

VII

The rush of air from the opened door passed like a solemn sighing through the big room, but it did not need that sound to send the chill through Alp and Jack Chapel. The face of the girl was enough. She went straight to Chapel.

'Have you done anything wrong?' she whispered.

Why was all the concern for Jack Chapel? Was there not another man in the room? Through a haze of jealous agony Lou heard Jack answer: 'In my time ... things bad enough, I guess. Why?'

It was the grave and perfectly controlled voice which Alp envied. He was almost glad that the girl had not come so directly to him with that whispered alarm, for he knew that a sudden blanching of the face would have answered her. But Jack Chapel was quite controlled.

'I don't mean what you've done long ago, but lately... I haven't any time ... a robbery...'

There was a little pause – a heart-breaking little pause – and during that space of a second or so Alp stared intensely at the girl. She was without color. There seemed a cold film of blue shadow around her mouth, and her eyes were unnaturally dark and deep. There was accusation in the glance she fixed upon Chapel. It was rather a prayer for his good. It seemed impossible that Jack Chapel could lie to that face.

Then he heard Chapel's voice, rather stifled. 'Robbery? I'll say this: that I've never taken a penny that I didn't feel was owing to me!'

Lou Alp sighed with relief. After all, had not the queer fool said something like this when he was about to commit the robbery? Had he not actually left part of the money behind, and the greater part at that? But he had no time for his own thoughts. There was a sobbing, small breath of relief from the girl.

'I knew ... oh, I knew,' she said. 'But I had to ask you. And I had to ... to tell you that Marshal Gaines is here, and that he's coming up to see you.'

'Who?'

Lou could see that the name shook his companion.

'Marshal Gaines. But I'm so glad ... so happy ... that there's no trouble.'

She was gone like a shadow and, as she went through the door, she looked back as she had looked at Lou once before, only this time the look was for Jack Chapel. And what a look it was! What a flash of eyes! What a tremulous smile! Bitterly Alp remembered that not once had she glanced at him this time. Her whole care was for Jack Chapel, and he, the wounded man, could fend for himself as best he might. His companion turned slowly toward the bed, smiling faintly.

'Who's Marshal Gaines?' asked Alp, leaning forward.

'She's got eyes like a man,' was the singular answer of Chapel. 'Eyes like a man's eyes. But her smiles! That's all woman. Have you noticed her smile, Lou?'

'Forget her smile,' groaned the sneak thief. 'Who's Marshal Gaines?'

'Marshal Gaines?' echoed Chapel carelessly. 'Oh, he's just a gent that I know.'

The words froze the trembling heart of the thief to motionlessness. 'That you know?' he whispered at length. 'Then, for heaven's sake, does he know you?'

'Better'n you do, a lot,' replied Jack Chapel.

Lou Alp fell back in the pillows with a chalky face. 'What does it mean?' he asked.

'It means we're done for,' said Chapel.

'No, no, no,' whined Lou. 'No, no, no!' He began wringing his hands; then he stretched them out to Jack Chapel. 'Gimme a lift out of the bed. I can't go back to the pen, pal. I can't go! Who got me into this? You did! Who tried to keep away from the whole thing? I did! You got to save me. You got to!'

'Shut up,' said the larger man. He winced before this exhibition of cowardice and looked at the other with new eyes. 'Is this the stuff you're made of? Shut up, or she'll hear you!'

'I don't care,' gasped Alp. 'Gimme a lift to the window. I can stand the drop to the ground. There's snow on it and it'll break the fall. Then, my leg's good enough. Gimme a help and I can wiggle along. I'll get away from this infernal trap.'

'Shut up, will you?' snapped Chapel. 'I got you into this. I'd get you out if I could, but I can't. Now stop whining. I told you who the gent is. It's Marshal Gaines. There's no hope.'

'None?'

'None!'

A singular change came over Alp. He arranged the pillows behind his back. His natural color returned. 'Pass me the makings, will you?' he demanded. 'I thought there was a show but, if there ain't, let's see what the music's like.'

The sudden change of front made Chapel blink. 'You've got something, Lou,' he admitted admiringly. He himself was gray about the mouth, and his jaw was set.

'Tell me about Gaines.'

'It'd take all the rest of the night. I'll tell you this much. If I knew that Gaines was out on my trail, I'd stop runnin'. I'd turn around and go in and give myself up to him to save a lot of trouble for both him and me. That's the sort he is. He's so good that, if I had two guns and he didn't have nothin' but a knife, I'd throw up my hands and let him take me. Why, man, I ain't a gunfighter, and Gaines is a devil. He took "Sandy" Crew. He took Gus Landers. He killed Peters and Galbright, and... I could reel 'em off by the yard. That's Gaines.'

'Well,' sighed the sneak thief, 'it's something to be taken by a bird like that. Thing that makes me sore is to be nabbed by some greasy cheap flatty, like's happened to me. Well, lead on your man-eater and let's have a look at his teeth.'

He twisted his cigarette deftly into shape, lighted a match, and waited with a steady hand for the sulfur to burn away. Then he lighted his smoke and inhaled a deep breath.

'That's nerve,' admitted Chapel, and brushed the perspiration from his own forehead. 'That's nerve a-plenty. Here they come.'

They heard the rhythm of footfalls coming unhurriedly up the stairs. Once, and once only, the eyes of the sneak thief darkened as he glanced toward the window. Then his glance went back to the face of Chapel and lingered there with a hungry content. In this crisis he felt his superiority. The larger man was going through a torture.

'The girl,' asked Chapel. 'What'll she think?'

'Nothing,' said Lou coldly. 'After a day or two she'll brush us out of her mind. No trouble at all when they see they've made a mistake. Girls can forget anything.'

'Do you think so?' said Jack through his teeth. 'But not this girl. She'll remember. Lou, what'll we get for this?'

'Oh, about five more years for you, same for me, maybe, or less seeing you started everything and simply took me along.'

'Five and ten ... fifteen ... forty-one,' said the other, rather incoherently. 'Too long! She...'

He stopped, for the knob of the door turned slowly, then opened and Moore entered with a man behind him. Lou Alp prepared himself for a shock meeting the eye of this savage marshal, this man so terrible that even Jack Chapel gave up at the mere thought of him. But what he saw was a dusty little man with misty, long-distance eyes. He carried his hat in an apologetic manner in both hands, fingering the brim as though he felt that he was out of place, but Lou was fascinated by the action of those nervous broken hands. He recognized in them a quality of deft and easy precision.

'Here they are, Marshal,' said Moore. 'Here's Jack Chandler and his partner, Louis Angus. Jack and Lou, here's Marshal Gaines, my old friend. He wants to talk to you boys. There's been an outrage. Holdup down the valley. Thirty-five hundred dollars walked off by a holdup artist. Between you and me, Marshal, I don't see what good this talk will do you. That holdup was worked by one gent. Here's two of 'em.'

The marshal nodded. He stepped from behind Moore and glanced at Chapel. Alp braced himself for the shock of the recognition, the flash of steel, as the marshal covered his man. He was stunned by the difference between his expectation and what actually happened. The marshal passed Chapel over with a glance and turned at once to Lou Alp, lying there helpless in the bed. It was embarrassing. Alp blinked and then smoothed his face to a smile.

'How are you, Marshal,' he said. It was always a policy of his to be ingratiating with police. And here was simply a new form of flatty.

'I'm doin' fairly well,' said the marshal, advancing as far as the foot of the bed. 'Got a touch of rheumatism, though. Settled in my left hip a couple of years ago and I ain't much in the saddle when these cold snaps come on.'

'Oh, you'll do well enough,' boomed Moore from the background.

'Sorry to bother you boys,' went on the marshal, 'but I got to look over the strangers in these parts. I'd be sayin' that you're kind of new around here, Mister Angus?'

'Kind of,' admitted Alp.

He observed a spark that came up behind the eye of the marshal, and the spark grew into a small and hungry fire. It made Alp feel distinctly ill at ease. The marshal's form was growing rapidly in his eyes.

'Well,' said the marshal, 'it ain't often that we get visitors around here in the cold spells. How long you think of staying on, partner?'

It occurred suddenly to Lou Alp that there was a double meaning in what the marshal was saying. He was addressing to the thief words apparently quite innocent in the ears of the other people in the room, but to Lou they might mean many things. At least he surmised that double meaning, and he decided to try out his theory.

'I dunno,' he declared. 'Maybe a month. Maybe a year. Maybe more.'

The marshal shook his head. 'I dunno,' he said, 'but I kind of feel maybe you're makin' a mistake. Take a gun wound like that, and it don't stand up none too well in stormy weather. I know.'

Lou Alp shifted his eyes to the puzzled face of Jack Chapel. Plainly his companion was bewildered by this friendly dialogue and was waiting for the denouement.

'Know what I'd do if I was you?' went on the marshal.

'Well?' asked Alp seriously.

'I'd climb on a hoss as soon as that wound would let me and get away from here. I'd get down to some warmer climate. Otherwise you'll find rheumatism settlin' in your leg and making you lame, maybe for the rest of your life. Understand?'

'Maybe I do,' said Lou, and his eyes grew larger. 'Maybe I do.'

'You look like an intelligent sort,' said the marshal carelessly. 'I wouldn't give that advice to everybody. Take your friend ... Chandler' – and he turned to Chapel and looked him over – 'if he had a wound like that in the leg, I'd leave it to his blood and good bones to bring him through safe and sound, even up here in the winter and in the mountains. Fact is, seems to me that some gents is all cut out for mountain life, winter or summer ... and some ain't.'

This statement of Gaines's was prompted by the fact that he had learned of Chapel's innocence of the crime with which he had been charged through letters from the prison authorities. The real murderer had confessed. Chapel understood.

Moore began to laugh thunderously. 'There you go on your rheumatics,' he said. 'Get you on that and they ain't any means of pryin' you loose from it. Come on downstairs and have a drink, Gaines. I guess you've talked to these boys long enough?'

188

'Sure. I guess I have.' The glance of the marshal went back and dwelt gently upon the face of Alp. The latter changed color. 'I'm sure I have,' continued the marshal.

'And you don't no ways think that they took the coin?' chuckled Moore.

'Nope. What I'm really lookin' for, Moore, is somebody that thought the big boss owed him some money, about thirty-five hundred of it. Well, glad to've met you boys. S'long.'

Without another word he was gone. Chapel turned to Lou with a white face.

'He didn't know you, after all,' said Alp cheerily. 'Ain't that a load off? He didn't know you, the batty-eyed old fool. He missed you clean.'

'He knew me,' said Jack, 'better'n you do. Why, three years ago I went on a hunting trip with the marshal. Not only knows me, but he knows that I ought to be in prison on a charge of murder.'

'He can't know that. He'd...' began Alp.

'But he does. I got a letter from him while I was there.'

'Then he's gone down to frame us!'

'That's not his way. And he seemed to take a fancy to you, Lou.'

'You fool! Didn't you hear him plain as day tell me to get out of this country as soon as I could ride a hoss, and stay out?'

'You mean?'

'I mean that he knowed me. Heaven knows

how. He's giving you a chance to make good, but he's letting me go to the devil.'

VIII

However incredible the miracle was, yet it happened. Not only did the marshal leave the house of Moore, but he never returned. Afterward Lou and Jack heard frequent reports. The marshal let it be known throughout the countryside that he was going to get the daring outlaw or bust in the attempt. It was reported that he had brought several clues into the wind, and it was known that on two occasions he had made long rides through the mountains. But still the perpetrator of the outrage remained undiscovered.

What it was that urged the marshal toward this elaborate camouflage, Lou and Jack did not know, unless indeed it was that out of old friendship he had determined to give Jack another chance. One of the few failures which the marshal had ever made was being scored in this case, and people of the mountains wondered at it. Sheriff Meigs took a hand and followed separate clues, but those clues never brought him to the house of Moore, and Lou and Jack were safe.

The days went on with Alp improving by leaps and bounds. By the end of the first week the wound was only a red blur on the surface of the skin. In ten days he had taken his first careful step; within a fortnight he and Chapel were thinking of their departure.

Yet those days of recovery were by no means altogether happy days for Lou Alp. It was a period of storm and stress, with the storm composed of small things no louder than the laughter of a girl or the fall of a woman's foot. After that first day he saw the hopelessness of hope. Every morning, when he wakened, he made a firm resolve that that day he would bar her out of his heart. But before he had even seen her, at the first sound of her step or her voice, the hard lines in which he had set his face in preparation for the meeting dissolved, and invariably he smiled when he saw her.

If she had been oblivious of him, it would have been easier, but she paid him every attention. In fact, the girl and Jack Chapel were meeting, as it were, over his body. His welfare and the progress of his healing wound composed a topic which apparently possessed undying interest for them. He used to lie in his bed and read through the hypocritical warmth with which they made their inquiries. Always his condition was the starting point, and always the talk ended in something a thousand miles removed from him. Usually it brought both the talkers out of the room, and then a time of misery would begin for Lou Alp.

All day long, while he was bedridden, he found himself listening with terrific concentration for all sounds of life that passed through the walls of his room. When his door was left open, it was a double trial. Sometimes he could hear them talking, their voices reduced to an echoing murmur up the long hall. Sometimes the piano tinkled directly beneath him. Or again, and this more and more often, he caught the sound of their singing. They had learned some two-part songs. Jack Chapel had a strong, somewhat rough baritone, and the girl's voice was a light, sweet-toned soprano. It seemed that his strength covered the meagerness of her voice, and her quality smoothed the harshness of the man. The result was altogether pleasant. Lou Alp admitted that fact with the cruel and cold justice which had come to temper his mind more and more since the first day. But all things else were nothing compared to the sound of the girl's laughter. He could almost hear that even when the door was closed. He had a seventh sense for it. He could feel the rhythm of the sound before it was audible to his ear. He could tell it by a sudden quickening of the pulse and falling of the heart. Yet it was a mellow laughter, though it went through the heart of Lou Alp like a sword of fire.

It is very bad for a man to think of himself

during any prolonged time. It is exceedingly evil for a man to set his heart on one desire, while his body is helpless to advance him toward his wish. A prisoner goes mad longing for green leaves. Yet the green may be on the other side of the wall, and half an hour in the sun would make him sick of the open day. Perhaps it is not the green of the leaves nor the yellow of the sun so much as the very thickness of the wall that torments the prisoner. Under ordinary conditions Lou would no doubt have cast the thought of the girl away or have pushed the memory of her into an obscure pain, recurring now and then.

Yet, perhaps, what a man once feels truly, he can never forget. Lou Alp was truly in love. Somewhere in that small, mean soul was fuel which fed the flame until it burned as brightly, as intensely as any noble passion in the heart of a noble man. The flame was too much for Lou. It crumbled that shell of a man. It tormented him. If he had been a poet, he could have translated his suffering into song and found relief. Or if he had been strong in manhood, he could have poured the truth frankly before the girl, and then roused himself with a muscular effort.

There was not a strong muscle in the body of Lou Alp. There was not a strong thought in his brain. She became to him what the drug is to the famished dope addict. He was in a fever, and the sight of her face was snow on his brow; his mind was filled with noises, and the sound of her voice brought him blessed peace. She fed the fire and she stacked it. If at times he blessed her as a devotee blesses his patron saint, at other times he writhed on his bed and cursed her with equal fervor.

There were not two possibilities. In the end there was only one result, and that result was a consuming, a devout hatred for Jack Chapel. Not that he really looked forward to winning the girl for himself if he could push Jack out of the way, but every time the girl smiled on Jack it cost Lou a pang, which he swore his companion should repay. Every time he heard them singing, every time the girl laughed in a high-hearted happiness, then Lou turned his face to the wall and begged God for a chance to blast this man, body and soul.

He did not reason on to final results. He only knew that Jack Chapel caused him pain, and therefore he wished to destroy the man. If it could be viewed abstractly, this devilish passion of Lou Alp's, was it not strange that such a girl as Katherine Moore, who had never in her life done as much evil as would give shading to a single day of an average man, was it not strange that she should have been the cause of such black viciousness?

She did not guess it, and Jack Chapel did not guess it. Once the sneak thief had determined that in some way or another he would destroy his former friend, he masked his purpose with truly fiendish cunning. At the very moment when he as closing his mind and his heart to all gentleness, he appeared to open his whole life to Jack. He told him stories of his childhood, and the dark, vicious days in the streets of Manhattan. He told him of adventures, some mean and all exciting. He told him things which would have caused an average man to turn away in loathing, but Jack was not average. He had on occasion called this fellow 'partner,' and in his Western eyes that was a sacred word, no more capable of recall than the fire of heaven. Moreover, a confession always subtly implies a reform and a change. Indeed, it is this hope of making the world believe him a better man or a man capable of better things, if he has the chance, that makes the suspected murderer make a clean breast of his past and sign his own death warrant. He will sign the paper that sends him to the gallows in the hope that his confession will draw one word of regret, one word of sympathy.

In this case the sneak thief was correct in his deductions. Jack answered the confidences of Lou with confessions of his own, and the two men seemed drawing close toward a true friendship. There was one bitterly sweet result of that. The more Lou wormed himself close to Jack, the more often the girl was with Lou. And to the man who is hungry, both the alms of charity and the alms of scorn are welcome. Lou accepted her presence with a deep joy and, knowing that her presence was due to Jack, he cursed Jack for it.

In the end, if he could have thought of no better way, Lou Alp would have stuck a knife into the back of Jack Chapel while his friend slept. But it did not turn out so. There was a better way, and Lou found it.

He had been searching his mind for days and days, hunting for some weapon which would strike down the larger man. One thing had repeatedly come home to him. The past of Jack, if it were known, would come like a wave and snatch him away to the prison as it withdrew. But if his prison record were known, the same danger that threatened one of them would threaten the other. Lou Alp was wanted, hardly less than Jack Chapel. He must find something that would overwhelm Chapel without scratching so much as a finger of the hand of he who struck him. Otherwise where was the satisfaction? Where would be the deep after-joy of seeing the girl in her despair, and remember her happiness of the past and all the pain which she had poured into his brain?

And then it came to him. It was the robbery. In that, at least, he had had no hand. Why could not that be worked? There was the lightning which he could direct at Chapel without singeing his own skin.

Suppose, therefore, that someone were to search the house for evidence of that crime. He would find thirty-five hundred dollars in the bedroom which Chapel now occupied, for Alp had insisted that he keep all the money until they were both well clear of the house. Also, the searcher would find the two revolvers which Jack had taken from the guards. Was not that proof enough?

But suppose that they then asked if he, Lou Alp, were not mixed up in this crime? Very easily answered! He had been through the mountains with Jack Chapel. He had met the man accidentally and they had struck up a friendship without asking about the past. On the trip they had stopped at a village. There they had heard about the coming of the pay-roll. The next day Jack had disappeared. Lou waited for his return. Late in the afternoon he had come, showing signs of having covered a long distance in a short time. They had gone on together in the storm. Then the accidental shooting occurred.

Or make it even stronger. After the return of his companion, Lou protested against the robbery in the first place and against keeping the money in the second. He argued violently. Jack Chapel flew into a rage, offered him part of the money for his silence, was refused, and then deliberately drew his revolver and shot down the unoffending Lou whose passion for law and order had drawn him to this dangerous pass. Thinking of this portion of the story, Alp felt tears of self-sympathy rise in his eyes. There he was on the ground, bleeding. Compassion seized the murderous robber as he saw his companion and late friend lying there in the snow. He felt remorse. He lifted the inert body. He carried his friend to the house of Moore and for a long time, filled with gratitude for that last act of grace, Lou refused to give the information. But at last the truth must be told, and he tells it. Surely that story would be smooth enough. Besides he would perfect it before it became necessary to tell it to the officer of the law.

To whom should he send the information? Not to Marshal Gaines, but rather to Sheriff Jesse Meigs who was the known rival of the marshal in that district, and who would consider it a choice morsel if he could take the man who had escaped the hands of the celebrated marshal. The plan had more and more good points which gradually unrolled themselves before the calm eyes of Lou Alp. There would not even be a whispered reproach from Jack Chapel until Jack was helpless in the hands of the law. He would make a bargain with the sheriff that his evidence should not be used against Jack until the last moment. In the meantime he would slip away and disappear, leaving behind him the money and the guns, sufficient evidence in itself to send Jack to prison for highway robbery, if not to bring out a lynching party to hang him up by the neck. The malice of Alp went even as far as this. Necessarily so, for if Jack survived, the day of reckoning sooner or later would come.

Yet for several reasons he decided to tell the marshal only enough to hint at the crime, only enough to bring the dogs of the law on the traces of Chapel. He wrote briefly:

If you want to find the dope on the holdup that fooled Marshal Gaines, come to Moore's house and look in the room where Jack Chandler sleeps. You'll find thirty-five hundred bucks and two guns.

He addressed the envelope, writing the address as he had done the note with his left hand, for Jack Chapel knew his writing. Using the cane which Kate Moore had given him, he hobbled slowly down the stairs and then out the front door and into the wilderness of shining snow outside. It was only fifty feet to the road, and by the road was the mail box. He lifted the iron flap and dropped in the letter.

IX

The rest of that day passed smoothly. There was only one real task for Lou Alp, and that was to exaggerate his limp. For, of course, when his leg was entirely healed, he and Jack Chapel must go on together. Now it was above all things necessary that he keep Jack in the house until that letter reached the sheriff and brought the man of the law to the house of Roger Moore. How long it would require for that he had not been able exactly to deduce, but he imagined that at least two full days would be required, unless the sheriff left the town as soon as the letter reached him and rode at full speed with his men.

That thought gave Lou another qualm. He should have warned the sheriff that Jack Chapel was a dangerous man, that there might be more than one man's handful of work in taking him. He had prepared to submit meekly enough to the marshal, but that was because he knew Gaines. Driven to the wall, and particularly now that he had so much to hope from life, Jack Chapel would probably fight like a devil incarnate.

The worry of it held on into the night for Lou Alp. In the afternoon he had retired to his room, pretending a feverish aching in his leg. In reality his mind was on fire with doubts, and he sat before the fire which Jack Chapel had built for him and kept rubbing his hands. The rest of his body was warm, but his hands were moist and cold always these days. A continual tremor possessed them. This afternoon he heard much noise and bustling in the house. There was, to Lou, an appearance of stealth about the noise, but he laid that feeling to his uneasy nerves. Everyone in the house was smiling. Everyone seemed to have bright and misty eyes. Everyone had a loud voice and a gay manner. There was a sort of reckless happiness, so strong that it pervaded the atmosphere as keenly as the cold.

Lou Alp canted an ear toward these sounds and regarded them with keen suspicion. It even occurred to him that all the rejoicing was because the girl and Jack Chapel had let the others know of their engagement, and the rest of the house had kept the secret well from him. Why? Did they guess how he felt about Kate Moore? Had they penetrated beneath his bright, shifting glances? Was that the reason for their singular gentleness this day, and the kindliness of their eyes? The thought put a whip upon him and made him writhe.

Supper that night was a trial indeed. The merriment, which had gone ringing up and down the halls all day and which had seemed to cover itself stealthily, now burst out full-fledged. Roger Moore dug out his oldest and most musty stories. Mrs. Moore wore a flush in either cheek which made her seem ten years younger and turned her white hair into a mockery. Jack Chapel was continually laughing with everybody, at everybody. Once he slapped Lou on the back with a force that made the teeth of the sneak thief rattle. Joy was closed upon the world, and Lou Alp shuddered in its presence.

In some manner he got through that nightmare meal and was in his room again. He stirred the embers of his fire and roused it with fresh wood. There he sat, nodding over his plans until very late. Just after supper everyone downstairs had gathered in the big front room and Jack Chapel and Kate Moore came up to plead with him and bring him down.

'Don't you know what day it is?' they asked in one voice.

He stared at them with blank eyes.

'He doesn't know!' murmured Kate Moore to Jack Chapel, and then they laughed together musically, idiotically.

It seemed to Lou Alp that they were flaunting their joy in his face to torture him with it. Finally they gave up their pleading, cast him a word of commiseration for his leg like alms thrown to a dog, and were gone off down the hall. Hardly had the door closed on them when he caught the muffled peal of their laughter.

Fools!

Later still, while the fire was dying down, he thought that steps went up and down the hall and paused at his door. He thought he heard guarded whispers. His mind was still clear enough and strong enough to dismiss such absurd conjectures, and finally, quite late at night, he went to bed and was instantly asleep.

Dreams haunted him. People seemed to come to him. Once his eyes snapped open and he could have sworn that there had been someone leaning over him. He could almost have sworn, from the jumping of his heart and the tingling of his skin, that there was someone in the room at that very instant. He dismissed the illusion. What earthly reason could there be for stalking him?

When he wakened naturally after such a disturbed sleep, it was quite late. He lay looking up to the lofty ceiling. There was a fresh scent in the room, as if the window had been left wide open and the odor of evergreens had blown into the chamber. Lou Alp was no passionate lover of fresh air, and he certainly was never guilty of leaving the window open in winter. Then he was aware that he was hungry, and he hunched himself up in the bed, preparatory to getting up. Yet he did not slip from beneath the covers. He remained there with his elbows propping him and blinking.

For this was what he saw. On either side of

the tall window leaned a great fir branch. From the mantelpiece over the fireplace dangled a long woman's stocking, bulged out of shape by its contents. On the table beside the bed there was a scattering of parcels large and small, wrapped in red paper and tied with gaudy green ribbon.

Lou Alp sat slowly erect in the bed. Then, like a sleepwalker, he got carefully out of bed and walked across the floor, in bare feet which did not feel the cold. He took the long stocking from its hook. He opened it and drew forth the contents, one by one. A bag of sugar candies, red, green, yellow, purple, blue; a necktie of gaudy stripe; some animal cakes, gilded with the colors of life; and on and on, his hand reached down the bag until he found a card and drew it out.

A happy, happy Christmas to the man who forgot.

The card fluttered from his hand, and falling into the fireplace began to blacken with the heat of the dying embers. And yet he turned again to the stocking and continued to draw out the silly knickknacks. A jumping jack which squawked foolishly when one pressed the button.

They had given him the gifts they would give a child in the house. Why? Because he did not know? Yet he seemed to expect something different, something more, and finally, at the very bottom of the stocking, his reaching fingers closed over the last thing. He knew it before he drew it out, and the form of Lou Alp shook, and his face whitened.

At length he let the stocking fall to the floor and there in his hand was a leaden soldier with red coat and stiff back, a painted musket at his side. Upon this Lou Alp gazed with a sort of horror, and raising his hand slowly he brushed numb fingers across his forehead. He had forgotten, but now it came back to him, so many things out of the past. But how had they known about the lead soldiers which in the brief time of his child life at home had been an inevitable part of every Christmas stocking? For some reason it humbled him.

He went with the lead soldier still clutched in his hand and opened the packages on the table, the largest first. It was a fleece-lined leather coat with a card scrawled upon in a great, rough hand: *'To Lou from Roger Moore. Good luck.'*

Then a bundle of home-knitted socks so soft and woolly that they crunched up in his hand and warmed his numb finger tips. *'To Lou from Mary Moore.'*

Then a big box of cigarettes, his own favorite brand of tailor-mades. *'To Lou from Kate.'*

Then a heavy little package, the smallest of

them all. The heavy leather tore its own way out of the flimsy wrappings of its own accord. Lou took out of the holster a neat little automatic, such a gun as he had often praised to Jack Chapel as the king of weapons, rather than one of these clumsy, wrist-breaking .45s. It came apart under his deft fingers, and was assembled again. A perfect weapon!

Then the card: '*To my partner, Lou.*'

No name to that. It came suddenly home to him that no name was needed, for probably Jack Chapel had never applied the term 'partner' to any other man. Lou Alp, dry-throated, laid the weapon carefully down on the table. He took up the little case of cartridges and loaded the gun with familiar swiftness.

There is a personality in weapons. The little automatic was particularly fitted for the sneak thief. One would expect to find it on him, and certainly he had skill in its use. Many a dick in Manhattan could have testified that Lou, in spite of his cowardice, when pressed to the wall could fight with tigerish ferocity. For there is nothing quite so terrible as the cornered coward. Under the surface lay the claws, under the velvet touch the steel.

Laying aside the loaded weapon, he sank down on the side of the bed. The chilly wind, prying through the crevices of the room, set him shuddering as though with an ague, but Lou Alp paid no heed to it. His face was

206

buried in his hands, and in one hand was the leaden soldier.

In that manner Jack Chapel found him sitting when, a little later, he opened the door softly. He shut it again, just as silently. The girl behind met him with a glance of eager curiosity when he turned away. Jack Chapel laid a finger against his lips, and then whispered: 'Hush! He's remembering.'

'Poor fellow,' said the girl, and her eyes misted.

'Poor devil,' said Jack Chapel.

They had between them such a great happiness that they felt they could give alms to all the world and still have plenty left.

X

Who knows what might have happened if Lou Alp had heard nothing of what they said? But he heard. The closing of the door, softly as it was done, had roused him as whisper rouses a cat. Instantly he was beside the door, on his knees, and this was what he heard:

'Poor fellow!'

'Poor devil!'

There is no man so low as to accept pity from a successful rival. If a great tide of tenderness had been rising in the heart of Lou Alp the moment before, it was now suddenly checked. He remembered that a treasure remained to Jack Chapel. The pity had a string to it that sent him reeling and gasping back into the room, as though a bullet had plowed through his vitals. He remained there in a silent frenzy, biting his hands, beating at his face.

Who has seen the frantic contortions of the cat that, playing with the mouse, loses the little creature? For such was the fury of Lou Alp. The fact that he despised himself for still hating Jack Chapel did not matter, it only intensified the hatred.

Going down for breakfast a little later, he found the old Negro servant hobbling up in the opposite direction. Lou nodded to him, and shrank aside, for he had an almost physical aversion for Negroes. But there was a great red-lipped smile, a flash of rolling eyes, and out of a deep throat the greeting: 'Merry Christmas!'

The words came back from the lips of Lou Alp, but they came as a harsh and hardly whispered echo: 'Merry Christmas.'

That chance meeting prepared him for what was to follow. In the dining room the people were already gathering. Mrs. Moore had on a new dress and, from the manner in which she kept looking down at it and then across at her daughter, it was plain who had made the gift.

The bald head of Roger Moore was covered

208

by a black silk skull cap which he touched now and then, as one will handle a novelty. But what Lou chiefly saw was the picture of Kate Moore and Jack Chapel in the corner. They were whispering together. They were almost holding each other's hands. Lou, shocked with surprise, realized that the parents of the girl must know what had been going on, that they actually approved of her affection for this unknown fellow, this chance acquaintance.

In the meantime all eyes had whipped across in his direction the moment he put foot through the door. There was a chorus of greetings.

'I dunno what to say,' muttered Lou Alp.

'You don't have to say a thing.'

'I forgot...'

What a joyous laugh there was.

'The best joke I ever heard,' cried Roger Moore in his enormous voice. 'A man who forgot Christmas!'

The words remained ringing in the ears of Lou Alp all during the breakfast, all during the rest of the day. But, after all, what was Christmas? Weren't there other holidays? What about Washington's Birthday? What about New Year's? Certainly all those were holidays which closed banks and stores with as much definiteness as any Christmas that had ever happened. Yet no one would laugh at him for forgetting such days. And here was

Roger Moore with a brand-new jest added to his stale collection, happy as a child with a new toy.

'Don't apologize,' the old fellow said. 'You made us all a present, without knowing it. I wouldn't have missed this for a year of life!'

Wherein was the day different? For it was different. It came tinglingly to Lou Alp himself. This was the one day in the year when the world forgot its taking and gave itself up to giving. Very strange! People gave things away and were happier because of the giving.

Here he sat, the sole member of that household who had not given away valuable things, and yet all the rest were happy and he was wrapped in gloom. It made him shake his head. How had it all begun, this giving away? Out of his childhood the old story came slowly back to him, the stable, the manger, and Mary with the child. The child who grew to manhood and gave everything and took nothing. The one perfect type of the selfless man, who lived for others and who died for others.

And what was the result of this giving, this senseless outpouring of effort? Buildings erected in His name around the world, and myriad's carrying His thought and one day each year set aside for giving in some small measure as He had given. The thought burdened and bewildered Lou Alp who had lived with his hand in the pockets of others. These people had given, and yet they acted as if they had received. Kate Moore, Jack Chapel, Mrs. Moore, Roger Moore, they all met him with open eyes and open hearts as though he had conferred a favor on each by his mute acceptances.

A bee buzzing in a small, closed room fills it with sound to bursting, and one large thought crammed the narrow brain of Lou Alp until it reeled. The thought kept him occupied all that day. Automatically he spoke, answered questions, smiled vaguely, and lived on the edge of the happiness which flushed the others and raised their voices. Nothing mattered. When the cook dropped the platter and spoiled the dinner set, there was only laughter from Roger Moore, and a smiling shake of the head from Mrs. Moore. When a gust of snow rushed through an opened window and soaked the carpet, there was an outburst of merriment, and everyone set about repairing the damage.

One would have thought that the howling wind was the voice of a friend, to see these people and to hear them. One would have thought that each of them sat in expectation of a legacy. And was there not, perhaps, a legacy left them by that man who had died two thousand years before? Again the thought appalled Lou Alp.

They were seated around the dinner table.

Roger Moore was at the head, Mrs. Moore at the foot, with her cheeks roses and her hair whiter than ever by contrast. Lou Alp sat at one side, and Jack Chapel and Kate Moore at the other. It was a large table, so heaped with food that the five people seemed utterly inadequate. The mountain of bittersweet in the center helped to separate one from another, so that Lou felt that a great distance lay between him and the two opposite.

Things came and went, plates were passed before him, and he ate mechanically, hardly tasting what he touched. Roger Moore was filling his glass with wine, a rare treat in the mountains.

'Watery stuff,' Roger Moore said, 'but it's sort of in style this time of year.'

Lou Alp did not hear or, if he heard, he did not understand. For the great thought was still rising and ebbing through his mind and crowding all other things out. All other things except the loveliness of Kate Moore.

How beautiful she was! There was about her a perishable quality. One might have wished that she be transmuted to marble and color, so that she could neither grow old nor die. No, death was not so much to be dreaded as the withering years.

Lou Alp attempted to push the thought of her beauty away by remembering what time accomplished. There was Belle Samson of Fourth Street near the Bowery. Belle at nineteen had been ravishing. The sort of girl people turned to look at and go on, half smiling and half sad. But Belle married Gandil, the saloon keeper, and at twenty-five her color was gone, the luster fled from her hair, her shoulders bowed, her fingers stubby. Still pretty, but without that other thing, that quality of a different world which stops the minds of men.

He could enumerate others. And then he squinted at Kate Moore across the table. It made no difference. He tried to dim those eyes with time. He tried to paint in the wrinkles on the brow and by the mouth. He tried to straighten the curve of the lips. But, when he had finished the picture which fifteen years would make of her, his hand fell away from the picture and his eyes saw the truth. No matter what she became, she would always remain, to him who loved her, what she was at this time. As if these young years alone truly expressed the soul within her. Afterward the husk of the body changed, but the spirit of beauty remained. Into the dark mind of the sneak thief the gentle thought made way, that love is an immortalizer, that time cannot undo that marvelous embalming.

XI

It had been an unfinished beauty, the face of Kate Moore, when he first saw her on the day of the shooting and the robbery. There had been lacking some master touch, and his weak hand had aspired, all unknowing, to supply the missing thing. But now the picture was completed. The room was lighted. There was nothing more to be wished. Every time she turned to Jack Chapel, the sneak thief remembered his first aspiration and knew that another hand had done what his own could not accomplish. Something as dry as soot choked him with hatred for Chapel.

They had come to mince pie and plum pudding when a knock was heard at the front door. The old Negro with a yellow face appeared at one of the two doors leading from the hall to the dining room, his lips parted to speak. He did not come to speech, for a hand brushed him roughly to one side and a big man, armed, stood in the doorway.

Lou Alp glanced to the other door. Immediately it was filled by a second man. Likewise he was tall and he was armed. There needed only one glance at either of them to know that these were trained man-hunters. The face of Roger Moore, starting up from his chair, would have supplied the information.

He choked down his morsel of pudding.

'What the devil, Sheriff...?'

The tall man who had first appeared raised his hand and took off his hat, which up to that time he had apparently forgotten.

'Maybe I look like the devil to you, Roger,' he said genially, 'and I'm a pile sorry that I have to break in on a party like this. I'll tell you how it is. I've got a little job to do here, and I've got to see that you folks all stay in your places while the job is bein' done. They ain't goin' to be no unpleasantness I hope. Jest you go right on eatin'. And then I'll slope and there you are. But don't nobody, man or woman, leave his chair till I get back!'

He disappeared, and a third man stepped up to fill the vacant place at the door. Neither he nor the other man offered a single offensive word or gesture, but it was plain from their shifting glances that they were keeping every member of that Christmas group in mind. But that was not what Lou Alp saw first of all. He saw Kate Moore, as she had sprung up, clutch the arm of Jack Chapel with both her hands, and the white, still face which she turned to her companion told Lou that she knew everything – everything. Jack Chapel had laid his past bare before the girl. Had he told her about Lou as well, curse him? But he had told her, and in spite of that she loved him. Once more the knife entered the flesh of Lou Alp, and he grinned in his agony.

Now another thing. They were settling back in their chairs, and Roger Moore was saying something about an outrage and that the sheriff couldn't run for dog catcher in that county after an affair like this, invading a private home at Christmas. But the big voice of Roger Moore was a blur in the ears of Lou Alp. He saw Jack Chapel sink back into his chair with a reassuring word to Kate that brought a tint into her cheeks again, and then the eyes of Jack went across the table, across the mountain of bittersweet, and dwelt steadily on the face of Lou Alp.

He knew! As sure as there was a God in heaven, he knew that he had been betrayed and who the Judas was. Lou Alp, with murder and horror in his heart, slipped his cold fingers over the butt of his automatic. Yet it did not come. The explosion hung fire, and then did not explode. There was death in the eyes of Jack Chapel and yet he did not lift his hand.

A vast wonder swept over Lou. Roger Moore was ordering everyone to fall to and enjoy the dinner in spite of the sheriff. Jack Chapel seemed to be obeying the order. He did not eat. He drained his wineglass, and then he turned to Kate Moore and began talking in a low, swift monotone. There was something almost fierce about his face, the set of his jaw, and the flare of his eyes, and Lou quaked with the thought that he was telling the girl the story of the betrayer.

But no. She raised her glance and gazed at Lou, and yet he knew that she did not see him. Her eyes were wide and starry with the look of distance. Her lips were parted as though she drank. Lou Alp knew that indeed she was drinking, drinking the words of the condemned man at her side. That was the reason, then, that Jack Chapel would not lift his hand for vengeance. That was the reason he let Judas sit unharmed across the very table. He needed those last, priceless moments to pour out his heart to the girl. The whisper became more than the rush of the storm past the windows, and like a storm it shook Lou Alp.

In a rush of inspiration he knew that man who sat opposite him for the first time, knew that Jack Chapel would let himself be taken without one word of accusation leveled at his confederate. What had the whole story of their relations been? It had been a giving by Jack and a taking by Lou. He had given Lou the very gun, which now threatened his life, if he made one hostile move.

Lou Alp closed his eyes and sagged forward in his chair but, in the darkness that swam before his vision, he saw a picture grow, a picture he had seen long before, forgotten, almost. It was a picture of one man among many at a table. There was light upon that single face. Lou Alp opened his eyes again and saw Jack Chapel's face. For the moment in the blur of his sight it seemed that there was a light upon the face of his companion.

Steps were coming heavily down the stairs from above, and the heart of Lou Alp beat steadily in unison with that sound. The form of the sheriff towered again at the door and, casting down a bag which he carried, it struck the floor with a clash of much metal within. Jack Chapel stood up by his chair. He laid his hand on the shoulder of the girl, but he sent his last glance across the table, and Lou knew that he was forgiven.

'Gents,' said the sheriff, 'I'm sorry to say it, but there's a thief in this house and his name is...'

The explosion of a revolver tore the next word to rags. Lou Alp was on his feet with the automatic barking in his hands. Roger Moore, with an expression of dumb surprise, slid gently under the table. Kate Moore had shrunk back against the wall, carrying Jack with her and circling him with her entangling arms. Mrs. Moore sat stupefied.

Not one living soul would ever know what beautiful gun play was going on before them. For Lou Alp was a master hand, when his hand was steady, and today his hand was steadier than it had ever been before in his life. He did better than hit the bull's-eye. He chipped the edges of his target. He sent a slug through the shoulder of the sheriff's coat and trimmed the edge of the other fellow's long mustache with his first two shots. So lightning fast was his work that he had fired twice before the others, trained gunmen though they were, had their weapons out.

A bullet crashed through the left shoulder of Lou Alp and drove him back against the wall. He fired again, aiming nicely, and gave the hair of the sheriff a new part. Another slug struck him in the hip. Two guns roared at once, and Lou sank gently forward on his knees, still farther forward, and finally lay on his face.

The sheriff was the first to cease firing. His long legs brought him first to the side of Lou. He jerked him over upon his back.

'Yes,' said Lou Alp, 'I done the job. And then I shoved the coin in Jack's room, because I wanted to frame him. He didn't have nothin' to do with it.'

Jack Chapel burst in between and gathered the shattered body in his arms. The whisper reached his ear only.

'My gift,' said Lou Alp. 'Be good to her.'

THE ONE-WAY TRAIL

'The One-Way Trail' first appeared under the George Owen Baxter byline in Street & Smith's Western Story Magazine *in the issue dated February 4, 1922. Even this early there are scenes and moments to be found in this short novel that clearly distinguish the kind of Western story written by Frederick Faust. There is action, motion, constant momentum, but the author's concern is not really focused on these but rather on what is most important and most intimate and most meaningful in our lives, what alone ultimately matters. Love, friendship, loyalty, courage are affirmed, yet beyond even these is the prospect of redemption. It comes about through human interaction in stories such as 'The One-Way Trail' and the others collected here. They are not really plot-driven but depend on human character almost entirely for their motive and progression – the spiritual capacity for sublimity as well as despair, the potential for decency that exists in every human being, and the possibility even in the outcast, the criminal, the socially and politically disenfranchised to attain through one gratuitous act true nobility of soul.*

I

The Shifter picked up a chair from the circle around the stove and, drawing it back a little so that no one could easily pass between him and the wall, he sat down to think. With The Shifter thinking was a process quite unusual. He ordinarily acted first and did his thinking afterward. Thinking was so strenuous a task that he needed utter repose of body while his mind struggled.

Not that The Shifter was stupid. Far from it. But he was only twenty-two years old and, though he had crammed enough action into that narrow span of life to furnish sufficient excitement to a dozen able-bodied men, he had never encountered a problem which could not be solved by the adroit use of his hundred and eighty-five pounds of mule-hard muscle. Or, if muscle alone could not gain the desired end, he possessed sundry accomplishments of wrist, finger, and eye which, in the parlance of the country, were termed collectively 'gun sense.' Consequently, it was not strange that The Shifter had not overstrained his mentality. But today it was different – very different.

He had come back to his home town of Logan expecting to be received with smiles and open arms as a hero. He had come back that morning after an absence of four years, during which he had not forgotten a single face or a single voice. But the applause which greeted him was so muted as to be almost non-existent. Old Curry, the town loafer, had greeted him to be sure with a broad grin and a request for a five-spot. But that was about the only smile he had encountered. A few minutes later the sheriff had come up to him – Sheriff Joe Brown who had taught him to ride in his childhood. He had been both curt and to the point.

'Now, look here, kid,' he had said, 'maybe you've come in all ready to light up and celebrate, but my job around these parts is to keep things quiet. You lay to that! And if they's any uncommon trouble starts, I ain't going to ask questions. I'll just start for you, Shifter, and start *pronto*.'

With that, he had turned on his heel and strode off down the verandah. It was this that had made The Shifter go inside the hotel to find a chair and quiet so he could think. They were all against him. That was plain, and gradually he came to see why. They were afraid of him, afraid of The Shifter! He was like a stranger.

When they knew him as Harry French, before he went away, he had been as popular as any youth in the town. Now they seemed to think that he had changed his identity when he was given the nickname. They avoided his eye; they did not enter into con-versation with him; and, when he entered a group, the group dissolved at once and reassembled in another place. He would not have been so surprised anywhere else, but here they ought to know him. They ought to understand that all the stories that floated through the mountains about him were not entirely true. He was a gunfighter only on occasion and by necessity, not by choice. Could not his own people see that at a glance?

He dropped his chin upon his hard, brown fist and pondered. His thoughts flickered out of the hotel lobby, stuffy from the heat of the stove and the closed doors and windows. They danced off to that day, four years before, when he had fought his first fight and won his nickname. It was in the mining town of Ferris to which Harry French had taken the optimism and the fine good humor of an eighteen-year-old youth.

There, on a pay night in the saloon, he had been involved without fault of his own in a sudden hurly-burly of fighting men. Somebody had chipped his ear with a bullet as he strove to get out of the sphere of danger. The moment Harry had felt the sting of the wound, he lost all desire to escape. He had turned back and rushed that crowd, weaving from side to side, smashing out with either hand, bowling over stalwart miners at every punch, until at length a panic took the crowd. They had bolted for the door. The town bully had remained, drawing his gun and Harry, avoiding the bullet with a side leap, had downed his man with a heavy slug in the thigh.

That was where he had earned the sobriquet of The Shifter because of the restless footwork with which he had gone through the mob. It was an instinct that made him do it. Ever after, when he entered a fight and rushed his man, he came swerving and dodging like a football player on an open field. The result of this swerving attack was that in all his fights he had never been touched with a bullet.

Others of those battles came back to his mind now. Certainly there were many of them – too many! His great consolation was that he had never picked trouble, never forced a combat. Trouble had simply hunted him down and forced itself upon him. And now they looked upon him, even these men of his home town, as little better than a legal murderer who picked fights and then used his uncanny ability to destroy his foes. That explained the cold glances he received. That explained why the little hush had fallen over the circle around the stove since he drew the chair back to the wall.

He raised his head. Every eye was fastened upon him, and instantly every glance turned in another direction. They did not wish to be found staring, for a gunfighter would pick a fight at the very slightest provocation.

In fact, every one of those men, hardy fellows though they were, was sweating with anxiety as long as he was in their midst. What fools they were? Could they not see that his one consuming desire was to be friendly with them? Could they not see that he would pay for their esteem with combat?

Tears of vexation and self-pity rose to the eyes of The Shifter, and his scowl grew blacker as he studied the floor, looking down to hide that suspicious moisture. Footsteps entered, paused. The voices which had begun to murmur in conversation were solemnly hushed. The Shifter looked up to find a tall, raw-boned man staring at him with a face deathly pale. His hands were clenched to fists at his sides, and there was a set look of desperation about his face. The lips of the tall man worked a moment before sound came and, when he managed to speak, his voice trembled.

'You got my chair, French!'

Sudden understanding came to The Shifter. Here was Long Tom Cassidy, whom he had known like a brother four years before. Now Long Tom was ready to battle. The reason was perfectly clear. If an ordinary fellow had taken the chair, Tom would never have dreamed of raising an objection, for after all he had no power or right to reserve his seat when he left the room. It just happened that on this occasion, when he returned, he found every chair taken, and in his own recently abandoned place sat a killer of men. That was the reason he stood so straight and stiff. He felt that he would be shamed. He felt that he would be taking water if he allowed this terrible man to preempt his seat. Sooner than be shamed, Long Tom Cassidy was ready to die.

It came home to The Shifter of a sudden, and it made him sick at heart. What could he do? He would rather drive a bullet into his own flesh than shoot down Cassidy. But could he meekly rise from his rightful place and surrender it to another? Might that not be interpreted as disgraceful taking of water? Perhaps Cassidy had built up a reputation for skill with weapons in the past four years. Perhaps he might be capable of putting up a desperate battle, and the others would think that fear motivated The Shifter to make him move.

All these thoughts whirled in a blinding stream through the bewildered brain of The Shifter. He did not want to fight. His heart ached to go up and greet Tom with a hearty handshake, but he could not. Men would as soon shake hands with the devil. They sat about now staring with black brows from one to the other. Then, gradually, they began to shift their chairs out of the line between the two prospective combatants. Their sympathies plainly were all with Tom. At the least provocation they would join him against the gunfighter. The Shifter looked them over with the sad eye of despair and found not a single kindly response to his glance.

'You heard me talk?' Cassidy was saying, his voice gaining in strength and roughness.

'Tom,' said The Shifter slowly, 'don't be a fool. You ain't got this chair mortgaged, I guess?'

'Look here,' cried Tom, 'just save your words for them that'll stand 'em. I ain't your dog to be booted out of a chair and then jawed because I want it back!'

A spark of rage was fanned into a red gust of temper in The Shifter, a familiar red blur which had preceded all of his battles. But he controlled himself, leaning back in the chair and running the tip of his tongue over his white lips.

'Cassidy,' he said, 'you're hunting trouble. Cut it out. I'm not going to fight about a chair, even if you want to.'

'Then,' said Cassidy suddenly, 'get out of it!'

The Shifter stared at the big man for a moment in silence, thinking harder than he had ever thought before. He decided to surrender. It was hard to do. It would bring doubt and some suspicion of cowardice upon him. But at least it would prove to the people of his own home town that he did not wish to force trouble on peaceful men.

He leaned to rise.

What happened then was simply misapprehension and bad luck, though unquestionably the first movement of a man leaning to rise from a chair and the first movement of a man leaning to get at his gun are the same. At any rate Tom Cassidy, on edge with excitement, interpreted the movement in the second way and grabbed for his own gun.

That gesture The Shifter noted from the corner of his eye and saw that he would be forced to fight or die. His leap was of a tigerish speed. It carried him out of the chair and far to one side, where he landed with his gun in his hand. In the meantime the bullet from Cassidy's weapon had crashed through the back of the chair he had just left and dug through the wall behind. Long Tom whirled to fire again.

There was one alternative left to The Shifter and that was to run for the door. He would have done so had he not noted the effects of the first fire of Cassidy. The man was a little slow but terribly sure with his bullets. He would shoot The Shifter squarely through the middle of the back as his man went through the door. Flight would not do, then. Reluctantly, holding his fire to the last instant, The Shifter twitched up the muzzle of the gun which had been hanging idly at his side and fired.

II

In the pause that followed Long Tom Cassidy seemed like a very poor actor on the amateur stage. He did his gestures one by one with foolish awkwardness. The gun dropped from his hand and rattled on the floor. He gripped violently with both hands at his left thigh, and then he sank down on the opposite side.

The others had pressed back against the walls of the room with a shout. For an instant there was only the wail of the northern gale outside the hotel. Then the bystanders rushed in between and surrounded their fallen townsman. A quick examination of his wound showed that the bullet had passed through the flesh only, leaving bone and sinew untouched. He was carried from the room, groaning and cursing, just as the sheriff entered. As he had promised, he paused at the door only to jerk his hat lower over his eyes, then he went straight for The Shifter, a gun in either hand. As for The Shifter, he remained standing idly against the wall with the revolver hanging loosely from his finger tips.

'Stick up your hands, Shifter!' commanded the sheriff. 'Stick 'em up!'

Only the muzzle of The Shifter's gun twitched up in return.

'I'll put 'em up when I get good and

ready,' he said slowly. 'You, Brown, keep on the far side of the stove. Understand?'

'I'll make this the last fighting you do, bucko,' growled the sheriff, but he remained on the far side of the stove.

The Shifter was white, as always, when he grew wildly angry. 'I used to think you were a man, Brown,' he said. 'But I see you ain't. They don't raise 'em that way around Logan. I come back here ready to act peaceable as a pet dog. First thing I know an idiot starts a fight about a chair. I leave it to the gents standing around here. Did I pick that fight?'

There was no answer.

'What?' shouted The Shifter. 'D'you mean to say I started it?'

There was no answer.

'Wasn't I getting up out of the chair just they way he ordered me to do? Wasn't I taking water from him, when the hound pulled on me, and I had to jump to save my neck?'

But still from that circle of dour faces there was no response. The Shifter knew, at once, that he was beaten. He looked back at Joe Brown.

'Well, Sheriff,' he said, 'I see I get no backing. These blockheads can't see straight. If they do, they can't remember what they see. Point now is: what d'you mean to do?'

The doubt was all on the side of the sheriff. As for The Shifter, there was not a shadow of a doubt that he was enraged to the very verge of starting an attack. Many an old tale of his doings in battle floated back upon the memories of the others in the big room. If they wanted The Shifter, they could take him, but the price would be a terrible thing to pay. The sheriff ran his eyes around the circle and wondered. It might be that his reputation as a man-taker would be lost in this affair. But if the fight started, he himself would be the first target for that tall, gray-faced youth. It was a very convincing thought.

'I'll tell you what I'm going to do,' said the sheriff, making his voice larger than his spirit. 'I'm going to run you out of this town, Shifter. And I'm going to make it hot for you if you ever try to come back. If I had a shade more again' you, I'd lock you up now. But I figure Long Tom Cassidy made a fool play. Anyway, Shifter, out you go and on the run, too!'

The sheriff ran his eyes around the circle of listeners, and his heart warmed. There was an unmistakable air of relief on every face.

'I'll walk, Brown,' answered The Shifter. 'I was never built for running.'

So saying, he deliberately shoved his revolver back into the holster, tilted his sombrero to a more rakish angle, settled his bandanna into a more flowing knot, and slowly sauntered across the floor with his pale-blue eyes wandering from side to side, daring them all, or anyone, to make the first move to detain him or to hurry him. But not a hand was lifted, not a voice was raised, until he reached the door and, with his back turned squarely toward them all, he opened it and stepped out into the staggering gale.

Then, inside the room, a loud buzz of comment rose. The younger men milled together, talking loudly of going after him and bringing him back, and they even went so far as to cast black looks of suspicion at reliable old Joe Brown. But the older men shook hands with the sheriff one by one.

'He didn't do enough for hanging,' they assured Joe, 'and it'd be a joke to put him behind the bars for anything else.'

'He's sure gone bad,' said the sheriff wisely, 'and, if he shows himself around these parts again ... well, I'll make things hum for that young man.'

But The Shifter had not the slightest intention of ever showing himself within gun-shot of Logan again. He was decidedly through. They, his own people, had denied him. They had refused to give him a chance or a hearing. They had set themselves shoulder to shoulder against him and, if he had not been hurt to the very heart, he could have laughed at their folly.

He went straight to the horse shed. A bony, Roman-nosed roan lifted an ugly head and glared at him above the side of the stall. The

Shifter tossed a saddle over this unprepossessing beast and dug his knee into the ribs of the big horse as he tugged the cinches taut. Glorious – for that was the name of the homely brute, unless it were shortened to Glory – attempted to catch his master with a rear heel, tossed up with wonderful dexterity on the end of a long leg. Failing in this, he swung his head around but received an elbow in the nose as he attempted to sink his big teeth in the shoulder of the master. In another moment he was outside, bucking like a demon and running straight into the teeth of that terrific north gale.

Inside a quarter of a mile Glorious settled down to a long, easy canter, defying the force of the wind and even pricking his ears into it. In fact, Glorious was never so happy as when he was under way on a long journey and a hard one. His feud with his rider began with every saddling and ended with the first furlong or two of the gallop. For Glorious did not hate The Shifter in particular but mankind in general.

Out of a brief and terrible career as an outlaw in horse-breaking contests, he had passed into the capable hands of The Shifter, and he was gradually settling down. He had been long schooled to detest human beings, but the kindness of his owner was gradually neutralizing the acid in his disposition. The Shifter had found the long-legged brute invaluable. If there were savagery in the heart of Glorious, there was also uncanny wisdom in his brain. He could tell a rotten bridge by a glance and the first tentative tap on his forehoof. He knew by inborn instinct which stones on a mountainside would give sure purchase and which would roll at the first pressure. Mud or snow had no terrors for him. He could have kept his feet in a landslide or have ambled easily on a trail well nigh too narrow for a man. Also, his fierceness was becoming very largely bluff. The Shifter had shrewdly guessed that in another six months, in spite of small eyes and Roman nose, Glorious would be as affectionate and trustworthy a mount as stepped through the mountains.

He drew the big horse down to a steady jog in anticipation of the long and hard trail that lay before them, for The Shifter intended to take the one-way trail across the Kendall Mountains to Vardon City. It was well-nigh a disused route. There were other trails across the mountains. The sole advantage of the one-way trail was that it was the shortest. Running down from the loftier peaks of the Vardon Mountains in the north, the Kendall River cut a narrow trench through the mountains of the same name, a gorge with sides as sheer as the walls of a room almost. Along one side of the gorge a difficult trail had been cut, dipping up and down, twisting in and out. In half a dozen places it was wide enough for passing, but mile after mile it stretched as a narrow little ledge where a man on foot was in danger and where a man on a horse continually risked his own neck and the life of his mount. In recognition of this fact there was an unwritten law that the trail should be used only by travelers from the south to the north to avoid any more head-on meetings such as had, in the early days, been the cause of more than one tragedy.

Ordinarily even The Shifter would not have thought of using this route, particularly now that the north wind was tearing through the gorge, ready to pry between the rider and the cliff wall beside him. But this was not an ordinary day for The Shifter. His mind was in a turmoil of rage, and he welcomed the prospective danger of the one-way trail as a relief. He only wanted to get out of his home town by the shortest and the most expeditious means, and consequently he directed the big, ugly head of Glorious toward the mouth of the gorge.

The wind was increasing steadily, stringing long, pale drifts of clouds across the sky, clouds in such rapid passage from the north that they flicked across the face of the sun in swift succession and dimmed it only momentarily, like a winking light. The Shifter bowed his head to the gathering force of the gale and rode on.

Behind him, about a mile away, came four horsemen, closely bunched and maintaining his own pace. When he halted, they halted likewise; when he cantered, they urged their horses into a gallop. It did not need much penetration to tell that these were townsmen come out to make sure that he was leaving that section of the country. The upper lip of The Shifter curled away from his teeth as he glanced back at them, and for a moment he felt one of those wild, hot impulses to turn his horse and charge back on them. But he restrained himself. No, his plan for life hereafter was to be free from violence. He would go into a section of the mountains where he had never been heard of, and there he would settle down and carve for himself the repute of an honest, patient, and law-abiding citizen. This idea was strong in his mind as he jogged up the last grade, turned about the shoulder of a mountain, and came suddenly upon the gorge of the Kendall River and the beginning of the one-way trail.

III

It was unlike any other gorge he had ever seen. Though he remembered it well enough from the other days, it came upon him now like something seen for the first time. Other things had changed greatly in four years, but the one-way trail along the valley of the Kendall seemed more terrible than ever. The walls went upon either hand to the very summits of the range, as though the chain of the mountains had been stretched from each side until they snapped asunder along a smooth line of cleavage, or as though – to use an extremely old metaphor – a giant axe had cleft through a thousand feet of solid, virgin rock.

He looked down. The Kendall flowed through shadows, save where a shaft of sunlight was here and there reflected from the polished face of a cliff and brightened the water, and in those places he could make out the foam-white surface of that troubled water. When the shouting of the wind fell away from time to time, he heard the call of the Kendall go up the cliffs – wild voices snatched away a moment later in the renewed violence of the storm and blown to shreds. The trail was almost indistinguishable as it wound here and there, climbing with well-nigh imperceptible footings from one jutting crag to another. Sometimes it was merely a distant scratch along the blank walls of stone.

He looked back. The four watchers had bunched their horses closely together and were pointing after him apparently in great excitement. That decided The Shifter. He favored them with a deep-throated curse and then touched Glorious with the spurs. The big horse leaned far forward into the heart of the wind before he could take the first step, and then they jogged out onto the trail, with Glorious pressing close to the wall and snorting his fear of the dizzy fall on his right.

In half a mile he had lost his first terror and was giving himself to his work with consummate skill. The first sharp turn, following the winding of the valley, had proved nearly the death of both of them for, as they went about it, the storm smote them squarely from the inside, and Glorious tottered on the very edge of destruction. Only the quick action of the rider, as The Shifter flung himself violently to the left, gave Glorious a chance to regain his balance, and he found his footing once more. But that lesson did not need to be repeated. Thereafter he negotiated every turn of the trail like a seasoned diner-out approaching an unknown vintage. Glorious literally smelled his way to safety around every corner and then took the turn with his head lowered and his long, snaky neck stretched out. He made such a ridiculous appearance in the midst of this maneuver that Harry French several times burst into laughter. But Glorious merely shook his head and trudged on, regardless of the mockery.

As Madame du Deffand said, when she was told of the martyr who took ten steps after his head was struck off, it is the first step which is the hardest. Within ten minutes Glorious had negotiated all the variety of dangers which the one-way trail presented and had reduced his work to a perfect technique, the chief point being that at all times he kept his long body pressed closely to the wall even when the trail was comfortably broad.

Once his mount had gained this surety of going, The Shifter forgot to a great extent the dangers of the way. Even to the fierce pressure of the wind, now and again falling away and then striking at him with treacherous suddenness, the rider paid little attention. He almost lost himself in his thoughts. They ran, almost entirely, to the new life that would begin at the end of this trail. It was a melancholy series of reflections, taken all in all.

He felt that his past life was behind him, that twenty-two years had been wasted. When a boy reaches that age, he feels that a very great deal indeed has been passed. So The Shifter considered the future with a gloomy sobriety of mind. Out of his past every remembered face was a dead thing, every remembered voice was a ghost.

The Shifter was brought out of these dreary reflections, these grave plans for the future, by a sharp prick of reality. He turned a corner of the trail with his head bowed into the teeth of the wind, and he did not raise it again until he was astonished by the stopping of Glorious. Then he looked up and found facing him a youthful rider on a big, brown horse. And the trail was not three feet wide!

Even two men, in passing, would have leaned in against the wall, so dizzy was that fall which must be avoided. It was impossible for even the most adroit and cat-footed mustang to turn in this space. For horses as large as Glorious and the brown, it was absurd to attempt such a maneuver. Neither could they back the horses to a possible turning place, for behind each was the bend which had just been rounded. If the horses could barely make way around those turns going ahead, it would be an insured fall if they were forced against instinct to back up around them. Besides, it might be a mile in either direction before a more advantageous position were reached.

Both The Shifter and the other sat their horses in silence, drinking in the full extent of the catastrophe, while the animals swayed a little from side to side under the outrageous cuffing of that north wind. The Shifter adjusted himself in the saddle, so that that cunning right hand of his would be perilously near the holster and ready for use, while he studied the stranger. The man was apparently between twenty-five and thirty, perhaps even more. He was well built, rather stocky and broad shouldered, compared to the athletic ranginess of The Shifter, but brown with outdoor life and sufficiently deep of chest to promise unusual power in a hand-to-hand effort.

The head, however, was not so formidable as the body. It was distinctly small, and the face was small likewise, with handsome features extremely regular in cut and oddly contrasted with the aquiline cast of The Shifter. The eyes, too, were set closely together, and in their restless quality they suggested a certain unhealthy cunning that troubled The Shifter.

Yet, whatever the physical possibilities of the stranger, he was now in a blue funk. Never had The Shifter seen a man so obviously in the grip of the frozen hand of terror. He sat in his saddle with mouth agape, staring, his face bloodless. When he attempted to speak, Harry French made out only a meaningless gibberish.

For one thing, it plainly declared to The Shifter that he was the master of the situation. This trembler would make no stern opposition to his will and his ways. But also it was a thing so disgusting to watch that The Shifter blinked and looked away. He was embarrassed also. Some hard-faced, formidable man would have been preferred to this coward, for then they could have fought it out. The better man would have gone on.

'Well,' asked The Shifter, 'what d'you make out of this business? What'll we do?'

242

'What do I make out of it?' the other shrilly called back, his face reddening with anger as suddenly as he had grown pale. 'What I want to know is what you mean by riding up this trail in the face of a wind like this? Are you crazy?'

The Shifter paused a moment before he answered. He had been vowing, in his inward thoughts of the moment before, that hereafter he would take plenty of time before he spoke or acted. Now he began to act accordingly.

'Seems to me,' he said mildly, when he had regained mastery of that treacherous temper of his, 'that I'm the one that has the right to ask questions. This here is a one-way trail, I guess. I'm riding it the right way, and you're riding it the wrong way. Got anything to say to that?'

The other hesitated. Then he answered authoritatively: 'Plenty to say. I'm in a hurry. I got to get to the end of the gorge. That's why I'm riding this way.'

'Same way with me,' said The Shifter, his anger steadily rising in spite of himself. 'I'm riding this trail because I'm in a hurry.'

'In a hurry!' cried the other, and his face swelled with red passion. 'In a hurry ... so you buck into a wind like this! Why, it was all me and my hoss could do to keep to the trail with the wind behind us. In a hurry!'

He regarded The Shifter with a fierce

contempt, and the younger man closed his eyes for an instant and commended his heart of hearts to patience. In his entire life he had never met with a man who so keenly aroused his hatred.

'Look here,' he said coldly, 'they's one thing plain. These two hosses can't get by each other. I'm not saying who's to blame for it. But I'll give you a fair break. One hoss has to die and drop down into the Kendall River. No other way out. The other hoss goes on through, and the gent that loses has to finish his trip on foot. We'll throw a coin, partner, to see who loses and who keeps his hoss.'

So saying, he drew forth a broad, half-dollar piece and juggled it in his hand. But his heart was by no means as light as his manner. There was not a sinew in the big, ugly, powerful body of Glorious that The Shifter did not love. Only there was nothing else to be done.

'Throw a coin to see which hoss dies?' The stranger sneered as he spoke. 'Say, friend, d'you think I'd risk a hoss like The General, here, against a skinny old ramshackle like your roan?'

'You've said a tolerable pile,' said The Shifter through his teeth. 'And you've said a pile too much. If you got talking to do, try out your tongue on something beside my hoss.'

The other changed his manner at once. 'In

a way,' he said with a lofty condescension, 'I'm in the wrong, and I've brought this mess about. Well, I'll pay you the price of your hoss. I'll pay you a good price, too.'

The Shifter smiled. 'D'you think a hoss means just so much money to me?' he asked. 'Why, stranger, a hoss is a life, just the way you and me are lives. You can't buy a hoss. You may pay somebody a price, but you ain't paying the price to the hoss. A pile of gents sit the saddles on hosses that they don't own a hair of, because they ain't never taught the hoss to love 'em.'

'Bah!' snorted the other. 'You talk plumb ridiculous. This is my hoss, got my brand on him, bought with my money. He's just hossflesh. To be used, like soap or oil or coal.'

'All right,' said The Shifter, breathing hard, 'maybe that's all he is to you. I'm sorry.'

'For what?'

'For the hoss.'

'What d'you mean?' exploded the stranger, pushing his brown horse closer to The Shifter.

But he got no farther in his tirade. The Shifter suddenly swung forward in his saddle, clinging with trembling knees to the sides of Glorious, and his face was gray and drawn. Save for his eyes, he seemed to be in a panic, but the eyes bore an ample assurance that he was in a red fury. The stranger shrank, and his own eyes grew dim and wide.

'Now talk business,' said The Shifter. 'Shall I throw the coin?'

'All right ... all right, if it's got to be that way. But lemme get close enough to see the coin fall.'

So saying, he pressed nearer, until the head of the brown was near that of Glorious, and on the inside. What was about to come The Shifter had no means of guessing save that, as he took the half dollar on top of his thumb, preparatory to snapping it into the air, he saw that the hand of the stranger on the bridle rein was trembling and gripped hard.

He snapped the coin high, raised his head to watch its twinkling rise and, just when it hovered brightly at the height, the brown horse was driven at him by a yell of the stranger. He was perfectly helpless. With head thrown up, urged on by the driving of the spurs in his tender flanks, the brown came in with maddened eyes, driving between Glorious and the cliff.

IV

There was no time to whip out a gun and shoot, no time to fling himself from the saddle, no time even to throw his weight in toward the cliff to steady Glorious, for the rush of the brown forced the roan straight up and back, rearing and toppling on his

246

hind legs, while the voice of the other rider, yelling with savage satisfaction, urged the brown on. The Shifter looked down. Far below him, with nothing between, rushed the Kendall. The upward and backward lurch of the roan was driving him swiftly to the toppling point. Already, he was clinging fiercely with his knees to keep from pitching headlong out of the saddle.

He saw, to the side and before him, the convulsed face of the stranger as he pressed the brown in and, with his quirt, showered stinging blows over the head of the roan. Glorious, with a squeal of rage and fear and pain, rocked and balanced erect as a bear on his hind legs. The one great forehoof went up, flashed down. Again and again and again! He was fighting as wild stallions fight, not submitting tamely to destruction. To escape that crushing, slashing shower of blows, the brown horse in turn reared, a maneuver which brought a yell of terror from the stranger. The Shifter, at the same instant, flattened himself along the neck of Glorious and gave weight to the rush as the roan drove forward on all four legs and now charged like a fighting dog at the throat of the brown.

Higher the brown reared, to strike with battering forehoofs even as Glorious had done, but Glorious drove in like a savage terrier, and now the weight of his shoulder ground in between the brown and the cliff.

There was a shriek from the stranger as the brown reeled back. The Shifter, realizing that their roles had been changed, struggled furiously at the reins to draw Glorious back, but it was like tugging at a stone wall. Higher went the brown, staggered, and, with a terribly human scream of fear, pitched sidewise into the abyss. The Shifter caught a glimpse of a face hideous with terror, the lips writhed back over a shriek which did not come. Then he swayed far out in the saddle, reached with both hands, and with the right he caught the falling man by the shoulder.

The whole length of that arm was whipped through his grip, the sleeve being torn away like cobweb under the terrific force of his hand. But the strain checked, in a measure, the impetus of the fall and, as his right hand caught a firm hold on the wrist, The Shifter flashed his left across and secured a hold lower down. The whole weight of the falling man came with a single jerk – for all of this, of course, happened inside a tenth part of a second – upon the strained shoulders of The Shifter. Glorious, swung over by the sudden side strain against which he could not brace himself, toppled on the very verge of the cliff. Snorting with fear, he fought to regain his balance and, looking down, The Shifter found himself suspended for the second time over the gulf of the cañon. He might throw away his life and the life of his horse for the sake of a man who, he knew, was a treacherous cur. But the sight of that fear-frozen face hanging there a double-arm's length away made him retain his hold. Never had he passed through such a moment. The opening of his hand would save himself and send another human being to death.

Then Glorious, struggling hard, caught his balance again and swayed toward the face of the cliff. In a moment the crisis was over, and the stranger lay senseless on the floor of the trail beside the roan. The Shifter himself was trembling like an invalid newly risen from bed when he climbed slowly out of the saddle and kneeled above the rescued stranger. One pressure of his hand assured him that the fellow lived, though the heart beat faintly and the lungs merely stirred. The Shifter rose, climbed into the saddle again, and pressed slowly on down the trail, speaking in a shaken and changed voice to Glorious. He could not force himself to stay until the stranger returned to his senses. He could not stay to hear thanks from the lips of this detestable coward.

After that the trail seemed as broad and as safe as a high road. What matter if the wind were increasing? What matter if the evening were coming on? What matter even if the rain began to whip out of the sky and rattle against the slicker which he put on? All of this was nothing. If Glorious slipped on a wet stone in the dimness and reeled on the verge of the precipice, it was almost a thing to be laughed at, for The Shifter and his horse had seen the very face of death that day on the trail, and now nothing mattered.

It took more than two hours to do the remaining six miles of the trail, with all of its ins and outs and ups and downs and hardly a place where they could do better than walk. The rain was coming down in streams of stinging force through the dull twilight when The Shifter rode into the muddy streets of Vardon City and heard the downpour drumming heavily on the roofs on either side, while the light from the windows was split into yellow sprays in passing through the torrent of rain. It seemed to The Shifter a harborage and a refuge of perfect peace after the terrors of the one-way trail. He secured a room at the hotel without difficulty and went up to it at once to lie down to rest – to rest and to think for, oddly enough, his first step into a life of kindliness had almost brought him to his death.

He lay on the bed with his eyes closed wearily, and through his mind passed the picture of what the other Harry French would be doing at this moment, the other Harry French who had existed that very morning. He would be down in the lobby of that old building holding the center of the stage with his stories, with his laughter, with his mockeries. He would be beating down the glances of quieter men with his own defiant and bold eyes. After all, was it not better to live like that, to be feared and respected and followed and admired even by those who dared not imitate him? Was it not better than to lie here in the darkness brooding over what the future might hold for him?

He rose drowsily to answer a soft tap at the door. He swung it wide. There in the hallway stood a middle-aged man in an immensely wide-brimmed sombrero and, behind him, solidly packed, were half a dozen more. Every eye was focused on the face of The Shifter with an intensity with which he was bitterly familiar. The leader planted his riding boot inside the door so that it could not be closed. His right hand rested prominently on the butt of his revolver.

'You're Harry French?'

'Who are you to ask?'

'I got a right to ask questions, son. I'm the sheriff, John Clark.'

The thoughts of The Shifter danced away into the obscurity of strange reflections. Since his resolution to lead a peaceable life he had been forced into a brawl by a man he tried to avoid, had been driven from his own home town, had been nearly murdered on a mountain trail, and now a sheriff with a formidable posse was invading his hotel room to ask him questions.

Sheriff Clark who, of course, could not follow the trend of these thoughts was astonished to see The Shifter burst suddenly into ringing laughter. Then the latter drew back politely.

'Come in, gents, and make yourselves to home. Sorry I ain't got anything to offer you to drink. But I ain't a drinking man, and I hate moonshine, anyways.'

'Gunfighters and card sharps mostly do,' said the sheriff. With this insult on his lips, he kicked the door still wider and strode into the room with his men packed behind him.

As for The Shifter, he saw that a side leap would take him to his gun and belt where they lay on the bed, and then it would be a comparatively simple matter – for him – to jump through the window onto the roof of the shed beneath and so down to the ground and only a few steps from the horses. From the entrance speech of the sheriff he gathered that the visit foreboded him no good. Or were they simply about to invite him to leave the town and ride on?

The sheriff was walking slowly around the room. He reached the gun belt and picked it up.

'I'll keep this a while,' he said and drew the gun from the holster.

That is, he made the beginning of a movement to take the weapon, but the gesture was never completed. The toe of The Shifter's boot at that instant connected with the sheriff's wrist, drew a curse of pain and surprise from that worthy, knocked the gun spinning into the air and, when it descended, it fell into the agile hand of The Shifter.

He stood with his back to the wall, with a semicircle of armed men before him, every man ready to shoot. Again The Shifter could have laughed, if it had not been for the fierce and rebellious pain in his heart. For the second time on the first day of his good resolutions he found the protectors of social quiet arrayed *en masse* against him with their guns in their hands.

The sheriff was nursing his injured wrist with his other hand, still cursing, but he showed no fear, it must be admitted in his favor, and barked forth a steady series of orders to his men. 'Watch that window, Bud and Joe. It opens out over the roof of the shed. Block the door, Charlie. And just light that lamp, will you, Pete? We need more light than what we get out of the hall. There's plenty of time to get his gun.'

'Sure,' said The Shifter coolly. 'A sheriff can have my gun any time for the asking but not for the taking.'

'Why, you fool,' retorted the sheriff, while the flame welled up in the chimney of the lamp as Pete lighted it, 'd'you know you've resisted arrest?'

'You lie,' said The Shifter almost wearily. 'Nobody's told me I'm under arrest. You started to grab my gun, and I kicked it out of your hand. I'd do it again. Keep off there, you with the red hair! You can go as far as the law allows you but, if you take a step farther, I'll singe your whiskers for you!'

This last was addressed to a big man who started to edge in along the wall. His progress was instantly arrested.

'You see?' said the sheriff. 'I told you what he was! All right, Shifter. I'll tell you now that you're under arrest.'

'That's easy to say,' answered The Shifter calmly. 'But what's the charge? You can't railroad me, partner.'

'The charge is murder on the one-way trail,' said the sheriff, his voice suddenly trembling with emotion. 'Murder of my son, Jack Clark!'

V

The pale-blue eyes of The Shifter narrowed as he stared at the sheriff, but there was no similarity between that brown, hard-featured countenance and the face of the man he had drawn back from the peril of falling into the chasm of the Kendall River.

'Murder?' repeated The Shifter calmly. 'Murder of a gent on a brown horse ... big-shouldered fellow with a sort of smallish head and a ... a foolish face?'

The sheriff clamped his teeth together. 'You hear him, boys?' he said to the others. 'He's identified Jack! I've found 'em cold-blooded and steady as iron before but never as bad as this.'

There was a murmur of assent from the others.

'He's not dead,' said The Shifter. 'He's out on the one-way trail.'

The sheriff shook his head. 'You save that talk for the judge. Meantime, will you give up your gat peaceable?'

'Partner,' said The Shifter as calmly as ever, 'I never play a game that's sure to be a loser. Here it is.'

He handed over the weapon. There was a general sigh of relief from the others. 'Hold out your hands,' commanded the sheriff and then, over The Shifter's readily proffered wrists, he snapped the handcuffs.

'What you say'll be remembered for the jury and the judge,' he said, 'but if you want to talk, go ahead. We'll all listen ... and we'll all remember.'

'D'you think,' said The Shifter, 'that I'd've let you get me so dead easy if I was afraid my yarn wouldn't hold? I'll tell you the straight of it. I was coming north along the trail and at about the middle of it, while I was bucking a hard wind, I come on a gent riding the wrong way. There wasn't no chance to pass, and there wasn't no way of getting to a turning place except by backing one of the hosses about a mile. You know that couldn't be done on the one-way trail with the wind blowing the way it was today. They was only one way out and that was to kill one of the hosses and let it fall over the cliff. By rights, him traveling the wrong way, his hoss had ought to've been killed. But I offered to toss a coin for it and, while I was throwing the coin, this yaller-hearted skunk that you say is your boy rode his hoss at me and tried to knock me over the cliff, and he damned near done it. But old Glorious up and beat him off with his forehoofs and then jumped for the throat of the brown hoss like a fighting dog. I tried to pull him in, but it wouldn't work. He had the bit. And he jammed the brown hoss right off the trail. They fell together, your son and the hoss...'

There was a deep groan from the sheriff.

'But I grabbed him as he was falling,' went on The Shifter hastily, 'and I pulled him back onto the trail. He fainted plumb away from the scare. I made out that his heart was still beating, and then I rode on down the trail. And that, gents, is the straight of the story, I swear it! Either he's in Logan by this time, or else he's still on the trail.'

There was something so convincing about the manner in which this story was told, incredible though some of the mentioned incidents were, that the men of the posse looked from one to the other after the fashion of men whose conviction has been shaken and who are willing to hear more reason. But the sheriff, though his eye had brightened, shook his head.

'We'll give you the chance, son,' he told The Shifter. 'We'll send a man to ride the trail, and we'll wire down to Logan to see if Jack has come in yet. But the fact is that Jack has had plenty of time to of got to Logan long before this. Soon as I had word that the fool boy had took the one-way trail in the wrong direction, I wired on ahead to Logan and asked if anybody had entered the trail from that end. I got back word right off that you were just starting up that way. Well, Shifter, next we heard was that Jack's brown hoss had come rolling and tumbling down the Kendall, all smashed to pieces. But no Jack had come through. Then we see you big as life riding out of the one-way trail. And you didn't have no story to tell till just now. Why didn't you talk out as soon as you come in? Wasn't it worth talking about?'

The Shifter shrugged his shoulders. 'Go ride the trail,' he said calmly. 'You'll find him. You can leave me in the lock-up till he's located. I guess that's square all around?'

Everyone had to agree that it was. They took Harry French – still following him in a compact body as though even his manacled hands were to be feared – downstairs to the street and up the street through the crashing rain to the edge of the village. Here they turned to the left and approached, down a graveled road winding among trees, a house larger than any other which The Shifter had seen in Vardon City. But when he came close under it, he suddenly remembered many things out of his boyhood and particularly this building, so large that it could be seen from the head of the Kendall Gorge, big among the little shacks of the town.

It turned out to be the home of the Clarks which also served as the town jail. The stout cellar wall offered a greater security than any other building in the town and saved the village the expense of a public structure. To the sheriff himself it was a double advantage, for on the one hand he received a generous fee for lodging the guests of the county and, on the other, the fact that he owned the jail was a sort of automatic assurance that he would be reelected to the office of sheriff so long as he cared for the position.

Through a hall of mid-Victorian magnificence The Shifter was conducted to a door which opened on a flight of dark, damp stairs, and down this he was brought to the jail proper. A fencing of steel bars had been constructed like a great netting throughout the cellar and was divided and subdivided into a dozen cells, though more than half of that number had never been occupied at one time. At the present moment there was not a single tenant on any of the little cots. The Shifter was assigned to the central cell which had the advantage of offering him no concealment from spying eyes. Moreover, in case he attempted to break out, he would have two barriers of steel bars to cut through instead of one. All of these facts the sheriff pointed out to his companions who wandered about here and there admiring the interior of the jail with a sort of proprietary pride.

'There ain't any town of our size in the mountains that can show a better jail or a safer jail,' they declared more than once, and the sheriff smiled with becoming modesty as he unlocked the door and ushered The Shifter into his place of confinement. One of them came back to The Shifter when the party was about to leave and, leaning against the bars, he nodded wisely to the prisoner from whose hands the manacles had, of course, been removed.

'We know you, French,' he said. 'We remember you from the days before you got to be known as The Shifter. Maybe you've turned out bad ... as bad as we've heard. And maybe you ain't so bad, after all. But you can lay to it that you'll get a square deal in Vardon City. Here's wishing you good luck.'

The Shifter shook hands heartily through the bars.

'I'll tell you what,' he said, 'Vardon City ain't through with me. I'm about to settle down, partner, and I've made up my mind that I'll settle down right here. If you folks don't like me to start with, I'll make you like me before I'm through.'

The other grinned. Then he whispered shyly: 'Don't let the sheriff get you worried so you try to bust out. He's just nacheral gloomy. You see?'

With this word to the wise and a broad wink, the good-natured fellow left The Shifter to his thoughts and retired to retreat with the rest of the party. Alone with the cellar dimly illumined by the light from a single lantern which swung from a rafter in a corner, The Shifter immediately set about examining his surroundings. He had entered the jail in perfect confidence but, when he heard the steel-barred door slam behind him and heard the heavy lock click, his heart had leaped into his throat, as it does when one jumps into cold water. He was trapped, and no matter how harmless his actions had been, the fact that he was helpless was in itself alarming. The size of the lock on the door made him yearn for a key to open it, in spite of his good intentions to let the law take its own course in its own way.

In the meantime his cautious explorations

revealed several things of interest: that the bars which surrounded him were new and unrusted, that they were thick and set close together and resisted his grasp and strong pull, as though each were a wall. Above and on every side he was hemmed in by a resistless opposition. He lifted with ease one of the broad, thin boards which formed the flooring of the cell and found what he had dreaded to find – that the network of steel bars ran under the boards. Truly, he was securely held, and the thought sent a numb thrill of uneasiness into his brain.

Suppose something happened to Jack Clark on the one-way trail? Suppose, in the downpour of rain, his foot had slipped on a wet rock, or in the dimness of twilight he had fallen and...? But here The Shifter's brain refused to work any further with the grim possibility. Upon the known safety of Jack Clark depended his own life. So much was clear.

He had lain down and composed himself for sleep when this possibility entered his mind and brought him bolt upright on his cot. As he sat there with his head in his hands, he was suddenly startled by a feeling that someone was nearby, watching. He looked up with a jerk and found that the sheriff had stolen into the cellar, his footfalls covered by the noise of the storm which still yelled and drummed outside the house. He stood in uncanny silence, his face pressed close to the bars, his eyes on fire with savage hatred. The Shifter, cold with dread, straightened slowly to his feet.

'Well?' he asked, so dry of throat that he could hardly speak.

'We've wired to Logan again,' said the sheriff. 'Jack ain't there.'

'He's on the trail, then,' said The Shifter, gripping his hands and steeling himself to fight away the convulsive shudders which were spreading over him.

'We've rode the trail. We've had 'em ride all the way up from Logan. Jack ain't on the trail.'

'Then where is he?'

'Down in the Kendall River where you throwed him when you killed him!'

'Sheriff...!'

'I'll see you swing for it,' said the sheriff slowly. 'Aye, I'll see you swing for it. You've sent him to his death. You've sent me to mine. And I'll see that you go down with us. Sleep on that!'

He turned and stalked from the room with a long, slow stride but with his shoulders sagging, as though all in a moment an irresistible load of years had been poured upon him.

VI

The stairs from the cellar to the first floor

creaked one by one, one by one, under the step of the sheriff. Between every sound his mind rushed through years of life, years of planning and of hope which had been blasted this night by The Shifter. He had built his own future on the future of his son; with his son gone, his own hopes of success were withered at the root. Not that the heart of the grim man was tender for his offspring. He knew the boy for what he was – a coward, a knave by instinct, and something of a fool. But, nevertheless, he had planned to wrest success and wealth from the world through the use of this wretched tool, and he had been on the verge of victory when the tool was torn from his hands. That was why his eyes were fiery when he leaned at the bars of The Shifter's cell and looked at him.

It was an unsavory story, that tale of his life's plans. Ten years before, rich William Chalmers had died and left his daughter and sole heir in the keeping of John Clark as guardian. The fortune which went with her had been tied up in bonds – all but a small sum for her living expenses – and the very interest upon them could not be touched until Alison Chalmers reached her eighteenth birthday. The sheriff had taken the custody of the child with the best of intentions and in all good faith. The gradual wreckage of one business scheme after another did not alter him. Another man would have seen a chance of escape in the fortune which the girl held as her own, but the sheriff was not of that kind of stuff. He had no idea of using the fortune of the girl with or without her will.

True, he did conceive the idea of marrying Alison to his son, but he conceived it without malice aforethought. It is true too that, even as he planned the thing, he knew that his son was really unworthy of the girl, but in Alison he also saw the salvation of Jack Clark. Other fathers had made the same mistake before him.

Although at times he might shrewdly have guessed that his son was a coward and a knave, as a rule he closed his eyes to the truth and strove to make himself think that Jack only needed the passage of time to make him into a real man. He could not be wrong. The boy's mother had been a gentle wife whom the sheriff still loved and looked back on with a deep devotion. The sheriff had never been accused of cowardice or of the instincts of a bully.

More than once the very flesh of John Clark had crawled when he heard or saw evidence of the mean spirit of his boy, but always he shook his head and returned to reasoning and self-delusion to cover up the fact. It was sad, and it was shameful, but, after all, it was natural. He could not despise his own son. Jack must be a good man – in the making.

The sheriff would do what he could. When he was done, he depended upon the girl to come to his aid and finish the job.

There was one great, almost insuperable obstacle. Alison hated Jack. More than once this fact had made the sheriff draw back from his plans and shake his head. He wanted the girl to be happy. He wanted to secure her future just as much as her own father could have wished it, but what he could not eventually see was that happiness could never be based upon bed rock if she were to be married to his son. Middle-aged people have a strong predisposition toward believing that the ideas of the young are changeable. Time will tell the tale is too often their creed. And that was the creed to which the sheriff held. Time would change Jack, and time would also change the girl. He himself would oversee the marriage and make sure that Jack treated Alison well. Under his oversight he did not see how matters could go wrong.

He forgot his own youth. He forgot a young man's opinion of marriage. Love was something which he left out of his estimate in the full assurance that habit could take its place. The bitter truth is that men who have loved their wives are too apt to think that a man *must* love a good woman and that a woman can grow accustomed to any man.

All of these things John Clark had pondered upon many, many times. He was struggling honestly to do the right thing throughout. That struggle occupied a great many of his waking hours. There was only one point in his conduct in which he was dubious. That point was whether or not it was right to hold Alison back from communion with other boys and girls of her age. On this subject he debated with himself long and earnestly. His conclusion was wrong, but it was a conclusion honestly reached and honestly maintained. Many and many a time he had said to himself it was fitting that Alison have the right to her own society among the young people of Vardon City, and he knew that she would quickly become popular among them. But he knew also that, pretty as she was, she would be very apt to be impressed with one of the youngsters of the town. This must not be. It was cruel to keep her at home, but by keeping her at home he swore to himself that he was reserving her for an assured happiness when she should marry Jack and when she should achieve the position of head of a happy household under his own supervision.

No doubt this was blind argument. No doubt it was folly. But the sheriff was honest in his conclusions. The result was that he kept her at home, saddling her with household duties above her years. He knew it was painful to her. But he promised himself that in the future she would be amply rewarded for the pain which she now underwent. After the marriage – why, her life would start anew. In the meantime he kept her closely at home. After the days in the public school were finished – and he was glad when they were ended – the sheriff saw to it that she left the house very seldom. He discouraged all intimacy between her and the young men of Vardon City. If he needed an excuse, he found it readily.

'She's not very well,' he used to say to people. 'You see how pale she is.'

All the time he knew that the pallor, the silence, the downward-cast eyes, were the result of his own regime which he imposed upon her. The full realization of this struck him when he stepped through the door to the hallway. There was Alison carrying a lamp in one hand and a tray of food in the other for the prisoner. He had not heard her coming. It was characteristic of her, this softness of foot. She stole through the house like a phantom, never lifting her eyes even when she was spoken to, even when she answered.

Bitterly the sheriff realized that this was his work. He saw her now for the first time as he stared at her in the dim hallway. How pretty, indeed! There was a woman who would make some man happy. Possibilities of warmth of soul and of manner were in her. Almost against his will he had checked and changed those impulses. He should have given her freely to the companionship of those of her own age. He had not done so, and for that reason he felt that he had done a hard and cursed thing. Well, now had come the time when he would make amends, most generous amends.

He loved the girl. Many a time he had had to pretend a harshness with her in order to give instructions that kept her at home at her drudgery. But all of those instructions had been for the sake of Jack and, now that Jack was gone, all was changed. Jack was gone, and there remained only one cause for his living. That was to make life happy for the daughter of his old friend. In his sad heart he felt a store of inexhaustible tenderness. How astonished she would be when he began to draw upon that store and pour it forth upon her.

Curiously, sadly, he gazed upon her. She was like a new creature, considered in this different perspective. Yet, he was bothered by those downward eyes. She did not lift them when she saw him but came to a patient halt in enduring silence. Sight of that pale face with the purple-shadowed eyes fell like a whip on the soul of the sheriff. It was his work, and how completely it was his work, only he could tell. But he would make amends, now that Jack was dead and his hopes undone. He would make amends in some way. With that good thought a chain was burst somewhere in his heart. Tears rushed to his dry eyes, tears which the loss of Jack had not brought.

'Alie, dear...' he began.

Her eyes rose. She cast on him a glance of utter astonishment, utter fear, and shrank a little to one side as though to give him more room for passing her. She was used to curt commands, and this caress in his voice startled her. The sheriff turned and stumbled blindly down the passage. He heard the cellar door close behind her as he reached the stairs.

Now he needed quiet to think matters over and rearrange the scattered remnants of his hopes. So he trudged up the stairs to the second story to seek his little private office. He lighted a match as he entered, fumbled until the lamp jingled under his hand, and then lighted it. As he replaced the chimney, his left hand froze about the glass, for he was acutely conscious of another presence in the room. Then he whirled with his hand on his gun and looked straight into the grinning face of his son.

So completely had he made up his mind that the boy was dead that now he blinked in a ghostly fear. Then he straightened, caught Jack by the shoulders, and shoved him with a low cry of rejoicing against the wall.

'Hey!' cried Jack, writhing in that iron

grip. 'Let go, will you? Let go. I ain't made of leather. What's all the fuss about?'

The sheriff stepped back, still choking with relief and happiness. 'We gave you up. What happened, Jack? How come you to get out of the trail? Did you fly? We got a gent down in the cells that I was getting ready to have hung ... and here you pop up with a dry skin.' He laughed, his voice trembling with pleasure.

'A gent on a roan hoss?' asked the son.

'That's the one.'

'I wish you'd hang him, anyway,' Jack went on surlily. 'He was the cause of killing the brown, and he near killed me, too. Tried to ride between me and the wall. He done it, too, and pushed the brown over the cliff. I jumped just in time, but I hit my head against the rock. When I come to, he was gone, and it was getting dark. So I turned and got back here without nobody seeing me. But ... you don't have to turn that skunk loose, do you?'

The sheriff nodded. 'No matter what happened, it was your fault. You had no call to ride the one-way trail south.'

'Who'd've thought they was such a fool in the world as to ride that trail north ag'in' such a wind? Anyway, I was in a hurry.'

The sheriff sat down, mopping his forehead clear of perspiration, though the room was cold. He said weakly: 'It seems all like the insides of a dream. I'm just waiting to wake up. But what made you in such a hurry?'

The eyes of Jack glanced, ferret-like, from side to side. 'I told you I had to have that three hundred,' he said sullenly. 'I did have to have it. It was a matter of life and death!'

'Three hundred!' cried the father angrily. 'Where'm I to get three hundred every time you turn around. You spend more'n I do the way it is. What made it a matter of life and death? Whose life and death?'

'Mine!'

The father stared. 'Yours? What you been up to? What you been doing, Jack? I know you've played the skunk more'n once, but I never knew you had the nerve to do something that needed killing to pay you back.'

Under the stream of sarcastic abuse, the lip of the boy lifted and curled with a wolfish malevolence. Like a wolf, he could not long look his father in the eye. His head lowered, and he crumbled to the floor.

'It's Kruger. He ... he cleaned me out of the money with his slick card playing. He just makes the cards talk in a poker hand. I didn't have no chance with him. When I couldn't pay, he wouldn't hear of waiting. Said ... said that he'd come gunning for me if I didn't show up with the cash. He gave me till yesterday to get it. I tried cards, I tried everything, even you, to raise the coin. But I couldn't, and I didn't want to kill a man because I owed him money, so I decided to

271

slip out and...'

'You didn't want to kill a man!' cried the sheriff, writhing in his chair with shame and anger. 'You didn't want to kill a man! Why, you ran to save your skin, and you know it!'

Jack ground his teeth and flashed one evil glance at the older man. 'Nobody else could talk like that,' he said, 'and you know it. I got to stand it from you. But one of these days...'

'Well?' shouted the sheriff. 'One of these days what?'

'You'll be sorry for it,' concluded the son lamely. 'Now, the point is, what'm I going to do?'

'You're going out and face that rat Kruger without the money and tell him he has to wait for it. That's what you're going to do!'

Jack Clark turned a sickly yellow. 'He ... he's a gunfighter!' he said thickly.

His father was even more yellow of face than he. For a moment he gazed on Jack with unutterable contempt, but then sadness succeeded scorn.

'Yaller,' he said at last, 'and so yaller that I suppose it must have been born in you just that way. Well, Jack, if you won't fight him, you'll have to run again. But I've made up my mind to one thing. I'm going to make a change with Alison. I'm going right down now and bring her up here and ask her once for all if she wants to marry you. If she says yes ... all well and good. If she says no, then

I won't hold her to it.'

Jack Clark burst into a stream of protestation. 'Good Lord,' he cried, 'ain't she rich? Can't she be the making of both of us? Are you going to throw a whole fortune away because you're a little peeved at me right now?'

'Peeved at you? Well, Jack, you can call it that if you want. But down I go and get her. She's too good for you. I know that. But I'll...'

He said no more but turned and, striding through the office door, he shut it on the clamorous complaints of his offspring. He hurried down the stairs, fearful of letting the good impulse escape before it should have been turned into a concrete fact. But, when he opened the door to the cellar he stopped, his hand freezing to the knob, his whole body shaken with something akin to fear, so great was his wonder – for from the dim shadows of the cellar below him he heard the melody of a girl's laughter.

VII

It must be Alison, and yet – Alison laughing? It was impossible! To be sure, in the old days when her father was alive, she had been a merry little child. But, now that he thought upon it, it was years and years since he had heard her laugh. It was a sufficiently horrible thought, this one that a young girl had not laughed for so long a time that he could not remember, but the sheriff did not dwell on the horror. What chiefly occupied him was wonder at what could have amused her now so heartily.

He slipped a cautious step or two down the stairs and peered below the floor level and through the little forest of upright bars, each faintly marked in place with a sketchy, silver penciling of light from the lantern and from the lamp that Alison had put down. There she was, turned in profile before him, and what an Alison he saw! The fairy godmother had struck her with the wand. The fairy had stripped the drab away and clothed her in sudden beauty. Her fingers were clasped about two bars of The Shifter's cell. She stood with her face close to the bars, her head lifted a little, her eyes bright, the last radiance of the laughter slowly dying from her face. As for The Shifter, he sat on the edge of his bunk with his hands clasped about his knees, teetering slowly back and forth. Certainly he was an amazing young man to sit there so calmly charged with murder.

'But you haven't told me,' said Alison, and the quality of her voice was richer and deeper than the sheriff had ever dreamed of hearing from her lips, 'you haven't told me why you are here?'

'I'm here,' said The Shifter, 'because someone disappeared, and they say I'm the cause of it.'

Her forehead puckered. Then she started. It was wonderful to the sheriff to see the play of emotion in her. He had known her for so long as having simply a white mask of a face. The chrysalis had been so suddenly broken, and here was a woman before him, young, capable of joy and sorrow, tears and laughter. The sense of her filled the gloomy cellar like a light.

'Does that mean ... you're accused of...?'

'Yes. But don't say it. It's a hard, black word. It couldn't sound pretty, even from your lips. Well, what are you thinking about? That you shouldn't be down here with a man like me?'

He rose to his feet, more serious than before.

'Oh, no. Of course,' she said, and she stretched out her hand toward him with a graceful little gesture of trust. 'I know that you are innocent. I know that. I'm only wondering how you can be saved ... how you can get away.'

'By unlocking the door of the cell,' he suggested.

'Yes. I think I might be able to get the keys. They're in the sheriff's office.'

'And he's the man you're so afraid of?'

'I'd risk it. If it would be any help to you...?'

'No, no!' exclaimed The Shifter. 'I won't let you do that! Why, that old devil would make your life a plague. Besides, it wouldn't do me any good.'

The sheriff crouched lower against the stairs and gripped his big, bony hands together. It was true. To this youngster he was a veritable devil. He looked at The Shifter with a pang. The makings of a man were in that boy. He had heard enough before of the fighting exploits of The Shifter, and from that last speech he could guess at his generosity and true, quiet courage. Indeed, there were plentiful makings of a man in him, such a man as the sheriff had dreamed once of having in his son. The thought sickened him. He remembered the snarling, shivering man in his office upstairs. Truly, the good angel was close at the side of the sheriff now, pointing out the truth to him.

'Besides,' The Shifter was saying, 'I'm not going to break away. They can't hang an innocent man. It can't happen. The truth always comes out at the last minute. I've seen it. Looks pretty black for me, I know. I've been tolerable hard. I've done my share and more of fighting. But I'm through with that. I'm going to get out of this mess. Then I'm going to settle down ... right here in this town, where I've made such a bad start. I'm going to show 'em that I'm all right. I'm going to make 'em like me, just as I've made a pile of others fear me. But making people afraid of you is bad medicine. Look here, you ain't afraid of me, are you?'

'Afraid of you? Why, that's silly!'

'You're a steady one, right enough,' said The Shifter, drawing closer to the bars. 'You're the sort of stuff a square gent is made of. You'd stick to a friend through thick and thin.'

'If I ever found one, of course I would.'

'You have no friends?'

'No. They all think I'm queer ... the people in Vardon City.'

'The people in Vardon City are a pile of fools, and I'll show 'em they are! Why, the...' His wrath exploded inwardly, and it made his face a bright red. 'I'll tell you what. When I get out of this, d'you know what I'm going to do?'

'Tell me!' said the girl.

How very eager she was, and how close she stood to the bars. The Shifter in turn came close. Their hands were nearing.

'I'm going to get you away from this old scarecrow of a sheriff and take you off where you'll have white folks around you ... some place where you'll learn to laugh and dance and always have a good time. Understand?'

Her smile was a trifle vague. 'I don't know,' she said. 'I suppose there are such places!'

'Why, right here in Vardon City is such a

place. But the point is, would you go with me?'

'Would it be right?'

'I'd make it right!'

'I don't know. I ... I think I'd have to go, if you asked me to.'

'Do you mean that?'

'Yes.'

'You'd be happy, then?'

'Oh, don't you see? I've never been happy before, it seems, except just now, talking to you!'

The sheriff saw fire gleam in the eyes of The Shifter, but then the gunfighter drew back a little, drew inside of himself and ground his knuckles across his forehead.

'What's the matter?' she asked tenderly.

'I'm trying to think,' he said in a shaking voice. 'I'm trying to think what's right for you. That's what comes first. If...?'

The sheriff waited to hear no more. He dragged himself up the stairs and into the hall again, closing the door with trembling fingers. He was so suddenly weak and sick at heart that he slumped against the wall.

Yes, The Shifter was just such a youngster as he had hoped to have in Jack. Honest, clean of mind, clear of eye and heart, brave, kind, reliable. No matter how wild he had been, he would turn out all right. If he took this girl away, he would make her happy as a queen. He would make himself over for her sake. She would have the molding of him. They would work together in the honest partnership which makes a home.

What would become of Jack? That was the lightning bolt which shattered the dream. What would become of Jack, the gambler, the idler, the shiftless do-nothing? Jack must be saved. How could he be saved? Only through the girl. It was brutally clear to him. She must not be sacrificed. She must not go down!

So the blasting realization grew on him as he climbed the stairs. His own son – *his own* – was no good. He reached the door of his office. He opened it. Jack was rolling a cigarette with a trembling hand. He started when he saw his father and, as he jumped from the chair, the cigarette was torn to pieces in his fumbling fingers.

The sheriff, as he closed the door, looked over his boy with a glance which for the first time in his life penetrated surely through the exteriors and reached to vital matters inside. He could begin to see the truth, not easily but with a slow and grim grappling. All that he saw made him sick at heart. He himself had made a sad mess of matters, he told himself. He had wasted his money in foolish business ventures. He had done one thing after another wrong in a business sense. But one thing at least could never be said of him. He had never done anything wrong in spirit. In his heart of hearts he had always tried to do right by everyone. The more he thought of this, the more bitter became his insight into the truth of his son. Why had he ever been cursed with such an offspring?

'You're afraid of Kruger?' he said.

'Me? Afraid of him? You see, governor...'

'Don't talk to me!' cried the sheriff in anguish. 'Good Lord! A son of mine showing yaller like you're doing ... well, you've showed it, and that's an end! But I'll tell you this, Jack, you're in worse trouble than you know. If you go down in the village and let folks know that you're alive, and that another gent has been in danger of hanging because of you, you'll get some hard words.'

'But I'm not going down into the village,' said Jack wildly. 'I'm not going to let folks know that I've come back from the pass.'

The sheriff started. 'You're going to let folks go on thinking that The Shifter killed you?' he asked, repressing his detestation of this man who was his son.

'Why not? What does it matter? Only means that he'll be in jail a couple of days. Anyway, the truth'll come out before he comes to trial. But all I ask is that you don't tell 'em till I get clear of the country. You'll do that, Dad? You won't let 'em know? Kruger would come after me like a hungry dog. And he's a killer ... a killer!'

He was shuddering with fear as he spoke,

and his father shuddered, too, but with a different emotion.

'D'you know what it means to be in a cell under the accusation of murder?'

'I don't know. I don't care. I only know that I got to get clear of this country before Kruger ... curse him! ... knows that I'm here.'

The sheriff drew a great breath. 'What do you intend to do?'

'I'll go up in the hills,' said Jack. 'I'll take a blanket and a can of beans and go up in the hills. I know where I can find shelter. I'll rest there a day or two. Then I'll strike out.'

'You'll leave Vardon City for good?'

'Until you get rid of Kruger.'

'I'll never get rid of him. Jack, I've tried you out for a good many years. Listen to me while I talk plain earnest. I've tried you out, and you ain't no good. The Shifter is a real man. Sized up alongside of him, you simply don't count. That's what's opened my eyes. I tell you this ... you got to get out and stay out. Get out of Vardon City. Get out of my life. I'm through with you. You'd let The Shifter hang, if you could. Well, that opens my eyes to you. Get out and stay out. That's final!'

He turned his back and closed his eyes to the frantic outburst of protestation. He had only one way of closing the mouth of his son. He took out a well-filled wallet and tossed it behind him without looking. Over it he heard Jack whine like a starved dog.

Then there was a stream of curses. At length the door closed on the son who was going out of his life.

VIII

Left to himself, the sheriff stepped to the window and stared into the blackness until he could make out the tops of the trees around the house swinging to and fro in the full current of the wind, for the night had turned wild again, and the storm struck the sides of the house in rattling gusts and then rushed wailing away across the forest. He turned back, shivering, and took down a heavily lined raincoat from the peg. It would be cold outside in that driving blast of rain. He himself was already cold to the heart.

This, however, could be remedied. From a closet he drew forth a brown jug of ample dimensions and, uncorking it, he poured into a water glass a great potion of colorless moonshine. He was normally a very temperate man, but now he drank it off with a toss of the hand and frowned as he felt the alcohol scorch his throat and burn into his vitals.

He was better for it, however. It numbed the thing which was torturing him. It freed his mind. It was even possible to consider the whole affair without heat. The main thing was to undo the wrong to Alison. For that he must have time for thought. Above all, he wanted to be among friends. He buttoned up the raincoat closely beneath his chin, jammed a broad-brimmed sombrero over his ears, and stepped into the hall. The suction of the wind caught the door out of his hand and slammed it with terrific force, so that the floor shook beneath his feet, and the long, desolate echo rang through the lower regions of the house.

Jack must be gone by this time, and the sheriff thought of the boy shrinking when the storm cut against his face. That was the trouble. He had raised Jack too tenderly. If he had the thing to do over again, he would do it differently. Force was the thing – force, force, force! He dinned that thought into his brain every time his heel thudded on the stairs going down to the lower level of the house. There he paused in the hall. A door had opened somewhere in the rear of the house, and a ghost of song had floated toward him, instantly cut off again by the closing of the same door.

It roused a sense of stern revolt in the sheriff. This night of all nights he wanted to hear no music. He strode back down the hall, opened the end door, and listened again, frowning. This time he heard it clearly as the ringing of a far-off bell, every word distinct:

What made the ball so fine?
Robin Adair!
What made the assembly shine?
Robin Adair!

What a voice sang it! A very soul of joy and tenderness was poured into the music, and for a moment the face of the sheriff went blank. Then he rallied, gritting his teeth, and stepped to the kitchen door. When he jerked it open, Alison looked up at him with a dish in one hand and a dishtowel in the other, looked up with the last note dying on her lips and a smile beginning in its place. The heart of the sheriff was touched profoundly.

'Alison...' he began and paused, horror stricken as he realized how much he had taken from this young life – how much a single, short conversation with a condemned man had restored to her. Then he saw that she was waiting patiently, her head obediently bowed – waiting for him to continue his speech. It was the attitude of a slave – the crushed spirit of a slave – and he had done the crushing. 'Alison!' he cried, 'I've been wrong! Wrong from the start! Understand that, girl?'

At this she glanced up at him, glanced up with something akin to fear widening her eyes. Plainly she did not understand and, because she did not understand, she was afraid. His thought flashed back to her father, his best friend. Heaven be praised that her father could not see her now!

'What I mean,' he continued, making his voice as even as he could, 'is that I intend you should be happier, Alison. You need happiness. I've had a wrong idea. I'm going to try to make up to you all the things that I've been wrong in. You understand, honey?'

Her smile was cold and wan. Her nod was one, he could see, of perfunctory acquiescence. 'Yes,' she said, and her voice had no meaning whatever.

All at once he shrank from her. She was like an incarnation of all his sins. He must escape for more thought. He would go down to the hotel, where the old-timers who knew him would be congregating on this evening of the week. With that thought he rushed out of the house, went to the stables, saddled his horse, led it out, mounted, and rode at a mad gallop down the roadway and into the main street of Vardon City. There he checked the gait to a trot then splashed to a halt under the sheltering roof of the hotel, which projected from the top of the verandah and stretched across an enclosed driving entrance, where a dozen saddle horses and buckboards were already tethered.

He swung down from the stirrup numb of brain and body and, with bent head and sagging stride, he moved slowly up the steps and into the big room which had once been the bar, but where now only soft drinks were dispensed and where the card tables were packed in from wall to wall. There was only a scanty gathering in this social center of the town tonight. But those who had ventured through the whirling wind and the driving rain were hardened old adventurers whom the sheriff had known half his life, men in whom habits had become riveted by long usage. He surveyed their faces for an instant with stern satisfaction. These were men of his own kind. Then he stepped toward the stove and stood before it with his hands extended, until a steam of hot vapor rose from them.

There was a slowly increasing stir among the others. The veterans had greeted him with grunts and nods, after their fashion. Now Bud Morton, still carrying a juvenile nickname through sixty years of hardy action, approached and dropped his hand on the shoulder of the sheriff.

'I sure grieved a pile when I heard what happened,' he said. 'But what's done is done. Buck up, old man. You still got a long life ahead of you. If it ever comes to a pinch where you need help or a friend, you can call on me.' He turned and glanced toward the others. 'And here's a dozen more would stand by you, John.'

There was a profound hush of sympathy in the room. It was far more eloquent than words. The sheriff could not turn his head.

There was only one right answer to this speech and that was to tell them that there was no call for sympathy to be expressed to him. His son was alive and well.

Alive and well! Alive and a self-confessed coward. Far better, indeed, that he should be dead and mourned than that he should be alive and in this condition. He himself – John Clark, known through five states as a fearless man – would rather die than have the shame of his son known, but what could he do? He shrank in all his soul from letting the good men of Vardon City continue to think The Shifter a murderer. Conversely, he dared not proclaim that his son was alive for yonder in the corner he marked the cold, steady eyes of Kruger, the gambler.

In one particular at least Jack had been right. Kruger was a gunfighter. The whole town knew him as such, and the doughty old sheriff would think twice before he invited trouble with the man. He would think twice before he invited trouble, but he would not wait to think even once before he accepted it. That was the difference between himself and his son. That was the difference between courage and cowardice.

He said to Bud Morton, without turning his head: 'Thanks, old-timer, thanks!'

Then he scowled down at the stove. How could he explain to them the truth without giving the information to Kruger? Always he felt those cold eyes of the gambler staring at him, probing him from that poker face.

'There's one good thing,' said Kruger, 'and that's the fact that you got the killer so quick. He'll pay for Jack. He'll pay plenty.'

The sheriff raised his head and flashed a glance at Kruger. After all, the man had generous instincts, for otherwise what kept him from telling the sheriff how much was owing to him from his son and demanding payment of the gambling debt, which of all debts is the most sacred? The sheriff remembered how his son had picked up the purse he threw him with a snarl of acknowledgment. What a blind fool he had been to be in ignorance so long as to the real character of the boy.

He must get away from the hotel. These old friends who collected here every week on this day were torture to him. The very fact that he knew them so well was an additional pain. He wanted to be away, aye, in the very midst of the breath and the rain of the storm, so that he could think. He had been an idiot in the first place to come among them.

'Me, too,' Bill Culbert was saying. 'I've knowed the same thing, partner. I've had my loss, and I've lived through it. Keep your head up, John, and don't figure that this is the end of everything.'

Well could Bill Culbert say it. His own son had died a hero's death, saving the lives of men in a mine into which others dared not to go down. Well could Bill Culbert speak, but he, John Clark, was the father of a coward. He turned abruptly.

'Thanks, Bill, old-timer,' he said as evenly as he could. 'But I'll be riding on. I guess I've had enough of this stove.'

He whirled toward the door, strode hastily down the steps, and mounted his horse. Looking through the window, he saw that the men had drawn together, and that they were talking earnestly. No doubt they were talking about his supposed bereavement. Pray heaven that they should never guess at the truth of the matter. He spurred fiercely out into the rain. He must have time and space for thought, and the storm was a fitting accompaniment to the tumult in his brain.

IX

The moment the sheriff's tall form disappeared through the door, the men in the room had been drawn together and called to attention not by any voice from one of their members but by a clarion call from an unexpected quarter. It came from old Nick, the bartender, who smote his hand flatwise upon the bar and cried: 'Gents, line up, stand up! What're we going to do for old John Clark?'

They looked at him in surprise and then muttered to one another. What had gotten into placid old Nick? But there he stood with his face lighted, and not pleasantly lighted at that. He was a formidable figure as to chest and stomach and formidable as to hand, also. It was rather fat than brawny now, though there was strength left in it, and many a man – aye, even of those at that moment present – could have testified to the power which once dwelt in that hand in the days of his prime when Nick, disregarding the threat of guns, had more than once stepped in between brawlers and hurled them indiscriminately through the door to roll in the dust outside.

'Fighting is fine for them that likes it,' was one of the maxims of Nick, 'but my bar-room ain't the place for gents to get their exercise and sharpen up their shooting eyes. If you want a roof for gun play, try the sky.'

'Gents,' he said now when he found that he had successfully focused their attention upon himself, 'I've served drinks in a good many towns and worked behind a good many bars in my day. I've done my turn in towns where the gold was coming from the ground so fast that the boys burned their throats out turning the dust into whiskey and getting it down. But I never seen a town act up so plumb orderly and peaceful as Vardon City. That's why I stuck when I come here twenty years ago. And why was it peaceful? They ain't any doubt about why. It was the sheriff. It was old John Clark. Did I have gunfighters smashing up my furniture in here in a way that would have turned the stomach of an honest man that come in here for a quiet drink? I didn't, because the gun-fighters was always scarce in Clark's county. Did I have stick-up artists come along and clean out the money box on me? I didn't, because stick-up artists sure hated the ground where John Clark walked. Did I have slick card sharks come along and trim all the boys that played in my place? I didn't, because old John Clark was always a-sitting right over there in the old armchair in the corner … that one with the initials carved all over the arms … and John could spot a card crook a mile away. Well, boys, it's sure a pleasure to serve drinks in a town that has a sheriff like John Clark, and here's what I'm coming to. For the sake of what he used to do, and for the sake of all the drinks that have spun across this here bar, I sure move that we take a job off Clark's hands and fin-ish up this wild young man-killer, this Shifter as they call him. Are the rest of you with me, or are you not?'

There is an accumulative power in words. They build out of nothing. They lead no-where. But out of them comes an effect. They have, at least, the value of mass. They have the emphasis of quantity. And the emphasis, in the case of Nick, was pointed by a fierce energy which came out of his heart. Therefore, the effect of his words was more than could have been guessed from a hearing of the words themselves, unbacked by all those connotations which spring out of gesture, tone of voice, flash of eye. In the case of Nick there were tremendous flashes of the eye, great swellings of the chest, convulsive poundings on the bar, polished smooth by the innumerable glasses which in the past twenty years he had slid across its surface.

What, above all, gave the words of the bar-tender point, was that no one in the crowd had even remotely suspected him of containing in his heart such emotion. When one has jested with a man, shaken his hand, and clapped him upon the shoulder for an indefinite period, it is very difficult to take the same man seriously but, when he actually does become serious, the effect is most astonishing.

The effect was, at least, astonishing now as regarded the old and hardened cattlemen who listened to the eloquence of Nick. First they stared at him; then they gasped at him; and at length they glanced at one another as though to check up their own impressions by the impressions of their neighbors. When they found that their neighbors were taking this fellow seriously, they turned back to Nick with corrugated brows which were in themselves an ample token that they meant business. They began to feel, in short, that John Clark was more than a mere sheriff. He was a representative of the whole population of Vardon City and, as such, he was a representative of each and every man in the town. Each man of those within the room remembered how many times in the past the sheriff had stood by him in such and such an emergency. Each and every man was, in his heart, a little ashamed to think that the veteran bartender had outdone him in loyalty to the guardian of the law.

Shame, then, was the bellows from which air was blown upon the fire, and shame is a power well worth taking into consideration. Too few are those who think upon it seriously, but shame is that thing which makes the soldier step out before his mates and dare the impossible. Shame is the spur which the bright spirit doth raise. Indeed, even the stern Milton would probably nod his head in agreement to the misquotation of his great line. At least, it operated powerfully upon the good men of Vardon City, although there was some argument on the head.

'Speaking personal,' said Bud Morton, shaking his gray head from side to side as he spoke, 'I always figured that Jack Clark was no more like his father than a half-blood colt of a mustang mare is like a Thoroughbred sire. He's mean by nature, a sneak by

293

training, and a hound by general principles.'

Harry Peyton came to the rescue of the Clark family and particularly of its son. 'Look at most youngsters,' he said, 'and, if you look close enough, you'll find that, no matter how well they mean, they ain't no good in practice.'

'Now you're talking wise,' said Morton. 'Anybody here can step out and say that I'm the sheriff's friend. I've proved it with powder and lead, which out-talks words a good many ways, but I'm also here to state that, no matter how much I like the sheriff, I ain't overfond of his son. If the rest of you would dig down into your vitals and talk true, I think you'd say the same.

'I've seen him quiet, and I've seen him loud. I've seen him talking friendly, and I've seen him talking mean. I'm cussed if I ever seen him talk or act the way I like to see a man. He always made me figure that he was only one part a man. At that, I've always give him the best part of the guess. I've always tried to see his father in him. But I ain't never been able to see much of John Clark in Jack Clark. Them two don't seem to string together.

'Why are we figuring to hit this gent they call The Shifter? We figure to go after him because he met Jack Clark on the one-way trail. What are the facts? The facts are that The Shifter was going the right way, and

Jack Clark was riding the wrong way on the one-way trail. Well, boys, work it out for yourselves. It ain't hard to do. Suppose you or me was to meet a gent riding the wrong way on a trail when they wasn't room for two gents to pass. What would we do? I ask you that. What would we do? Why, we'd simply up with a gun and get rid of the gent that was superfluous. And this ain't the first time, because there's Hugh Neer. Didn't Hugh Neer take the wrong way of the trail, and didn't he get shot by Billy Jordan, and didn't Billy come into town and boast about what he done, and didn't all of us shake Billy's hand? I ask you that?'

It was a long speech to be made in the name of a defendant not present. Certainly, had The Shifter known of it, he should have presented his thanks to Bud Morton. But as it was, The Shifter was thinking of far, far other things than speeches made in his defense. In fact, he was clinging confidently to a doctrine absurdly old and that doctrine held no man could be lost for a crime which he had not committed.

However, there is no argument so old that it will not meet with a refutation; there is no argument so old that it will not draw out an enemy; there is no argument so strong that someone will not take the opposite side. This is human nature. We delight in opposition. We plague our dearest friends with epigrams. So it was in the present instance. There arose from the ranks of the crowd one who was willing to stake his wits against the wits of all the others, not because he felt that he was inherently right, but simply because he desired to fight the great majority. This is the impulse which drives men to support lost causes. What wonder that it showed itself here, in the person of the gray and venerable Jefferson Smith?

Jefferson Smith was, so to speak, a tartar. In other words, he generally did the opposite of what people expected. Because he was the opposite of their expectations, it is not strange to hear that he was generally detested. What we hate is not, as a rule, what is dangerous to us, but what is new to us. So, to speak plainly, Jefferson Smith was quite generally hated. He was so generally hated that good wives, if one must be perfectly frank, dreaded his shadow over their doorway. He was so generally hated that men cared not at all if their secrets fell into the hands of the ordinary run of mortals, but they cared extremely much if those secrets fell into the hands of Jefferson Smith. Because Jefferson Smith was able to impart to the smallest thing that aroma of the important which may not exist in fact but which is very apt to exist in inference. He was one of those men whose inferences are more important than their statements.

It was this Jefferson Smith, then, who rose in what had been the ancient and respected barroom of the hotel at Vardon City. He rose and looked about him, and by his very rising he called to him the eyes and the attention of the spectators. They turned on their heels, they turned in their chairs, and they beheld Jefferson Smith rise and roll his eyes and tug at his slender beard, for it is not for nothing that in the West a man has shot a five-cent piece at thirty yards and blown its center out. It is not for nothing, either, that a man has killed three hard-fighting warriors of Colt forty-five and bronco. So every man in the old barroom of the hotel turned himself toward Jefferson Smith and watched him with the eye of one intent.

Which side would Jefferson take? Both were fairly represented. If not, every one knew that he would throw himself with the minority. It was generally conceded that by his weight he could determine the whole affair – the life or death of The Shifter was dependent upon the careless malignity or the careless generosity of this fiery old fellow. He allowed them to remain in the dark about his intentions for only a short time.

'Gents,' he said, 'it seems to me that we're all wasting a pile of valuable time about a mighty small thing. Are all of us going to stand around here and spend the night chattering about a youngster like The Shifter?

Bah! I've heard of him. We all have. We've heard him talked about as a man-killer … a bad one.' Jefferson turned his eye deliberately over the little crowd, and deliberately he picked out his two worst enemies. 'Gimme Calkins and Bud Morton to stand with me, and the three of us will take on thirty of such half-baked badmen. I say, boys, that we ought to ride up the hill to Clark's place, take this Shifter out of his cell, string him up to the highest tree we can find, and leave him there flapping in the breeze as a sign to others of what Vardon City does to the badmen who come its way.'

He pointed his speech with action as he stepped toward the door. 'Who's coming with me?' he said. 'Or do you want me to go alone?' And that was decisive.

X

Alison had not gone to bed. She sat with her face so close to the window in her room that sometimes the pane pressed cold against her nose. Beyond the glass, as her eyes grew accustomed to the night, she could make out vague outlines here and there. Sometimes the sheeted rain was an effective curtain that fenced away the rest of the world. Sometimes it shook away in a change of the wind, and she saw the looming forest. Whatever

she saw was noted only in semiconscious-
ness. Her mind was busy, terribly busy, with
the host of thoughts that had been crammed
into it this day.

The Shifter – Harry French – was a gunfighter, a known badman. It seemed impossible that this could be the case, but then
she was sadly ignorant of men. It might be
that she liked him so much simply because
he was the opposite of Clark and his son. She
admitted this to herself, nodding her head
wisely but very sick at heart. She admitted it
to her reason, but reason did not satisfy her.
If The Shifter were really bad, then she felt
that there was no such thing as goodness in
the world. The very sound of his voice
thrilled her with happiness; the very memory
of it was a joy.

'But I don't know much about things,' she
said to herself aloud. 'Most likely I'm wrong,
because I don't know much about men.'

She had not entirely obeyed the command
of her guardian to keep away from The
Shifter. She had stolen down into the cellar
after she had finished with the dishes, and
The Shifter had risen with a smile to greet
her.

'Somebody's been talking to you, I guess,'
he said bitterly when she shrank away from
him, watching with frightened eyes. 'Somebody's been telling you that I'm a regular
snake, eh? Full of poison?'

'I only wanted to know,' she answered, 'if you'd like to have some books or magazines to read?'

'I'd rather have you to talk to,' answered The Shifter at once. 'You're a pile better than all the books in the world.'

She retreated a little, and yet instinct was singing in her that there was nothing to fear in this man – nothing at all to fear.

'All right,' he called gloomily, 'if you're going to believe 'em, go ahead and stay away. I'll manage somehow. Good night.'

She could not muster courage to answer him. Something was choking her. So she turned and, once her back was toward him, a cold panic sent her scurrying up the steps and through the hall and up again to her room. Here she had been crouched beside the window ever since, harried back and forth by thoughts of The Shifter and his bright, steady blue eyes. She could visualize him so keenly that the eyes of the vision became intolerantly bright and brought her heart up into her throat.

It was at this point that she heard the sound of the knocking at the front door. The sound came dimly up the stairs through the clamoring of the storm. Perhaps the sheriff had forgotten his key. The thought of the sheriff in a passion was quite sufficient to blot all other considerations from her mind. She fled down the stairs like a deer and, panting, pulled open the front door against the drag and suction of the wind. Then the draft nearly drew her out into the night but, as she balanced on tiptoe, she made out that on the porch was not a single figure but a whole group of bewhiskered men glistening faintly through the night in their wet slickers.

'It's the girl,' said one voice. 'I'd forgot about her. It's the girl. That makes it bad!'

'Who are you?' she asked. 'Uncle John is not here. I think you'll find him in the hotel.'

Instead of answering, one of the men pushed in. He was a little man, not as tall as she, in fact. He had a sharply pointed little gray beard and glittering little gray eyes. He was withered with the passage of sixty years or more, but he had dried up without growing feeble. He was weather brown. His wrinkled skin looked as tough as leather. His active, gleaming eyes filled her with dread just as she trembled when the eyes of a rat glittered out of a shadowy corner at her. He stared through and through her. He seemed to be poking into veiled corners of her nature. There was nothing that could be hidden from this terrible little man.

Others came in behind him. Some of them were big, all of them were quite old, and all of them had brows wrinkled with knowledge of the world and its men and women and events. The silence with which they trooped in was strange and rather terrible. Alison shrank back toward the wall.

'You can come in, of course,' she said. 'I'll build a fire for you in the front room ... and make you some coffee. You must be terribly cold ... and wet!'

The little man turned toward the others.

'I'll handle this,' he said.

Then he turned back to Alison and laid his hand on her shoulder. His voice was smooth and kind. It was wonderful to hear. It sent a drowsy sense of security drifting through her. The hand on her shoulder was light as the touch of an affectionate child.

'Now don't you go bothering about us, honey,' he said. 'Don't you go bothering to fix up coffee. We'll get along without that. Thing for you to do is just to trot back up to your room and go to bed. We know the sheriff ain't here. But we've come to do something that he'll be glad to have done. We're all old friends of his ... you see?'

He patted her shoulder lightly as he spoke, and yet it seemed to the sensitive eyes of the girl that there was no reality in his smile. He was not talking to her but around her, just as the sheriff often talked when he wished to keep his true meaning from her. Being a specialist, as one might say, in pain, she recognized the same tactics in Jefferson Smith. The claws were buried not so very deeply beneath the velvet. Yet behind her own blank gaze the wise little man was not able to penetrate to the hidden meanings. She seemed to him perfectly simple, and he gave a little more credence than he ever had before to the tale which the sheriff had spread throughout Vardon City that the mind of the girl was weak. For that very reason he was tenderer and gentler with her.

The other men stepped quietly into the hall and closed the door softly behind them. It embarrassed them hugely to find only this reputedly weak-minded girl as a garrison in the sheriff's house. It was like attacking a helpless woman in a way. They scowled fiercely at one another, those hardy old veterans of the frontier. It would be better to have the sheriff himself present to overmaster and bind before they went after his prisoner.

In the meantime, Jefferson Smith continued to engineer the affair as general of the party. 'I'll go upstairs with you,' he said. 'You can show me the sheriff's office. Can you do that?'

She nodded and turned, passing slowly and with bent head up the stairs, for she was deeply in thought. She knew it was by no means ordinary for a group of men to call in the absence of John Clark and calmly ask to be shown into his office. That office was his sanctum. He hardly allowed Jack, his own son, to step inside those precincts.

What was up? In the guilty, storm-reddened faces of the men she had striven in vain to read the secret. But undeniably there was something fierce behind their attitude, something in the eye of Jefferson Smith which reminded her forcefully of the eye of a cat that sits patiently at the hole of the mouse with steel-like claws ready to strike inescapably. She showed her guest to the door of the sheriff's office.

He paused there with his hand on the knob. 'All right, honey. Now you run along to bed. Good night. And happy dreams!'

She looked wistfully up into his face. In spite of his smiling lips, his forehead remained stern. What was going on inside his mind? But all she could do was nod slowly and then turn away down the hall as Smith entered the room. However, she had hardly taken a step when, immediately after the sound of the scratching match and the small flurry of light in the office, she heard the jingle of metal against metal, the unmistakable sound of keys knocking together.

It brought Alison whirling back to the door with her heart a-flutter, for those keys, she knew, were the keys to the prison in the cellar – and there was only one reason for wanting those keys, which was to get at the prisoner – to get at The Shifter. And there, through the partly opened door, she saw Jefferson Smith turning away from the desk with the big, shining bundle of keys in his hand, and on his face an expression of cold and sinister purpose.

The mind of the girl leaped at once to the result. She had heard of lynchings. The absence of the sheriff gave point to her flash of suspicion. She reached in, drew the door to her. Cautiously slipping the key from the lock, she fitted it again on the outside and noiselessly shut the door and turned the lock.

So softly had she worked that Smith, half blinded by the flare of the match close to his eyes, was not suspicious. 'House full of drafts,' she heard him mutter as he reached the door on the inside. Then came the sound of the turning knob.

There was such a terror in her, now that she had acted, that she could not move but leaned half fainting against the wall of the hall.

'Hello!' she heard Jefferson Smith cry. 'What the devil has...?' He wrenched loudly at the door. 'Hello! Help!' he shouted aloud. 'Hey, boys, the little vixen has tricked me and locked me up here like a rat in a trap.'

That brought her to her senses. The shouting of the storm still was louder than the voice of Smith, and there was no rush of footsteps from the lower part of the house, but at any moment it might begin. She turned and fled down the hall.

XI

Her mind was working with singular precision now. She raced down the back stairs to the tool room behind the kitchen and there, with swift and sure touch, she jerked open the big tool chest in the corner and drew out the steel saw and the oil can. More than once she had seen the sheriff work with it, more than once she had seen him handle stout iron.

Thus equipped, she hurried down to the hall, slipped through the cellar door, and paused a moment before she closed it. There was a sudden outbreak of shouting in the front part of the house. Then came a roar of footfalls on the front stairs. They had heard Jefferson Smith, and they were rushing to his rescue. *How long would the locked door hold them at bay?* she thought, as she tossed the key down the steps.

She ran straight to the cell. The lantern now illumined the big room very faintly, for it was turned low. The Shifter, lying asleep on his cot, was a blotchy shadow among shadows. The girl pressed her face against the cold bars. Her voice shook crazily as she called, and yet she dared not call too loudly.

'Quick! Quick! They've come for you! Wake up!'

The fear in her voice seemed to reach him even in his sleep. One bound brought him to his feet, staring wild eyed at her.

'They've come!' she stammered. 'Here ... here's the saw. I'll put on the oil...!'

'Who's come?'

'Jefferson Smith and a lot of others ... hard-faced men ... and they mean to take you away. They've taken the keys in the sheriff's office and...'

She watched his eyes widen, his face turn gray.

'A lynching party!' breathed The Shifter. 'Good Lord!'

The saw was snatched from her hand and began its small, shrill song as it cut into the steel bar, until she silenced it with a trickle of oil from the can.

'Hurry!' she pleaded. 'Hurry!'

Remembering a vital step which had not been taken, she rushed back to the cellar door and opened it an instant, barely in time to hear a great tearing and crashing sound in the upper part of the house, as though the storm had beaten in a section of the roof. On its heels came a shout of triumph.

They had broken down the door to the sheriff's office with their combined shoulder weight. With palsied hands she closed and locked the cellar door and blessed its solid thickness of stout pine wood as she did so. Then she fled down the steps again and back to The Shifter.

He was working like mad, his face covered

with tiny beads of perspiration but absolutely without color, and he acknowledged her return with a frantic rolling of the eyes. Again she picked up the oil can and poured the trickle on the shimmering blade of the saw. It was eating into the heart of the steel bar, but how slowly, slowly, slowly.

'Quick!' she sobbed. 'I hear them coming!'

An instant later the body of a man crashed against the cellar door. The Shifter cast the saw jangling on the floor and grasped the bar. It held as though it were a column of stone. The guarding door which kept out the manhunters groaned as they assailed it again. A gun exploded. They were shooting through the lock, but that massive, old-fashioned lock would surely turn their bullets without giving way.

'Once more,' cried Alison and, laying hold on the bar, she added her own small strength now made large in her frenzy.

He gripped the bar again. All his strength of body, from head to heel, went into the effort. There was a slight bending, then a gritting sound as of crystal against crystal, and suddenly the bar snapped with a humming sound and bent far to the side. The Shifter flung himself headlong into the gap. He could not go through at once. In fact, his struggles as he was pinned there threatened to tear him to pieces, but finally his hips were through, and then he lay sprawling on the floor at her feet, while at the same instant the cellar door was burst from its hinges and went crashing and bounding down the steps with a flood of yelling men pouring through behind it.

'Get him!' yelled the shrill voice of Jefferson Smith. 'Shoot to kill, boys. He's loose!'

She saw a flash of fighting rage come into the eyes of The Shifter. Then he caught up the fallen saw and flung it at the lantern which hung from the rafter a few yards away. The lantern fell crashing, and the big cellar was filled with sudden, thick darkness.

In that darkness she heard the pursuers bang blindly into the bars and shout and curse furiously. Then a hand gripped her.

'Is there another way out? Is there another way beside the one back into the house?'

'Yes ... yes. If I can only find it in the darkness! Oh, heaven help us!' sobbed Alison.

Deftly she guided him down the alley through the cells and then sharply to the right, until they ran into the rear wall of the house. The hubbub continued in the front of the room, a babel of oaths and frantic callings for a light. Here and there a match glowed, cupped in big hands, but those feeble cups of light were not able to throw a ray into the far corner where Alison fumbled for the old door.

At least, there was a sufficient glimmer of light for her to see that the way was blocked with a big box, and she pointed it out to the prisoner. His hands were instantly on it. It was flung to the side, while the betraying sound brought a yell from the trailers. One thrust of his shoulder and the door went open. Then she stood with him in the freshness of the night, with the wild rain whipping about them.

'Which way?' he asked.

'Here!'

She barely gave him the signal when he was off and she, racing beside him, was able to keep up because of her knowledge of the ground. Twice he tripped and fell headlong over obstacles in the yard and so enabled her to stay near him, and they reached the sheltering darkness of the trees side by side behind the house. The noise of the self-appointed posse now burst out of the cellar and into the storm-ridden night.

'Go back and get lights!' shouted the controlling voice of Jefferson Smith. 'We'll run the fool down. He can't get far on foot. Newt Barclay and Saunders, run for the stable and see that he don't get off with a hoss. If you see anything, don't wait to ask questions. Shoot to kill. Jerry, wait here and watch this door so he don't double back like a fox. The rest of you...' His voice died away as he turned back into the cellar.

'Now,' said The Shifter grimly to the girl, 'you've sure done your share. You've given me a running start, and I'll do the rest of it. Go back to the house.'

'Go back and face the sheriff? Oh, I'd sooner die. You don't know him. He'll kill me for this!'

'Is he that kind? But, you can't go with me.'

'Shall I go alone, then? I know the ground. I can show you where to go … a place they'll never search for you. Only one other person in the world knows about it. And … I won't be much in you way. I'll run every step!'

'Lord bless you,' said The Shifter. 'In the way? After saving me? I'll keep you in spite of everything. If I only had a gun … if I only had a measly little Twenty-Two. But bare hands are better than nothing. Which way, then?'

'Follow me.'

She led straight through the heart of the trees, keeping her word valiantly and running ahead over the slippery ground with a sureness of foot and a strength that amazed The Shifter. It was all he could do to keep close to the form which twinkled back and forth as she raced through the trees. In a moment more they came to a stiff upgrade with the trees growing in a more scattered fashion.

'Now we're fairly started,' she panted, slowing to a walk. 'They'll never catch us before we reach the place.'

A gust of wind pitched her into his arms, and he held her close for a moment then

311

whipped off his coat and wrapped it around her shoulders, for her thin house dress was already soaked from the rainfall.

'Come on,' said The Shifter. 'If they follow us, heaven help the ones I lay my hands on!'

XII

They labored up a weary climb, their feet slipping on the muddy slope, but never once did the courage or the spirit of the girl fail her, so that The Shifter was struck with wonder again and again.

'It's a short cut,' she told him. 'They'll never dream of coming this way, and the best of it is that the rain will wash out our footmarks. They won't last till the morning.'

'And what of you?' he asked. 'What will you do, Alison? Are you going to give up your home?'

'It's not a home,' she said. 'It's a prison. Oh, if you knew how I love even the rain and the wind because I'm free at last! My whole soul is breaking out and growing bigger. I feel strange to myself, I'm so happy. And I...' She stopped suddenly and caught at his arm. 'Listen!'

'Well?'

'Do you hear a wailing?'

'It's the wind. Yes, I hear it.'

'No, no. Not the wind. I've heard it before.

I heard it when the jail break came last spring, and the two men got away. Jefferson Smith has got out his hounds! Listen again!'

He could catch it unmistakably now, for as she spoke the force of the wind fell away a little, the crash of the rain on the rocks was lighter, and the chorus of the deep-throated bloodhounds swelled heavily up the hillside.

'We're almost there!' she sobbed. 'But what good will it do to go into the cave? They'll follow us even there!'

'Will the scent hold in all this rain?'

'Uncle John says that the Smith dogs can follow even the thought of a man. Yes, the scent will hold for them!'

'If we're near the cave, then,' said The Shifter, 'let's go there and sit down a minute to think. My head's in a whirl in this infernal wind. Come on!'

He helped her up an almost precipitous rise of ground, digging his toes deep into the mud for footing. They came onto a little shelf of land on the mountainside.

'This is it,' said Alison. 'At least this cave will give us a cut-off and gain time. It passes clear through the hill and opens on the other side.'

'Suppose we cut through it and then block the other end with stones. The hounds may be thrown off.'

'Yes, yes! At least we can try.'

She led the way, dropping to her hands

and knees and crawling through the black mouth of the cave. The Shifter followed and found himself in pitchy darkness. For perhaps twenty feet he crawled on behind the girl, bumping his head when he attempted to straighten. But at length he was able to see her rise to her feet, and he followed her example. The cave had widened to comfortable dimensions. The smell of wet ground was thick around them mixed with another scent, fainter and sharper.

'Alison!' exclaimed The Shifter softly. 'There's someone else here! I smell wood smoke. A fire has been burning in the cave.'

'That can't be true,' she answered instantly. 'There's only one other person in the world who knows about it, and that's poor Jack. He and I used to come up here when we were little ones. Jack showed it to me. The wood smoke may have drifted up here and stayed here without being blown out.'

'But...?'

He checked himself. There was no time to worry about imaginary dangers, for the voices of the bloodhounds swelled faintly from beyond. The Shifter struck on again through the cave, bending far over to avoid striking his head against any projection. For some ten yards the passage held straight on. Then it veered sharply to the right, and The Shifter, striding blindly ahead, struck solidly against the rock wall.

He recoiled with an exclamation, and on the sound of his voice he was paralyzed with astonishment to have a broad shaft of light flashed upon him.

'Hands up!' snapped a voice. 'Hands up, whoever you are!'

The Shifter obeyed.

'If you're hiding out here, partner,' he said eagerly, 'I'm not hunting you. Matter of fact, I'm in the same boat. And...'

'You!' broke in the holder of the electric torch, and now The Shifter could make out the outlines of the figure and even the glimmer of the revolver which he held in his right hand as he poised the electric torch in the left. 'I figured I'd meet you again. But I never dreamed I'd get a chance to get back at you so quick. Now, son, you'll pay me for my hoss you killed, and you'll pay me big!' He added sharply: 'Who's that with you?'

'Jack!' cried Alison, her voice ringing out joyously. 'Oh, then all the danger is over! Don't you see? It's Jack Clark. He's not dead ... he's not dead!'

'Good Lord!' groaned Jack, the torch wavering in his hand as he recoiled. 'Alison, what're you doing up here ... with him? What're you doing up here?'

The mind of The Shifter groped vaguely toward the truth. Here was the 'murdered' man, after all, safe and sound and lurking like a condemned criminal escaped from the law.

'You'd've hung up here?' he growled savagely. 'Stayed right up here while they was holding me for killing you? Clark, you'll pay *me* big for this.'

'Will I? And suppose I stop your trail right now? If I catch you running off with a girl, d'you s'pose I ain't got the right to stop you … with a bullet?'

The Shifter had been resting one hand against the rocky side of the passage. Now in his blind rage his fingers contracted strongly, and a great chunk of stone came away in them. All caution left him.

'You hound!' he cried and lurched straight at the holder of the light.

The sound of the explosion of the revolver and the mingling wail of the girl rolled faintly out from the cave and reached the spurring horsemen who were driving their exhausted mounts up that hillside on the heels of the dogs, held hard in leash by Jefferson Smith and giving tongue furiously as the scent grew hot.

Up to the very mouth of the cave the hounds dragged Smith. He pulled them to one side, and the others crawled into the black hole. The scent of burned gun powder was lingering inside to guide them. Far away they heard the muffled weeping of a woman. Morton had found an electric pocket lantern before he left the sheriff's house, and with this he now probed the passage with a dim

316

shaft of light. They turned the corner of the tunnel at a run and so came full upon a strange group.

A man lay sprawled on his face, motionless. Another stood above him, leaning against the wall and staring down at the stricken. And Alison crouched, weeping, nearby.

'It's me,' said The Shifter slowly as they rushed about him. 'He tried to shoot me. I hit him with this rock. And ... and I think this time you got some call to hang me, boys.'

Bud Morton turned the fallen man on his back, and a shout of astonishment rose from his lips as he saw the face of Jack Clark. It was a face half muddy and half pale, and from the side of the head a trickle of crimson ran down his face.

'Is he dead?' asked Jefferson Smith from the rear.

'No,' answered Morton, his hand lying over Jack's heart.

'He'd better be,' said Jefferson in a ringing voice. 'Of all the dirty pieces of work I've ever seen or heard of, boys, this is the rottenest. Don't you see it? To get square with The Shifter there, who killed his hoss and maybe licked him fair and square on the one-way trail, this skunk waited up here till The Shifter swung for the job or got lynched. Lynch The Shifter? Why, boys, we'll step up and tell him we're a pile sorry for what's happened.'

It required time to bring about the conclusion. In that time Jack Clark, a sadly humbled and humiliated man, went north, far north into a new country, to carve out for himself a new name and a new character. And, since there is possibility of change in even the worst of us, Jack succeeded beyond the dreams of even his father who went with him. There in the north they settled down as farmers in an unknown community, and the letters that drifted south to Alison were all of prosperity, home building, and finally of the marriage of Jack.

They will tell you the story even today in Vardon City, particularly when a stranger is guided through the main street and past the big house at the head of the thoroughfare, its gables barely visible above the surrounding treetops, for Harry French, late The Shifter, and his wife now live in the big house. Their greatest friend is that formidable gunfighter, Jefferson Smith, who takes all the credit for their romance on his own shoulders.

'I smelled a rat from the first,' he is fond of saying. 'And then I ran it down with dogs. No matter if the name of the rat was not the one I started after. The fact is that I found a rat.'

No one cares to dispute Jefferson Smith. Certainly not The Shifter who has laid aside his guns.

The publishers hope that this book has given you enjoyable reading. Large Print Books are especially designed to be as easy to see and hold as possible. If you wish a complete list of our books please ask at your local library or write directly to:

The Golden West Large Print Books
Magna House, Long Preston,
Skipton, North Yorkshire.
BD23 4ND

This Large Print Book, for people
who cannot read normal print,
is published under the auspices of

THE ULVERSCROFT FOUNDATION